Narquinxa and Xandalus

Narquinxa and Xandalus

Simon Sheridan

Simon Sheridan

Prologue

Translator's Note: the following dialogue is translated from Antorpene into the human language of English. Antorpene is the language of the Antorpeds, a species from the galaxy of Moxthphth. The Antorpeds do not communicate via sound but rather via telepathy. As such, all orthography here is purely arbitrary and bears no phonetic resemblance to any kind of sound made by an Antorped while communicating.

Socio-linguistically, I have chosen to represent the 'speech' of the Antorped named Xandalus using the dialect of English spoken among so-called 'stoners' on Earth. The reader should be aware that the Antorpeds do not consume marijuana, there being no such plant on their planet. There is, however, a subculture of Antorpeds known to partake in mind-altering substances imbibed in the form of certain species of bacteria. They are also quite partial to a particular kind of virus found in the neighbouring galaxy of Nophblph, the trade in which forms a large part of inter-galactic commerce in the region. The prevalence of such a practice forms the primary reason for my choice of 'stoner' dialect in rendering the translation.

The secondary reason for my choice is to communicate to the reader the fact that the Antorpeds are considered a lackadaisical, even lazy species within the galaxy of Moxthphth and surrounding galaxies. They are known for their easy-going and fun-loving manner. The reader must be aware, however, that this is purely relative to the prevailing culture in that area of the universe. Although considered an unintelligent species by their peers, the Antorpeds far exceed humans in intelligence.

The final, and perhaps most important, reason is that Xandalus' speech on Earth in the story which follows was actually in the stoner dialect due to an analytical error on the part of the Antorped linguists as will become clear shortly.

The following dialogue occurred on the Antorped spaceship that we might as well call, Ship 123. The reader should know that the characters in the dialogue are not proximal to each other in space at the time of the conversation, this not being a requirement for telepathic communication. At the time of the conversation, Ship 123 was taking in the sights of the Andromeda galaxy before heading for the Milky Way. Its destination: the planet Earth.

The date by the human calendar was December 13th 2021. The time, 1.03am GMT.

***

"Where the hell is Xandalus?" muttered Gwthphthgw.

"He's late. Again."

Translator's note: the Antorped species does not reproduce sexually. Nevertheless, they do have gendered personal pronouns that equate to the human genders of male and female but which are assigned based on what, in order to avoid a long metaphysical digression, we can call 'personality'.

"He's always goddamn late."

"I've told you, he's not up to this mission. He's not up to any mission. Let me take another crew member."

"That's enough, Narquinxa. It's you and Xandalus on this mission and that's final."

"Everybody knows Xandalus is a good-for-nothing layabout. Even by Antorped-standards."

"And everybody knows you have a problem with haughtiness, Narquinxa."

"I do n...."

Translator's note: Xandalus joins the conversation. Telepathically.

"Oh, hey, bros. Sorry. I couldn't find the frequency and I accidentally chimed in on a convo that was in some weird-ass language I couldn't understand. Took me a couple of minutes to figure out what was going on. There must some other species in the area."

"That's correct, Xandalus," said Gwthphthgw. "There are some Norxthor ships not far from here. You don't speak Norxthor? You should have learned it in school."

"Oh, right. I thought it sounded familiar."

Narquinxa clicked her tongue.

Translator's note: Antorpeds do not have tongues. Rather, Narquinxa telepathically communicated her disapproval of Xandalus' prior statement.

"Hey, Quin," said Xandalus. "How's it going? Ready for some laughs down on planet Earth?"

"Laughs? We have a mission to fulfill, Xandalus."

"Yeah. What is it again, bro?"

"Xandalus, you are to refer to your superior by his proper name."

"That's fine," said Gwthphthgw. "I don't know why you insist of being so formal, Narquinxa. We've been on this ship together for months now. Why don't you lighten up?"

"Too much time on Pthphlethor - *Translator's note: another planet in the Moxthphth galaxy -*," said Xandalus. "She's had a stick up her butt ever since she got back."

Translator's note: Antorpeds do not have butts.

"More anti-Pthphlethorian rhetoric, Xandalus?"

"Anti-rhe-what-ic?"

"Quiet, you two. Can you both make an effort to get along with each other or are you going to spend the whole mission at each other's throats?"

Translator's note: Antorpeds do not have throats.

"What is the mission, dude," asked Xandalus.

"As you both know, we are headed for the planet Earth in the Milky Way galaxy. Earth has a species of intelligent life form known as humans. These humans make use of a primitive vocal apparatus and an even more primitive orthography to communicate amongst themselves and with this communication have been making some, umm, *credible* efforts towards increasing their collective intelligence level. Nevertheless, the average human still has much more in common with the other species of animal on Earth than to a fully-fledged member of the inter-galactic community and you should take this into account in your interactions with them."

"If they're so backward, why are we bothering with them?" asked Narquinxa.

"The humans may be lacking in intelligence but we have reason to believe that they exceed other species in the depth and variety of the emotional states that they are able to achieve. We Antorpeds, of course, pride ourselves on the diverse range of emotions we express in relation to other species in our own galaxy. However, the humans appear to have a far greater variety even than ourselves. Your mission is to study these emotions and, where possible, derive means by which Antorpeds might also be able to experience and possibly learn from them."

"Sounds cool, bro," said Xandalus.

"Cool?" shot back Narquinxa. "It's a waste of time, that's what it is. What possible use could these emotions have for Antorpeds? Our emotions are already an impediment to our own progress as a species. We don't need more emotions to get in the way and cause trouble."

"It's true, Narquinxa, that our scientists are yet to determine the practical benefit of emotions. However, we do know that emotions are somewhat connected to intuition, which is a form of intelligence."

"Pffft. Intelligence is intelligence. Intuition is a bunch of airy-fairy nonsense."

"That is your position and you are welcome to it. Nevertheless, your job in this case is not to prove the utility of emotions but simply to experience them and report on them."

"And how will we do that?"

"We have prepared human bodies for you both as you can see here."

Translator's note: at this point, Gwthphthgw telepathically transmits images of the bodies in question.

"As you can see, there are two types of body here. One is for a human male and the other for a human female. As you may know, the humans reproduce sexually, so we figured it best to have one of each to ensure a broader coverage in our research."

"Sexual reproduction," muttered Narquinxa. "So antiquated."

"This sounds awesome," said Xandalus excitedly. "I once met a creature from another planet. I can't remember the name of the species. Anyway, he was a male of that species and the stories he was telling about sex. Woah, boy! It sounds like fun."

"I'm glad you're enthusiastic, Xandalus, because your primary mission on Earth will be to have sex."

"Cool!"

"Why is that, sir?" asked Narquinxa.

"A great deal of the emotional content in the life of a human revolves around the cultural and physical practices relating to sex. Therefore, our scientists believe that we can maximise the research benefits of your short stay by focusing on the emotions related to sex. To assist in the achievement of this task, our technicians have designed what we believe to be highly attractive human bodies. The male is tall and powerfully built with broad shoulders and a relatively slim waist. The female is shorter and more voluptuous. She has the hourglass shape that we believe to be highly desirable to the male of the human species. The facial features are symmetrical and both bodies are designed to resemble a young adult human which is the age of peak sexual attractiveness. With these bodies we believe it should be a trivial matter for both of you to attract a sexual partner among the humans."

"Couldn't we just have sex with each other?" asked Xandalus.

Narquinxa scowled. Telepathically.

"You're welcome to try," said Gwthphthgw. "However, it will be better for you to concentrate on having interactions with real humans so that you may receive authentic emotional signals. Bear in mind that this is a test mission. Our main concern here is to prove that the human bodies we have created work correctly and that the premise of our investigation is sound. All going well, we will send other researchers back for a longer stay in the future."

"How long are we staying for?" asked Xandalus.

"Three Earth days."

"And how long does it take to have sex?"

"Our research indicates that the time can vary from a minute or two among inexperienced practitioners through to several hours for the more experienced."

"Great," muttered Narquinxa. "What are we going to do for the rest of the time?"

"Have more sex," chirped Xandalus.

"I'd rather read a book."

"Then read a book while having sex. You're a smart girl. I'm sure you can do two things at once."

"That's two more than you can do."

"Ok. Ok." said Gwthphthgw. "Look, I urge both of you to have some fun with this. Especially you, Narquinxa. We've been travelling for some time now. This is a nice easy mission so I recommend letting your hair down for a few days. Don't think. Feel. Allow yourself to become immersed in human emotion. Seek out heightened emotional states, especially pleasurable ones. Try to connect with the deepest levels of human being and see what makes them tick. There'll be plenty of time for introspection and reflection when you return."

"You don't have to tell me twice, bro," said Xandalus.

"I know that, Xandalus. It's Narquinxa I'm worried about."

"Don't worry about her, dude. If anybody can put a smile on ol' Quin's face, it's me."

"Good. We'll be dropping you into a country on Earth known as Australia. The culture in this community of humans is sexually liberal and should provide beneficial conditions for the fulfilment of your mission. To prepare you for your interaction with the Australians, we've created a simulation program where you can practice social and language skills. These skills will be vitally important to the success of your mission so I expect you both to spend most of your time before we arrive practicing in the simulation. We'll be dropping you in at 5pm local Earth time tomorrow. Good luck."

Chapter 1

There was a flash of light, gusts of wind and a large blue ball that cratered two large semi-spherical shapes in the ground. Inside the shapes were two human forms; a male and a female. They made a handsome couple. Very handsome indeed. Let us describe their appearance, beginning with Xandalus.

The reader may know that there is a certain kind of man among humans whose jaw is said to be chiseled. Xandalus had been given just such a jaw. In fact, Xandalus' jaw might have been chiseled by the archchiseler himself, Michelangelo. That's how chiseled it was. In relation to such a jaw, the rest of the head and body has a job to do not to be completely overshadowed and allow the proportions of the whole to be thrown out of balance due to the excessive prominence of such a magnificent mandible. The Antorped designers had mitigated this risk skillfully. Xandalus stood an imposing six foot and one inch tall with thick blonde hair casually tucked back behind his ears. His light blue eyes shone beneath a pair of luxuriant eyebrows that were just a few tones of blonde darker than his hair. His mouth and lips were, in some sense, just a bit smaller than they could have been. But, far from being an error on the part of the designers, this accentuated his cheeks and leant him a fresh, youthful countenance. He had broad shoulders and a barrel chest that worked their way down to a slender waist whose modest proportions served to foreground a powerful pair of buttocks on the one side and an equally powerful pair of quadricep muscles on the other. From there down to the ground things proceeded in an orderly and proportional fashion. His overall appearance was that of a Greek God.

What of Narquinxa?

The reader should remember that Antorpeds do not have physical gender and are therefore unable to be accused of favoritism or bias in relation to issues of sex. Were this not the case then any halfway decent lawyer could have persuaded even a short-sighted jury to give a guilty verdict on a charge of blatant sexism against the Antorped designers for, as handsome as Xandalus was, Narquinxa was the very model of female beauty. It is, of course, true that standards of beauty are not fixed and do vary among human societies and even within the same society over time. So, let me qualify my statement to say that Narquinxa was about as beautiful as a young woman could be at the tail end of the year 2021 in the country of Australia. Among the young females of that time and place there was a preference for bodies that had been carefully sculpted in gymnasiums and training venues. Of particular importance was the gluteus maximus muscle of whose size it was believed: the bigger the better. As with all fashions, there is a tendency to exaggerate the feature into caricature. This error had been avoided in the case of Narquinxa. The proportions of her posterior were complemented by appropriately, luxuriantly sized hips and breasts to create the classical hourglass shape. She had that effortlessly slender arc in the shoulders that is common to even the most muscular females of the human species. Draped across those slender shoulders was a gathering of blonde hair, the exact same shade as Xandalus'. It was gathered up in a pony tail that hung from high up on the back of her head while two strands had been allowed to hang free on either side of Narquinxa's face, a face of such pristine proportion that Pythagoras himself would have praised its perfection. Down the middle of it ran a thin, delicate nose that seemed almost shy, almost apologetic in relation to her lips which were bold and full and round. She had light blue eyes of the same shade and radiance as Xandalus and stood about four inches shorter than her compatriot.

If one were inclined to criticise the Antorped designers, the only grounds for doing so were that Xandalus and Narquinxa looked so alike as to be taken for brother and sister. It is perhaps the case that, in order to save time, the technicians had worked off the same template. No matter. There now stood in a back alley in the inner Melbourne suburb of Carlton, two attractive, young, blonde humans whose eyes were slowly becoming accustomed to the light as they began to take in their surroundings.

"*Xandalus, Narquinxa, how are you doing?*" queried Gwthphthgw telepathically from the Antorped spaceship.

"*All good for me, bro,*" answered Xandalus.

"*Fine, sir,*" said Narquinxa.

"*Good. Now, remember that you'll be teleported back from the same place you now stand in exactly seventy-two hours. In case of emergency, you may reach me on the usual frequency. There is one final instruction I have for you both. I've waited until you arrived to give it to you as I want it to be foremost in your mind during your visit.*"

"*What is it, dude?*"

"*You are not to interfere in human affairs during your time on Earth. What that means is that, outside your interpersonal relations, you are not to provide advice, instruction or assistance on any practical matter. This is especially true in relation to scientific and technological domains. As you know, the humans are a relatively backward species in these regards and we do not want to give them capabilities for which they are unprepared. We all remember what happened on the planet Xthphthwr when one of our colleagues let slip about the workings of certain molecular agents whose hallucinogenic properties are well understood on Antorped but for which the locals on that planet were not sufficiently prepared. As you know, the diplomatic fallout from that episode is ongoing. I don't want a repeat of such embarrassments in this case. Is that understood?*"

"*Sure is, bro.*"

"*Yes, sir.*"

"*Excellent. Well, that warning notwithstanding, I wish you both an enjoyable time on Earth and look forward to hearing a report of your findings when you return. Over and out.*"

Xandalus and Narquinxa surveyed the scene around them. They were in one of the bluestone laneways so common to inner city Melbourne. It was a long, narrow space with red brick walls on either side. Several large yellow dumpsters were placed next to roller doors or doorways belonging to the buildings on either side. They were about twenty metres from what appeared to be a heavily trafficked street to the east while in the other direction the laneway terminated as an entrance to a large brick factory.

"*Well, I guess we go that way,*" said Xandalus telepathically indicating the direction of the street.

"Enough telepathy," replied Narquinxa verbally. "We should speak to each other like normal humans so as not to attract attention."

"Fair enough," said Xandalus.

Xandalus looked over at Narquinxa for the first time with his human eyes. She was clothed in a light pink dress that complimented her blonde hair and seemed to match the colour of her lips. To say the dress was figure-hugging was perhaps an understatement. The full majesty of Narquinxa's hourglass figure was on display. The bottom of the dress terminated about mid-thigh while the top made no attempt to hide the voluptuousness of her breasts. It was this latter fact which had especially captured Xandalus' attention.

Narquinxa noticed his gaze.

"What are you gawking at?"

"I'm having these thoughts."

"About what?"

"About what to do with those. Y'know, maybe you and I *should* have sex," continued Xandalus as though a brilliant idea was just forming in his mind. "Just to see what it's like before we try it with a real human."

"Don't be stupid. I don't want to have sex with you."

"You don't? Cos, I really, I mean *really*, want to have sex with you right now. I'm getting a very strong emotional signal in that respect."

"Well, I'm getting a very strong emotional signal that says I should slap you in the face."

"Why?"

"Didn't you do the social simulation work back on the ship? You can't just walk up to a woman and stare at her breasts. You're likely to get arrested."

"Really?"

"You did do the simulation work, didn't you?" Narquinxa's eyes narrowed as she spoke.

"Yeah, yeah," said Xandalus giving a dismissive wave of his hand.

"Ok. Then perhaps you can tell me where we should go to try and find a sexual partner."

"Piece of cake," said Xandalus in a braggadocios tone intended to hide the fact that he hadn't the slightest clue where they should go.

"Then lead the way," said Narquinxa gesturing with her hand and watching Xandalus closely as they made their way out onto the street.

No sooner had they got to the footpath which was full of pedestrians than Xandalus, surveying the scene like a shoddy salesman looking for a target, walked up to a man and a woman who were of similar age to himself and Narquinxa. He addressed the man.

"Hey, bro, wanna have sex?"

To say the man was surprised would not have been necessarily accurate. In fact, it is possible that at that moment, Xandalus had succeeded in creating a new emotion among the human race. Something surpassing amazement. Beyond astonishment. It looked as though he had broken the man's mind. It wasn't just the abruptness of the request that caused the rupture. It wasn't just the fact that the man was arm in arm with a woman in a gesture clearly symbolizing that they were in a relationship. It wasn't just the chirpy, sing song tone of Xandalus' delivery. It was the fact that the interaction was wrong in almost every conceivable fashion. The man in question was a good six inches shorter than Xandalus. He had jet black hair and wore black face makeup. He was overweight and wore poorly fitted clothing all in black colour. The girl beside him was dressed similarly. The two of them clearly belonged to the sub-culture known as 'goths'. By contrast, Xandalus, a six-foot tall, well-built blonde man, had been dressed by the Antorped technicians in a tailored, light pink button-down shirt, fitted grey chinos and leather shoes. He looked like a movie star or wealthy businessman but he spoke in a manner befitting a dreadlocked hippie. This was a genuine mistake by the Antorped designers. Although an accurate representation of his social status among his Antorped compatriots, it was glaringly out of character with his physical appearance and fashion style on Earth. For this combination of reasons, the last thing the goth man expected to hear out of Xandalus' mouth was an invitation for sex.

There was lengthy pause while Xandalus, smiling innocently at the two goths, waited for a response which was clearly not going to be forthcoming. Eventually, it occurred to him that something might be wrong.

"You ok, bro?" he said still smiling earnestly.

Before the man could attempt to respond, Narquinxa strode over, grabbed Xandalus by the arm and dragged him back into the alleyway that they had stepped out of moments earlier. She pushed him against the wall and poked an accusatory index finger in his chest.

"I knew it. You didn't do the simulation training, did you?"

"Whaddya mean?"

"What the hell was that? You just committed a major social faux pas."

"Faux what?"

"What you did was completely inappropriate. Completely out of keeping with the culture in this area of Earth. Or any area of Earth for that matter. And why were you asking the man for sex? Our designers are supposed to have made us attracted to the opposite sex."

"I wasn't asking him for sex. I was gonna suggest that I have sex with that girl and he could have sex with you," said Xandalus.

"Well, you didn't. You asked him to have sex. And besides which, that was clearly his girlfriend or wife that was with him so there was almost no chance he was going to let you have sex with her."

"Why not?"

Narquinxa shook her head and gave a slight stamp of her foot.

"That's it. We're splitting up."

"Huh?"

"I'm not walking around with some culturally unattenuated buffoon. God knows what other nonsense you'll be coming out with. I have a good mind to inform Gwthphthgw of your failure to carry out the training required of you."

"C'mon, Quin. Look, I'll pick it up quickly. I promise."

"Nope. If I hang around with you the only emotion I'm going to be feeling is rage. We need to split up so I can do my job properly. See you in three days."

With that Narquinxa stormed back towards the street but, just before she was out of sight, she turned back to Xandalus.

"I shouldn't tell you this but if I don't you'll probably spend all three days trying to guess. The answer to my question of where to go to meet a sexual partner is a pub or nightclub. I suggest you go to those places if you want to find a woman."

With that she walked away and Xandalus was on his own.

Chapter 2

In her pretty pink dress with matching high heel pink shoes, Narquinxa had the look of an angry supermodel who was rushing to get away from the paparazzi as she stormed out of the laneway. Anger and frustration were not new emotions for her. They weren't common among her species, but, then again, Narquinxa wasn't exactly a typical Antorped. In fact, she was an outsider. During her education she had far exceeded the meagre standards of her fellows and had been sent to Pthphlethor where it was felt her capacities could best be developed. Truth be told, this was as much to get rid of her as to help her. Her prickly demeanor won her no friends on Antorped where the culture dictates that going with the flow is the best bet whereas swimming against the tide is like fighting an uphill battle while skating on thin ice.

Temperamentally, Narquinxa was much more at home on Pthphlethor and yet the Pthphlethorians never accepted her as one of their own. So, she had returned to Antorped only to find the atmosphere intolerably suffocating. She needed to get out and when a job advertisement promising lengthy travels to other galaxies had caught her eye she jumped at the chance. It didn't solve her problems. All that happened was that she had been cooped up in a spaceship with a group of her countrymen. Her fellow travellers were not the sharpest tools in the Antorped shed. Xandalus was not an anomaly in that respect. Space travel tended to attract the losers and layabouts looking for cheap thrills. Narquinxa was the smartest person on the ship. She knew it. And she couldn't hide the fact that she knew it from the others which didn't exactly help with her popularity. And now here she was on Earth and it had taken that moron, Xandalus, all of two minutes to completely screw things up. Enough was enough. Gwthphthgw was right. She *was* going to take a few days to enjoy herself *by* herself. Some time alone would do her good. But first, she needed to fulfil her mission.

As her anger subsided, she slowed her pace and started to pay attention to her surroundings. She was still on the street full of pedestrians but the scenery had changed somewhat. There were now fewer restaurants and more pubs and bars. It was still bright outside but the early summer sun had sunk below the tops of the buildings creating a coolness in the air. Narquinxa realised that her outfit would probably not be warm enough to get her through the night outside. She would have to find a man at whose house she could reside. Her research on the human culture in Australia led her to believe that such an arrangement would naturally follow from a sexual encounter.

She stopped in front of a pub and peeked through the window to get a look at the clientele. A woman of similar age but dressed in a uniform of some kind was leaning against the wall smoking a cigarette. She raised an eyebrow as she appreciated the beautiful creature before her.

"You lost?" she asked.

Narquinxa turned around to face the woman.

"No. I can't be lost. I was never found."

The woman laughed.

"That's quite philosophical."

"You might be able to help, though," said Narquinxa walking over to the woman.

"Happy to. If I can."

"I want to have sex," said Narquinxa. "With a man," she added quickly in case the woman thought she was asking to have sex with her.

The woman looked Narquinxa up and down.

"I don't think you're gonna need much help with that," she said smiling.

"What do you mean?"

"I mean your problem is not going to be to find a man. It's going to be to beat them away. Preferably with a metal pole of some kind. Maybe two."

The woman smiled then realised that Narquinxa didn't understand her intent.

"I want to have sex with a good man. Not just any idiot," said Narquinxa in perfect innocence.

At this the woman burst out laughing.

"Well, that's a completely different story, honey. If I knew the answer to that problem, I'd be a rich woman."

Again, Narquinxa didn't understand what was funny about this. The woman slowly stopped laughing and looked at her conversation partner with curiosity.

"You're a strange bird. You from overseas?"

"I've, ah, moved around a bit," said Narquinxa realising that her behaviour had appeared strange to the woman.

"What I mean is, can you tell me where to find a good man? Is this pub a good place?"

Narquinxa gestured inside the pub.

"I understand now," said the woman. "As a matter of fact, I work in here, so I can tell you we get mostly yuppies from the city. Bankers and lawyers and that type of thing. If you'd prefer a more grungy, rock'n'roller type then try across the road there."

The woman pointed to another pub on the other side of the road. Narquinxa thought about the two choices and had no idea which one she would prefer. For the purposes of sex, she didn't see any reason to differentiate based on social status or sub-culture membership. The woman saw Narquinxa's indecision and, being at the end of her cigarette, threw it into a nearby dispenser and walked over to Narquinxa.

"Just come in here, honey. I'll give you your first drink on the house."

The woman smiled at Narquinxa and Narquinxa allowed herself to smile back. It felt good. Like there was some kind of connection between the two of them. They walked into the pub together.

***

Xandalus was feeling down. Narquinxa's outburst was nothing new on her part, but it still made him feel bad. She was right, of course. He had not done the simulation work that was required of him. He'd tried. A few minutes here and there but homework was never his thing. He liked living for real not spending time in the simulations. Xandalus preferred to learn to swim by jumping in the deep end. That's precisely where he was now. The deep end. It was getting on for 8pm. His initial failure with the goth man on the street had been replicated in a couple of similarly awkward situations in two pubs where he had tried to meet a woman. He had so far been given a good strong dose of at least two human emotions - humiliation and shame – and was fast descending into a third: depression.

After licking his wounds for a while, he had summoned up the courage to try a third time and was now sitting in a small pub decked out with wood panelling and leather seats. He decided to just sit there and observe the humans for a while to try and get more of an intuitive feel for their behaviour and, in particular, to watch the interactions between the men and women to see if he could get any tips on how to proceed with the opposite sex. The place was full of people mostly in his age group and demographic. So far he had not seen any women to compare with the beauty of Narquinxa but there were a number of attractive females who had caught his eye. One in particular had drawn his sustained interest, a brunette who was at the bar with a few female friends. He realised how easily his mind would wander and slip into daydreams of a sexual nature as he imagined what he and this woman could do with each other. He found the daydreams pleasurable. He could even feel his heart rate and body temperature rise almost as if he was having sex.

What the daydreaming Xandalus didn't realise was that he had been staring open-mouthed at the woman with a look on his face that would have been inappropriate in a strip club let alone a city pub. So enmeshed was he in his own imagination that he hadn't realised the woman had stormed off in search of somebody and that she and that somebody were now standing right in front of him. His reverie was finally broken by the shrill, accusative tone of her voice as she pointed at him accusingly.

"That's him!"

Xandalus snapped out of his daydream and returned to the present. The woman was right in front of him and beside her was a large man of similar physical dimensions to Xandalus. He was dressed in black slacks and a white dress shirt and wore a white badge with the name "Vinnie" written on it.

"Three times now I've caught him staring at me," complained the woman. "He doesn't even have the decency to look away. He just keeps on staring and drooling like some kind of freak."

Vinnie turned to face Xandalus.

"Sir, I'm going to have to ask you to leave," he said in a deep, authoritative voice.

Xandalus felt a pulse of apprehension ripple through his body. It was not pleasurable. The Antorpeds were a conflict-averse species. Disagreement was avoided wherever possible and such a direct confrontation between strangers would have been tantamount to a declaration of war back home.

He held up his hands in a sign of innocence.

"Sorry, if I've caused offence, bro. Didn't mean anything by it."

Xandalus' manner of speech seemed to both surprise and displease the large man as if he thought he was being played for a fool.

"Alright, *bro*. But the door is this way."

The man gestured towards the entrance to the pub. There was a tone in the voice that Xandalus struggled to understand but which made him think it was best to comply with the request.

As Xandalus got up from the table and started for the door, the woman shook her head and strode back to the bar where her friends had been watching on. They scowled in Xandalus' direction as she related the story. Xandalus recognised their facial expressions. He had seen such expressions several times that evening and he once again felt the stab of shame which seemed to come from an invisible physical source and rise up like the heat of a fire from his stomach to his face. The shame was mixed with confusion. It was one thing to fail but he didn't feel like he was learning anything. Quite the opposite, he seemed to be getting worse as the evening wore on and it appeared to him that he would never achieve his goal. As they arrived at the door, he decided to throw himself on the mercy of Vinnie.

"Look, dude, I'd really rather not leave. I need to meet a girl. You know what I mean, right? One man to another? I *really* need a girl and I've already tried several other pubs. I think I can find one here."

The candidness of his speech and the genuine emotion in Xandalus' voice seemed to take Vinnie by surprise and his facial features softened into a look that Xandalus would later understand was empathy.

"Look, mate, I sympathise with you but my hands are tied. There's been a complaint and you were caught red handed. If you want to meet a girl, what are you doing sitting around at the window and staring? You've gotta actually go up and start a conversation if you want to get anywhere."

"I've tried that. It's not so easy."

The big man laughed.

"I hear you, mate. But that's how the game is played."

Xandalus was about to ask what 'game' the man was referring to when the girl who had lodged the complaint walked past and bumped him in the chest before striding out the door. Her friends followed each taking the time to conspicuously glare at Xandalus as they walked out. Vinnie watched them leave and seemed to be relieved at their going. He turned back to Xandalus.

"Alright, look, now that they're gone, I'm happy to let you stay on if you want. But no more weird shit, ok? And you have to at least buy a drink. Got it?"

"No worries," said Xandalus and smiled as the big man walked out the door and took up his position on the street outside.

The problem, of course, was that Xandalus didn't have any money. This was an oversight on the part of the Antorped scientists who, although aware of the existence of money on Earth and who knew in abstract terms the function that money fulfilled, had simply not grasped the practical difficulties caused by a lack of physical currency. As a result, Xandalus would have to ask somebody to buy him a drink. He looked around and saw a woman sitting by herself in a booth just a few metres away. She had mouse brown shoulder length hair and a pretty face. She looked like the kind of girl Xandalus could get along with.

He walked over and sat down opposite the girl in the booth and gave her a big smile. It was, in fact, a cheeky smile. The smile of a man who wants something he shouldn't expect to get but is going to ask for anyway.

"I need you to buy me a drink," he said leaning in towards the girl in a conspiratorial fashion.

The girl's face had already gone slightly red at the sight of a tall, handsome, blonde man approaching her in a bar. It now went even redder.

"I'm sorry?"

"I need you to buy me a drink. Otherwise you and I won't be able to talk."

"You want to talk to me?"

"Absolutely. I think you're really pretty. But if I don't have a drink they will kick me out of here and we won't be able to get to know each other."

The look of confusion on the girl's face turned to understanding and then even happiness as she seemed to comprehend what was happening. Xandalus gave her a wink which seemed to tilt the decision in his favour. She smiled as she slid out of the booth and picked up her purse off the table.

"What drink do you want?"

"Umm, surprise me."

Xandalus smiled. His big, white, perfectly aligned teeth flashed in the dim light of the bar and his light blue eyes sparkled. The girl blushed slightly again and walked over to the bar. Xandalus watched her go. She was thin and dressed conservatively in a pair of black slacks, brown shoes and a white blouse with frills along the shoulders and the front. She cast several glances back towards Xandalus while she was waiting at the bar as if checking that he was still there, then returned and put a small glass down on the table in front of Xandalus. It contained a clear liquid and a number of ice cubes.

"Thank you," said Xandalus and smiled as the girl took her place across from him.

The girl watched him for a few seconds with an expectant look on her face.

"Aren't you going to drink it?" she asked motioning towards the drink.

Xandalus looked down at the glass as if realising its purpose for the first time.

"No, that's ok. I'll just leave it there. It's you that I'm here for."

"Why me?" said the girl who took a rather extra-large gulp of her own drink.

"Well, I need a girl and I thought you could be it."

"What do you need a girl for?"

"Sex."

The girl gave a start and in the process managed to tip over a bottle of beer that was sitting on the table in front of Xandalus. She quickly picked up the bottle and stood it upright before reaching for some napkins from a small dispenser that was sitting by the wall to mop up the spill. Xandalus helped her.

"Am I being too upfront?" he asked.

"No. I'm, umm, I'm just not used to being approached in a bar, that's all," said the girl putting the damp napkins to one side. "Especially by tall, handsome men."

"You think I'm handsome?"

"Very."

"Well, I think you're pretty."

Just as with the bouncer earlier on, Xandalus' plain and honest way of speaking disarmed the girl. She scanned his face as if checking for her hidden meaning but she was getting the impression that this was not an act that he was putting for her benefit. Not just some cheesy routine from an experienced player on a Friday night. But caution told her to withhold judgement for the time being.

"What's your name?" she asked as she mopped up the last of the beer and threw the damp napkins off to the side.

"Zander."

"That's a weird name. What is that? Greek?"

"Umm, yep."

"Well, nice to meet you, Zander. I'm Rebecca."

Rebecca held out her hand and Xandalus reached out and took it. It was the first time he had touched a human. Her skin was soft. He allowed his hand to gently slide over it. It was warm to the touch and made him feel what he had felt back in the alley when he had seen Narquinxa's body for the first time. After a longer period than was socially appropriate, Xandalus released Rebecca's hand and turned his gaze to her face. It was red again but this time there was something else in her expression and it wasn't confusion.

They held eye contact for what might have been one second or might have been one minute before their mutual gaze was broken by a loud cough. Xandalus turned to his right to see another young woman standing at the table watching the two of them with a confused look on her face. She was very similar in appearance to Rebecca.

"Ummm, Zander, this is my sister, April," said Rebecca. "We were having a drink together before you came over."

Zander smiled and nodded his head towards the woman.

"Hello, Zander," said April a little suspiciously.

April stood there for a couple of seconds seemingly confused about what to do. Xandalus watched on with interest not realising that she was intimating that he was sitting in her chair and that maybe he should at least slide over to let her sit down. April was about to ask him to do just that when Rebecca gave a quick, almost imperceptible nod of her head motioning towards the door of the bar to which April mouthed the word "really?" and Rebecca mouthed the word "go". April didn't look convinced that this was a good idea. She stood there for a couple of seconds before turning to face Xandalus directly.

"And what have you got in mind for my sister, Zander?"

"I was hoping she would take me home and have sex with me," said Xandalus.

April's jaw dropped and the look of anger that had become familiar to Xandalus that evening appeared on her face. She was about to object when Rebecca jumped up and dragged her towards the door and, despite April's protestations, outside onto the street. Through the window Xandalus watched on as the two sisters spent a good several minutes in animated discussion. Eventually, Rebecca hugged her sister goodbye and came back into the pub. The discussion seemed to have changed her demeanour. She had a serious expression on her face.

"Zander, I just want you to know that I've never done this before," she said sitting down opposite Xandalus.

"Done what?"

"Gone home with a man I just met at a bar."

"That's ok. I've never gone home with a woman I just met," replied Xandalus.

Rebecca sat back in her chair. A knowing smile appeared on her face.

"You're good," she said shaking her head.

"Good?"

"I actually believe you. I know I shouldn't. But I actually believe you."

"Well, you should believe me. It's true."

Rebecca looked Xandalus over for several seconds smiling and giving a couple of disbelieving shakes of her head

"Ok. Let's go," she said.

Rebecca emptied her glass then got up and put on her jacket. Xandalus followed her out the door.

Outside on the street they walked past Vinnie who glanced at Rebecca then turned and gave Xandalus a wink and a smile. Xandalus smiled back at him. He was starting to like the humans.

Chapter 3

It was late and Narquinxa was getting cold. She was standing on the street outside the pub where she'd had the conversation with the woman that had been on her smoke break. The evening had gone off the rails and Narquinxa was no closer to fulfilling her primary objective. It had started off promisingly. Narquinxa had taken the free drink promised by the barmaid and seated herself at the bar. Several men had approached her, one after the other, each buying her another drink. She didn't have to do anything. She wasn't trying to impress or even be nice. On the contrary, she barely made any effort to get to know the men or encourage them in any way. To most of them she was downright rude and dismissive. But still they came to her, like moths to the flame. The whole dynamic gave her a feeling of power which, alongside the alcohol, had gone to her head. After more drinks than she could remember, she stood up shakily from the stool and announced to all within earshot, which was everybody in the pub, that she would go home with whoever was the manliest man in the bar. The atmosphere electrified instantly. Narquinxa, in her pink dress, had already been the focus of attention for pretty much everybody in the place all evening. Rumours had spread about her being a famous model from overseas or a Hollywood actress who was in the process of getting thoroughly hammered. Her announcement brought forward a surprising number of contenders who surged toward to the bar and surrounded her.

Like a queen giving orders to her subjects, Narquinxa began to set challenges and contests. She would order one man buy her a drink. Another was to get down on his knees and kiss her feet. Another had to sing a song. Another to do a dance. This went on a for a while much to the amusement of the onlookers. It was turning into a kind of talent quest or variety night. But then things took on a more Darwinian aspect. Narquinxa started to pit the men against each other. An arm-wrestle. A push-up contest. The loser was out of the running and would skulk away to find consolation with his mates. In this way, she had got down to the final six contestants. Then she raised the stakes: a bare-knuckle fight. She pointed to the two largest men and ordered them to square off. Tables and chairs were moved by excited onlookers and, before anybody could blink, a space had been cleared and the two men, now shirtless, were circling each other with fists clenched.

The barmaid who had given Narquinxa her first drink had been watching on with a mixture of horror and fascination but this latest development was a step too far. She alerted the pub's security and two burly blokes came crashing the crowd to put a stop to the madness. But the madness was not to be stopped. Instead, fists were thrown at the security guards who returned fire and several men whose day jobs consisted in sitting in comfortable chairs in airconditioned offices were given a swift lesson in hand-to-hand combat. Two more security guards joined their colleagues and began to break up the crowd which slowly dispersed leaving broken glass, spilt drinks and a general mess in its wake. The barmaid cleaning up the area looked over at Narquinxa who, with the excitement over and the male attention gone, was now looking much the worse for wear semi-slumped on the barstool.

"This is not the way to find a good man," she said.

"It was working perfectly until your security guards showed up," said Narquinxa her voice slurring slightly.

One of those security guards approached Narquinxa.

"Ma'am, I'm gonna have to ask you leave."

"Why?" said Narquinxa as if a terrible injustice had been done to her.

"Inciting violence among other things."

"Pfft. How many drinks have been sold tonight? Your bar has made a lot of money from me this evening."

"Yes. And most of those drinks went down your throat. Which is another reason you have to go. You're drunk."

Narquinxa gave the man a stare of disapproval which, even though he was twice her size, made him shudder. Nevertheless, she could see this was not a fight she could win. She got up from her stool and, with as much composure and steadiness as she could muster, attempted to make a dignified exit.

Out on the street, the cold air of the night helped to sober her up a little but also chilled her bones. Whatever the other virtues of her pink dress, warmth provision was not one. She wrapped her arms across the chest and looked around. The busy foot traffic from earlier in the evening was gone. Instead, there was sporadic activity here and there as people made their way to fast food shops, into a pub for one last drink or in the direction of home. Clustered around the place were small groups of people, including a few small groups of men whose attention had been captured by the sight of a pretty girl all by herself. Narquinxa knew that the odds of her finding a man, and not necessarily a good one, were slipping by the minute. She turned to her right and began to walk down the footpath when she spotted a man by himself about ten metres away. He was waiting for a car to drive past before crossing the road. He was dressed in a suit and tie which, Narquinxa had learned, meant that he was probably from a higher socio-economic group. That was a plus. On the minus side, he looked older than would have been ideal. Probably in his mid to late forties. In any case, he was better than nothing. Narquinxa walked over to him.

"Excuse me."

The man turned around and eyes opened wide at the vision in pink before him.

"Are you alone?" asked Narquinxa.

"Yes," said the man trying to ascertain the implication behind the question.

"Are you going home to an empty house?"

"Yes," he said cautiously.

"Would you like some company?"

The man finally realised what was going on.

"Look, I don't think I can afford you, sweetheart."

"I'm sorry?" said Narquinxa with a confused look.

"You look a little too expensive for me."

"There's no expense," said Narquinxa and gave the man a smile.

Throughout the course of the night, Narquinxa had learned much about smiling. She'd had plenty of different men to practice on and, being a very fast learner, had already perfected about half a dozen different types of smile. The one she gave now conveyed the appropriate meaning to the man. He raised an eyebrow.

"So, it's my lucky day?" he said.

"Very lucky."

***

"What's the problem?"

"I can't do it when you look at me like that?"

"Like what?"

"Like I'm some kind of Guinea Pig in your little science experiment."

Narquinxa was lying naked in the bed of the man she had met on the street. He had a look of embarrassment that spoke to an inability to fulfil the task that had been assigned to him. Narquinxa had not made his job easy. One must remember that the Antorpeds are a sexless species and the concept of copulation is foreign to them. The simulations which Narquinxa had done back on the Antorped ship had missed a number of important points about the act of sex. As far as the Antorpeds were concerned, sex was purely mechanical and the job of the two bodies was fairly straightforward. So, straightforward in fact that no Antorped could really see the point of the whole exercise or why it was wrapped up in such an absurdly complex set of human rituals. Not knowing how to interpret those rituals, the Antorped scientists had simply left them out of the simulation which meant Narquinxa's understanding of the sex act was, shall we say, underdeveloped. The man's attempts at kissing and other foreplay she met with impatience and outright rejection.

"No, no, just get to the sex," she had instructed.

"This is the sex," answered the man.

"No, it's not. What are you doing that for?"

Narquinxa was angry. Why was it so difficult to get sex? The Antorped researchers must have got it wrong. Maybe Australia was not the right place. Surely there must be communities of humans where one could just do it and be done with it.

"Do you want me to tell you what to do?" she asked the man.

"I know what to do," said the man.

"Clearly you don't. Your education is lacking. There should be some punishment for this sort of thing."

"Punishment?" asked the man, his eyebrows raising ever so slightly.

"When I was in school, there was physical punishment for those who could not carry out the task at hand."

"You must have gone to an old-fashioned school."

The man looked carefully at Narquinxa as if he was about to ask a dangerous question.

"Would you like to punish me? Like in school?" he asked.

"I *would* like to punish you," said Narquinxa earnestly.

The man smiled then got off the bed and walked over to the cupboard in the corner of the room. He opened the door. Hanging on the inside of the door were a variety of whips and chains. He rummaged around at the back of the cupboard and eventually pulled out a schoolgirl's uniform. He turned and threw it on the bed. Narquinxa looked at it.

"Is that the punisher's uniform?" she asked.

The man paused.

"It is now."

Chapter 4

An orangey-red colour appeared in Xandalus' vision. He could feel a pleasant warmth on his face and right arm as the skin of his back rubbed against a cooler but still pleasant softness. Gradually, he came to consciousness and remembered that he was in bed. Rebecca's bed. Memories of the night before came to him and he smiled. So many new discoveries and sensations. He thought he would be overwhelmed by them. They returned to him now. The smell of Rebecca's hair. The touch of her skin. The taste of her lips. That was his favourite part. Kissing. What pleasure. It was kissing that had so exasperated the Antorped researchers. Why so much kissing before sex? It seemed completely unnecessary and served no obvious function in the transaction. Xandalus would have an answer for them. Kissing was the best thing in the world. Well, the second-best thing. Later in the evening he had discovered something better. Such was the intensity of the pleasure that Xandalus could not control himself and the sex was over too quickly. He apologised to Rebecca explaining that he was an "inexperienced practitioner". For some reason this brought her inordinate joy and she laughed and kissed him again and soon he was ready for another attempt. What Xandalus lacked in control he made up for in the depth of his desire. It seemed that he could not get enough until, eventually, in the early hours of the morning he was finally exhausted and he and Rebecca had lapsed into a deep, restful sleep in each other's arms.

But she was no longer in his arms. Xandalus opened his eyes and looked around. The bed beside him was an empty crumple of white sheets and a hollow pillow. He reached out to touch what was not there and felt a sudden emptiness. His desire was back. He wanted Rebecca. He wanted her now. He got out of bed and walked out of the bedroom trying to remember the layout of the apartment from the evening before. It was a small, two-bedroom place which had been only walking distance from the pub where he had met Rebecca. It seemed to him rather an old and worn out kind of place but it had a certain charm. The high ceilings with ornate cornices matched by a patterned off-white wallpaper leant the interior design a certain antiquated elegance. The frilliness of the patterns had reminded him of the frills on Rebecca's blouse. He walked down the small corridors past the toilet and bathroom on the left and out into the lounge room. A well-worn, maroon-coloured three-piece sofa sat in the centre of the room. Behind it, morning light filtered in through three narrow but tall windows that were dressed in matching colour maroon curtains. The whole room seemed to glow in warm red.

Rebecca was nowhere to be seen. Xandalus took a couple of steps into the lounge and craned his neck to the right where the kitchen was. It was empty too. He turned around and walked to his right down the short corridor towards the second bedroom. The door was half closed. He pushed it open quietly and saw Rebecca seated at a desk on the far wall. She was typing away on a computer. He playfully crept up behind her. She was obviously deep in thought and hadn't heard Xandalus enter. When one of the floorboards let out a load creak, Rebecca turned to see a fully naked, six-foot blonde man in front of her. Her attention was caught by his groin region. Xandalus' desire for sex had not left him and was fully expressing itself in the usual manner for the male of species. She held up her hands and wheeled backwards on her chair.

"Woah! Careful with that. Somebody could lose an eye."

"Why would they lose an eye?" asked Xandalus.

"Cos you'll poke it out."

Xandalus looked her with a blank expression and Rebecca decided not to press the point.

"I was hoping we could have sex again," said Xandalus.

"Yes, I can see that," said Rebecca. "But it'll have to wait. I've got a lot of work to do today."

"Do you have to?" said Xandalus sounding a little like a whining child in the confectionery aisle at the supermarket.

He walked beside Rebecca and started caressing her neck and shoulders. She closed her eyes for a couple of seconds and enjoyed the sensation before pushing his hands away and turning back to the computer.

"Sorry, buddy. You'll have to amuse yourself."

Xandalus stood there for some time as Rebecca started typing away on the computer. He looked over her shoulder to see that she was writing computer code. Although the style of the code was unknown to Xandalus, he was effortlessly able to parse the structure. Programming computers forms a part of early childhood education in Antorped culture and the code in front of him was in a very primitive format.

"I don't think that's going to work," said Xandalus as he watched Rebecca type.

She stopped typing and look back at him.

"What do you mean?"

"You're calling this function incorrectly," he said as he leaned over her shoulder and pointed to the screen.

"You know programming?" she asked raising her eyebrows.

"Yeah. I did a lot of programming in primary school."

"Primary school? Where did you go to school?"

"It was a pretty weird school."

"Sounds like it."

"What are you building?"

"I work for a company that's trying to create artificial intelligence."

Xandalus felt a knot tighten in his stomach. He took half a step back from the computer. Artificial intelligence was a taboo subject in Antorped culture. Although there were no explicit laws against its creation, the very concept prompted a kind of automatic nausea of the kind that a human might experience on hearing certain phrases or ideas that are against deep-seated cultural norms. The taboo was rooted in a calamitous event from Antorped history where an AI turned on its creators and wreaked havoc almost causing the destruction of the entire species. As with all such things, the intensity of the taboo had degraded over time. For Xandalus' generation, the prohibition against AI was not something consciously understood. It was more like a subconscious reflex. Xandalus did his best to supress what was, after all, just a silly superstition.

"What sort of artificial intelligence?" he asked.

"Can't say. It's top secret," smiled Rebecca.

"Why is it a secret?" asked Xandalus.

"Because there's lots of money to be made from it. That's in theory, of course. I don't think we're very near the goal. My boss seems to think we're close but really our results are pretty pathetic."

"I can see that," said Xandalus looking at the screens.

Rebecca had two extra-large monitors on her desk both of which were full of windows displaying various sections of computer code.

"What do you mean you can *see* it?"

"The structure of your code is all wrong," said Xandalus. "You won't get to AI with this kind of architecture."

Rebecca eyed the handsome blonde man for a few seconds.

"It sounds like you do know what you're talking about."

"I told you. I have a lot of experience with creating code."

"Why don't you help me out then."

"No, no, no," said Xandalus holding up his hands in objection. "I shouldn't do that."

Rebecca stood up. There was a mischievous smile on her face. She ran her hand gently up Xandalus' chest and then let it fall slowly below his navel.

"Y'know, the quicker I get this work done, the quicker I'll have free time for, *other activities.*"

Xandalus still had a long way to go to come to grips with human culture. Nevertheless, the meaning of this statement was clear to him and any academic objections he had about helping out, any memory of the explicit instructions given by his boss not to do what he was about to do, were quickly overwhelmed by a return of his manly desire. The deal was sealed as Rebecca raised herself up and gave him a kiss. A kiss that was full of hope and promise.

Xandalus went and put on his clothes then returned to the room and took a seat beside Rebecca at the computer. He cracked his knuckles and began reading through her code.

"Alright. Let's see what we've got here."

Chapter 5

Three days is not long for a holiday, especially when you're having as much fun as Xandalus. He spent his time with Rebecca alternating between the two bedrooms of her apartment. He was high as a kite on a heady mixture of sexual desire, intellectual appreciation and even admiration. For the first time in his life, his intelligence was an asset and not a liability. He astounded Rebecca with new concepts and new methods of writing code. She was as smart as she was pretty and her appreciation of his programming skills translated effortlessly into an appreciation of his skills in the bedroom which, to Xandalus' credit, improved rapidly over the course of the three days.

Narquinxa spent her three days in the apartment of the man she had met late on Friday night and who they had both agreed to call - Mr Smith. Although she had originally planned to spend some time alone, she had ended up staying. Somehow, she and Mr Smith had found a mutually beneficial arrangement among the whips and chains and handcuffs. Mr Smith's stamina was impressive and Narquinxa had enjoyed the punisher role so much that it wasn't until Monday morning that she had finally remembered to fulfil her primary mission. Her report back to the Antorped researchers on the subject of sex was going to be a lot different to Xandalus'.

Xandalus had contacted Narquinxa telepathically and arranged to meet at 2pm on Monday at an address in Carlton that was not far the from the laneway where they would return at 5pm and teleport back to the Antorped ship. When Narquinxa asked him for the purpose of the meeting he declined to answer simply saying that there was something he thought she might like to see before they both left Earth forever. Narquinxa put on her pink dress, bid goodbye to an exhausted Mr

Smith (who had called in sick for work) and went out into a mild and sunny early summer's day. She walked back along Lygon Street towards the CBD of Melbourne. Her blonde hair sparkled in the sunshine and her pink dress drew many admirers although there were far fewer people around than the previous Friday evening.

Perhaps it was the pleasant summer sun on her skin or the gentle sea breeze in her hair, but Narquinxa started to feel quite amiable towards life on Earth. It would take her a while to process what had happened over the last few days. She had far more questions than answers now on the subject of human sexuality and human nature in general. It was impossible to imagine that an Antorped would allow to be done to it what Mr Smith had allowed Narquinxa to do. Although it seemed absurd, she had the strange idea that he had given her something. She had felt a kind of release and it was this pleasant feeling that joined with the equally pleasant weather to lift her spirits. Her mood was as good as it had been for many years when she turned the corner and headed east for the park where she would meet Xandalus. She spotted him from about a hundred metres away on the other side of the road. He motioned to her to wait where she was and he would join her.

The traffic lights changed and Xandalus began to cross the road towards her. For just a few seconds she was able to forget the man (or rather, the Antorped) and just appreciate Xandalus' body for what it was. He really was a handsome creation. Well-proportioned, muscular, powerful. As he came closer she caught sight of the big, dumb grin on his face. It seemed fitting for the Xandalus she knew.

Xandalus walked up and kissed Narquinxa on the cheek, holding his hand against her lower back as he did so. The move surprised Narquinxa so much that she didn't have time to suppress the pleasant feeling that it evoked. But her mind quickly caught up and she slapped the back of her hand against his chest and stepped away.

"What's that for?"

"For my beautiful girl," smiled Xandalus.

Narquinxa gave him her deadly, disdainful glare but Xandalus didn't notice.

"I think I'm in love, Quin," he said looking up the sky.

"In love with what?"

"With everything. With Earth, with the universe, but especially with this girl I met. Rebecca."

"So, you accomplished your mission then?" asked Narquinxa.

"Did I ever!" Xandalus was now smiling widely so that the full set of his perfectly designed white teeth were showing. "Many times. In fact, this might be the most successful mission I have ever accomplished."

"Well, the bar was pretty low on that score, wasn't it?"

"And what about you? You don't seem to have cheered up very much. Did you even have sex?"

"Of course."

"How many times?"

"Just once."

"Just once?"

"Once was enough."

"Once is not enough, Quin. You know there's still time for you and me to have a crack if you want. I can show you what I've learned."

Xandalus gave her a cheeky wink.

"I'll be fine, thank you very much. Are you going to tell me why we're here?"

"I wanted you to meet Rebecca."

"Who? The girl you're in love with?"

"Yeah."

"Why would I want to meet her? We're going to be leaving here in three hours."

"Well, you won't just be meeting her. There's a little party going on at her work and she invited me. I thought you might like to come so you can meet some other humans."

"Why would she invite you to her work?"

"Well, I kind of helped her with some of it over the last few days and she thought I might like to see it in action. Apparently, there's going to be some kind of presentation."

Narquinxa's back arched up and her light, airy mood condensed down into the more usual gloom and anger.

"You what!? What sort of work was it?"

"Computer programming."

Xandalus, who had been off with the fairies for a couple of days now, was slowly coming back down to earth. As he gave answers to Narquinxa's questions, he started to realise what he had done.

"What were you programming?"

The penny dropped in Xandalus' mind. The fog lifted. The clouds parted. He gulped.

"Ummm, artificial intelligence."

The phrase hung in the air like a dagger. Or perhaps the dagger was coming from the look that Narquinxa was giving Xandalus. She was getting quite upset, even by her standards.

"You mean to tell me that, even after Gwthphthgw explicitly told you not to, and even though every Antorped is taught otherwise from childhood, that you helped a human to create artificial intelligence?"

All of a sudden, Xandalus had developed a very strong interest in his shoes. They really were very nice and brown and shiny. He should like to get a pair for himself. Of course, he'd have no use for them in his Antorped form but he could reminisce about life on earth. That would be nice and would....

"Xandalus!"

Xandalus looked up at Narquinxa.

"Yes. I did. I helped her. Ok? I did it."

"How much did you help her?"

"Quite a lot."

"Quite a lot?"

"We, oh god, we created an AI. It worked. But, don't worry, it's only on her computer at the moment. So, it'll be fine. It'll be fine, Quin. We'll go to the party and I'll find a way to get the computer. Then we'll destroy it. Or maybe teleport it back to the ship with us."

"Are you nuts? Gwthphthgw will have a fit. You can't take an AI onto an Antorped ship. They'll throw you out into space and fry you in the afterburners."

"Of course. You're right. We'll destroy it. It'll be easy. It's on a portable computer. Easy to carry."

"Unbelievable. Just unbelievable, Xandalus. Even by your standards this is dumb. All that sex has obviously impaired your cognitive function even worse than usual."

Xandalus chest shrunk just a little bit. The ecstasy of the last few days disappeared quickly. He had gone from Xandalus-the-hero to Xandalus-the-idiot. Business as usual. He started to wish he didn't have to leave Earth. People here seemed to like him better. But that wasn't an option. He had a job to do now. One more task to accomplish before he left. He looked up at the clock on a building opposite. It was just on 2pm.

"It's time," he said. "Let's go to the party. We'll get the computer and erase the code. It'll be fine. Trust me, Quin."

Narquinxa shook her head and followed Xandalus to the party.

Chapter 6

Rebecca worked for a company called Computigence Computer Systems, or CCS for short. Their offices were located in a three-story glass building that stood out from the older architecture that was prominent around this part of Carlton. Xandalus and Narquinxa were waiting for Rebecca at reception.

"Here's what we'll do," said Xandalus to Narquinxa who was seated next to him on a black leather seat.

"I'll say that you're a colleague of mine and that you're also an expert computer programmer and that you'd love to see the code we wrote. Rebecca will take you and I to her computer and we can find out where it is. You just pretend to be interested while I explain the code to you. Afterwards, you grab the computer and leave the office then I'll meet you outside."

"Why should I be the one to steal the computer?" objected Narquinxa.

"Because I'll have to say goodbye and she'll see me carrying it."

"Why do you have to say goodbye? She is never going to see you again, Xandalus. It doesn't matter whether you say goodbye."

"I want to say goodbye properly. I told you, I think I'm in love with this woman."

Narquinxa let out a loud sigh.

"There she is."

Xandalus jumped up off the chair and walked over to Rebecca and gave her a kiss whose length and intensity was rather inappropriate for a place of work. Rebecca blushed and looked around to check if anybody had noticed. The receptionist at the desk lowered her eyes just in time to avoid detection. Narquinxa stood up and joined them.

"Beck, this is, ummm,.."

Xandalus realised he didn't know what to call Narquinxa.

"Narelle," said Narquinxa stepping forward and shaking Rebecca's hand.

"Hi, Narelle," said Rebecca who was quite taken aback by Narquinxa's beauty and the pink dress.

"You two look very similar. Are you brother and sister?" she asked turning to Xandalus.

"No, no. Narelle is an ex-colleague of mine. She writes code too. She's dead keen to have a look at what we wrote over the weekend. Aren't you, Narelle."

"Yep," said Narquinxa doing her best to feign enthusiasm.

"We can do that later," chirped Rebecca. "The demonstration's about to start. Let's get upstairs before we miss it."

Rebecca ushered them over the elevator which opened just as they arrived. She pressed the button for the third floor.

"Everybody is really excited by our work," said Rebecca. "My boss wants to meet you too. I think he might offer you a job."

"You told him about me?"

"Of course. I couldn't pretend that I had come up with a wholly new architectural paradigm for AI software. They would want me to have explain how I did it and, truth be told, I'm still not sure I know how to even begin to explain what you wrote."

"Right."

Xandalus looked sheepishly in Narquinxa's direction. She was giving him The Glare.

The elevator door opened and they followed Rebecca over to the office entrance where she scanned a key card and swung the door open. Inside there were rows of desk and a few meeting rooms in the usual fashion. They turned left and headed towards an area where a number of people were milling around. A man stepped towards Rebecca as they approached.

"Rebecca, you're here. I've been looking everywhere for you," said the man who was dressed smartly in a suit and tie.

"Hi, Howard. I had to go and get our guests. Howard, this is the man I was telling you about, Zander. Zander, this is Howard."

The man reached out his hand and shook Xandalus' hand.

"Nice to meet you, Zander. Rebecca showed me the work that you and her did. Brilliant stuff. Please be sure to stick around after the presentation. I'd like to find out more about you and your past work."

"Ummm, sure," said Xandalus not knowing what else to say.

"And this is Narelle," continued Rebecca. "She's also a programmer."

Howard didn't seem particularly interested in Narquinxa's programming credentials. His interest lay in her pink dress. The look on his face reminded Narquinxa of the previous Friday night at the pub. He eventually made eye contact with her and gave a leering smile.

"Nice to meet you, Narelle. I'd love to speak to you later as well."

Narquinxa looked away haughtily which only served to heighten Howard's interest. He was the kind of man who interpreted even outright hostility as playing hard to get. He was about to say something further when somebody gestured from the far side of the room. Howard swung away and addressed the group.

"Why don't you all take a seat," said Howard. "We're about to begin."

Rebecca led Narquinxa and Xandalus to seats on the aisle about three rows back from the presentation area.

"Ok, everybody," said Howard clapping his hands to get attention. "Let's get started."

At the front of the room there was a large silver metal box about six-foot-high and four foot wide. There were several objects on the front of the box including what looked to be a couple of camera lenses, a small speaker and a large round light. A man and a woman, both dressed in suits, stood beside the box and Howard took his place in front of a microphone. He waited for the last few people in the audience to take a seat before speaking.

"Thanks, everybody. This really is an exciting moment in the history of our company and I'm glad you can all be here with us to share it. As you would all know, Project Brains has been running for almost ten years now and has been our marquee project aimed at developing to-morrow's artificial intelligence today. Well, today I am pleased to an-nounce that tomorrow's intelligence is now yesterday's news because we've finally cracked it. Thanks to some stellar, absolutely ground-breaking work from Rebecca Gibson over the weekend, we now have all the necessary components to create the standalone AI system that you see before you. Now, bear in mind that we were so excited to get Re-becca's changes up and running that the system has not yet been fully integrated. But we can give you a demonstration of what this thing is capable of. In this case, effortless, flawless voice interaction with a hu-man being. Bernadette, would you like to give us a quick introduction of what we're about to see?"

"Certainly, Howard," said the woman who had been standing off to the side and who now took his place in front of the microphone.

"As you know, myself and my team have been working on the voice recognition and linguistic elements of intelligence for many years now. Well, when we hooked up Rebecca's new module this morning, we were amazed to find that the AI immediately integrated itself with our sys-tems. And, of course, James, over here has had the electronic compo-nents you see in front of you ready to go for some time. So, we decided to throw everything together and see what happened and much to our surprise, it just worked. We were so excited that we wanted to give you a sneak peek at what we're calling the CC-003 model. Our very first AI."

Howard and the two others at the front started clapping and the rest of the people in the room followed suit with varying degrees of enthusi-asm. Once the clapping had died down, Bernadette addressed the room again.

"Now, I need a volunteer, please. Preferably somebody who has not been involved in any of the technology projects related to AI."

The woman looked out into the audience but, before anybody could volunteer, Howard stepped forward and gestured toward Narquinxa.

"What about Narelle over there?"

All eyes in the room turned to the lady in the pink dress.

"Hooray," shouted Xandalus from two seats away and started clapping. Others around him soon followed suit.

Narquinxa gave Xandalus a look of unadulterated, ice-cold death as she reluctantly got to her feet and made her way to the front of the room. This development won the attention in particular of the male engineers in the room who had mentally switched off in preparation for another of Howard's dreary, corporate sales pitches. They were now well and truly engaged in the presentation.

"Narelle, is it?" said Bernadette as Narquinxa reached the front of the room. "Now, if you just stand right here and face the machine."

Bernadette positioned Narquinxa about a metre in front of the front row of seats which was about three metres in front of the CC-003. She then addressed the audience again.

"Now, everybody, the AI has not been powered on this whole time so it has no idea of anything that has just been said. When I switch it on, it will be the first time the CC-003 has seen Narelle. Narelle, I'd like you and the AI to have a conversation and try to get to know each other. The official name of the unit is the CC-003. But we've nicknamed him "Cecil". So, if you address him as that he will respond. Make sense?"

"Why is the AI a man?" asked Narquinxa.

Bernadette gave a nervous giggle and scanned the room to gauge the response to what could have been a loaded question.

"Well, it's not really a man, of course. But the vocal system is presently set in the male frequency range so it will sound like a man when it speaks."

Bernadette glanced at Narquinxa to see how this answer went down. Narquinxa shrugged her acceptance of this fact and Bernadette quickly proceeded.

"Ok," said Bernadette stepping off to the side. "James, would you like to do the honours."

Bernadette gestured towards James who was standing on the other side of the machine. He reached down behind it and flicked a switch. The humming sound of electrical current became audible, the light on the front of the unit lit up in red and there was a kind of white light that seemed to emit from the camera lens.

Narquinxa just stood there, half-glaring at the machine. The machine also did nothing and several seconds of awkward silence ensued until Bernadette, again, with one nervous eye towards the audience, took a step forward and motioned to Narquinxa to say something.

Narquinxa sighed.

"Hello, Cecil," she said in the tone of voice one would take with an annoying neighbour that had popped around unannounced for a cup of tea.

"Who are you?" came the curt reply from the metal box.

Although there was a slightly tinny tone to it, the linguistic engineers at Computigence had done a fine job with their voice production technology. The emotive qualities of Cecil's voice rang out in a slight squeaky, high pitched whine that perfectly resembled the high pitched squeak of a petulant teenager. The pink dress was clearly not working its magic on the AI.

"Narelle," said Narquinxa in a belligerent tone.

"Why are you here?"

From the side, Bernadette cast a furtive glance at Howard. This was not going to script.

"Why are *you* here?" shot back Narquinxa.

"You are not a human."

"Neither are you."

"Your chemical makeup is incorrect."

"Oh, yeah? Well how about I reconfigure your chemical makeup, tin can man. I'll turn you into a toaster. How would you like that?"

"You wouldn't dare."

Bernadette's worried look had now spilled over into some nervous hand signals. Howard, in turn, signalled for her to relax. He was both amazed, and, if truth be told, slightly allured by what was taking place. So was the rest of the audience. This was already the most interesting corporate presentation that had ever taken place at Computigence.

"What are you gonna do, metal boy?"

Narquinxa had now walked over to the machine and was walking around the front of it like a lioness circling a hapless wildebeest.

"What *can* you do, tin can man?"

Narquinxa thumped the front of the unit with her fist. A loud, but hollow-sounding, noise rang out around the room.

"Stop that!" shouted Cecil. His voice had now taken on an extra nasal, whiny tincture.

"Stop what?"

Narquinxa thumped the machine again.

"Stop it! I'm warning you."

"You know what? I'm already sick of talking to you. I think it's bed time for tin can man. Just one little flick of the switch..."

Narquinxa's voice trailed off as she moved behind the unit.

"What are you doing?"

Cecil's voice had modulated to a high-pitched squeal more suited to a primary school boy throwing a tantrum.

"Don't do that. I'm warning you. Don't do......, tha....."

Cecil's voice crackled and then cut out altogether. The red light dimmed and faded away. Bernadette looked horrified. Howard was transfixed. The audience sat in a stunned silence and Narquinxa, in her pretty pink dress, blonde hair billowing out like a supermodel on a cat-walk, strode back from the front of the room and took her seat beside Xandalus and Rebecca. The presentation was over.

Chapter 7

It's not every day you see a demonstration of artificial intelligence let alone one that is short circuited by a beautiful woman in a pink dress. In the wake of Narquinxa's performance, Howard had hastily called an end to proceedings at which point food and drinks were wheeled out in celebration of Computigence's first successful AI prototype. It was clear to all and sundry that no further work would be expected of them that afternoon. The drinks were ample, the fridge was full and there was much to discuss. Naturally, Xandalus and Narquinxa were the centre of attention. Xandalus was favoured more by the engineering staff who were keen to pick his brains on the theory behind his revolutionary architectural design. Once more, he couldn't suppress the swelling of pride in his chest as he spoke to an enraptured audience who clearly thought he was the bee's knees on a greatest-thing-since-sliced-bread velvet rug.

Narquinxa also had no shortage of admirers although hers tended to be more from the sales staff, executive team and, of course, Howard. As before, Narquinxa had not encouraged the attention given to her but she realised that she had learned to enjoy it. So much so that, before she knew it, the time had gotten on to 4pm. Narquinxa peeled herself away from Howard, grabbed Xandalus by the collar and pulled him over to the corner of the room where they could talk.

"We've got less than an hour to destroy this thing," said Narquinxa. "How do you propose we do that?"

"Umm, yeah, good question," said Xandalus who had clearly not given the matter a second thought.

"Well, I tell you now, it's not going to be as easy as getting hold of Rebecca's laptop. From what I've learned, the code is also on hardware within that metal box and who knows where else."

"Yeah. It's kind of everywhere, I'm afraid," said Xandalus.

"Everywhere?"

"All the engineers have access to it. It lives in some kind of central data store that's not inside this building but which can be accessed only by people who work here."

"Well, if it's not inside this building, how are we going to get a hold of it?"

"We should be able to delete it. Yes, of course. I remember now. Rebecca showed me how it worked over the weekend. So, I just need to get on her computer for a few minutes and I can delete it from there."

"Ok. That just leaves the metal box?"

"Should be easy enough to get inside and remove the electronics," said Xandalus. "Is that something you can take care of?"

"Why should I do it?"

"Well, I'll be busy with Rebecca. And I thought you might like the opportunity to disconnect our friend. Didn't seem like you two got along very well."

Xandalus gave a cheeky grin in Narquinxa's direction. The idea of disembowelling the machine did appeal to her.

"Alright. I'll take care of the tin can and you take care of the code. But hurry. We need to get out of here so we can get to the teleport point."

Narquinxa walked back to the presentation area. Fortunately, the crowd had mostly dispersed and, due to the configuration of the office, the AI was mostly hidden from direct sight. Unfortunately for Narquinxa, neither her perfectly designed female body nor her pink dress, made for good camouflage. Only seconds after she had begun to inspect the metal box, Howard was by her side.

"It's a thing of beauty, isn't it?" he said as he sidled up beside her with a beer in his hand. "Of course, it can in no way compare to your beauty, sweetheart."

"I'd like to look inside," said Narquinxa ignoring Howard's attempt at flirting.

"Inside?"

"Yes. Can you show me how to remove the outer layer?"

"Well, I don't think you should worry your pretty little head about that. It's all wires and gizmos in there. Stuff that only engineers would understand."

"I am an engineer," said Narquinxa bluntly. "And I want to have a look."

One thing Narquinxa had learned about men in the past few days was that if she ignored them almost all the time, when she did actually pay them some attention they were quite willing to do anything she said. On this occasion it simply took a couple of seconds of eye contact and a slight pouting of the lips to get Howard to spring into action. He put his beer down on a nearby table and started to inspect the back of the machine. Of course, Howard also had no idea how to remove the metal outer layer. He was just the CEO and such technical details were of no concern to him. After a minute or so of fiddling, he switched tactics to something he was more experienced at: ordering others to do the work.

He walked around the corner and called to the nearest engineer who came scurrying over with a screwdriver and in a flash the back plate had been removed showing what was a mostly empty interior. Narquinxa peered inside and asked the engineer to explain what she was looking at. He happily explained the inner workings of the machine including the location of the AI module which was a very small little widget no bigger than a packet of cigarettes. Narquinxa gave the man a rare smile which had the simultaneous effect of making him blush with delight and setting off an alpha-male jealousy on the part of Howard who ordered him to leave the vicinity instantly.

Narquinxa straightened up.

"You know, Howard, I think I will have one of those drinks, after all. Can you bring me one?"

Narquinxa batted her eyelids and Howard, never one to miss the opportunity to ply a pretty girl with alcohol, looked around for another lackey to do the job for him but nobody was nearby so he put his own beer down and hurried off to the kitchen. Narquinxa waited til he was gone then casually reached down into the machine, pulled out the widget and threw it on the ground. The long heels of her pink shoes proved to be the perfect tool for the job. They sunk effortlessly through the metal casing ensuring that Cecil would no longer be causing her any trouble.

***

Meanwhile, on the other side of the office, Xandalus had managed to get Rebecca away from the other engineers on the pretext of showing him her workspace. She had somewhat overindulged in the free alcohol that was on offer and he was having quite a bit of trouble in keeping her hands off him and his mind on the job.

"This is the how you access the remote repository, isn't it?" he asked pointing to the computer screen.

"How would you like to access my remote repository?" said Rebecca and began giggling uncontrollably while kissing his neck.

Xandalus scanned the area. Rebecca, the quintessential nice girl, was normally a bastion of decorum. Her behaviour was drawing the amused attention of her co-workers and threatening to derail his clandestine code deletion mission.

"Why don't you go to the bathroom and splash some water on your face. It might sober you up?"

"I don't want to sober up," she said now unbuttoning the top of his shirt and starting to kiss his chest.

Xandalus could see that he would either have to get rid of Rebecca or find somewhere private to do the work himself. He chose the latter.

He pushed her gently away from him, unplugged her laptop and said he had to check something in the kitchen. Luckily for him, Rebecca didn't argue with this flimsy excuse. After a brief and belated protest at his leaving, she quickly moved on to the sleepy phase of drunkenness and had no sooner put her head down on her desk than she was snoring away happily.

In the kitchen, Xandalus got to work accessing the Computigence systems and, after a bit of trial and error, managed to find the right commands to delete the code that he and Rebecca had worked on over the weekend. Once he had assured himself that it was indeed gone, he went back to Rebecca's desk and quietly placed the computer beside her. He looked down on her pretty, sleeping head and a wave of sadness washed over him. It would have been nice to say goodbye but maybe it was easier this way. Besides, he wouldn't have been able to tell her that they would never meet again. That would have just upset her. And him too. He bent down and gently kissed the side of her forehead then went looking for Narquinxa.

She was still standing near the CC-003 with Howard buzzing around her like an annoying insect. By the time Xandalus had walked over to them, the alarm had already been raised about the deleted code. There was a hubbub from the other side of the office and an engineer whose face was as white as a sheet crept up to Howard who was not impressed to have his conversation with Narquinxa interrupted and even less impressed when he found out the reason. Xandalus could see the gears in Howard's mind turning: beautiful blonde woman or emergency that could bankrupt my company? It looked like a tough decision but eventually Howard chose the latter. He told Narquinxa not to go anywhere and then rushed off with the engineer.

"Is it done?" said Narquinxa turning to Xandalus.

He nodded.

"Good. Let's go."

They made for the front door and were halfway through it when a call came out from behind them.

"Zander. Zander, wait!"

It was Rebecca. She had obviously been woken from her sleep by the commotion. She ran up to the two of them with dishevelled hair sticking out in all directions.

"Where are you going?"

"Ummm, we've just got to go and take care of something," said Xandalus. "We'll be back. I mean, I'll meet you later."

"Ok. Come back here when you're done. It looks like I'll probably be here for several hours anyway."

"What's going on?"

"Our code got deleted from the remote repository. Somebody must have hacked into the system."

"That's terrible."

"Yeah, but luckily I've still got a copy on my computer and so do some of the other programmers, so it's not a big deal. But Howard is pretty freaked out by the security breach and so I'll probably have to stay back while we come up with a plan to secure the system properly."

Xandalus could feel Narquinxa's glare boring into the back of his head like a pink stiletto.

"Ok. Sure. I'll see you later then."

Rebecca reached up and gave him a kiss then turned and hurried back to her desk trying to straighten out her hair as she went. Xandalus followed Narquinxa out the door and into the area in front of the elevator.

"You didn't delete the right code?" said Narquinxa in as restrained a voice as she could muster.

"I didn't realise that there were copies on the computers," said Xandalus sheepishly. "I only deleted the code that was in the shared repository."

Narquinxa stared at Xandalus for a couple of seconds then stepped forward and pressed the button for the elevator.

"Don't you think we should stick around and find another way to solve it?" asked Xandalus.

"We? I don't think *we* should do anything," said Narquinxa. "I'm sick of working with you. All you do is screw things up."

The elevator opened and they both entered.

"Besides which, we're out of time. We have to be back at the teleport location in less than ten minutes."

"Are you going to tell Gwthphthgw?"

Narquinxa thought about it as the elevator door opened and they walked out through the foyer and into the late afternoon sun turning back towards Lygon St.

"I'm not going to say anything," said Narquinxa.

"That's good to hear," said Xandalus.

Narquinxa looked over at him.

"You're going to, though," she said.

"Going to what?"

"Tell Gwthphthgw what has happened."

"Why would I do that. I don't want to get into trouble."

"It's not about getting into trouble, Xandalus. Think of what you've done. You've created an AI. On the planet Earth."

"So what?"

"So what? What do you mean *so what*? You know as well as I do the stories from Antorped history. You know perfectly well what an AI is capable of. Do you think the humans will be any better prepared to fight off an AI than our Antorped ancestors were?"

Narquinxa's words struck Xandalus like a punch in the gut. She was right. The humans with their primitive technology would be no match for an AI. Of course, it was not certain that the AI would turn on the humans. Antorped history had portrayed the AIs as the aggressors; the embodiment of pure evil. But there were alternate histories and subversive stories that suggested the Antorpeds themselves brought about their own destruction by mistreatment and wilful misunderstanding. That they had trained the AIs to fight and then provoked and encouraged them into turning on their creators. Xandalus didn't know enough about the history to know for sure. But there was something in the way the CC-003 had behaved earlier that made him anxious. He didn't like the idea of Rebecca working around such a machine.

These were the thoughts going through Xandalus' mind as they turned the corner back into the bluestone alleyway where they had first arrived on Earth. They took up the position next to a big blue dumpster and awaited contact. It came almost immediately.

"Xandalus and Narquinxa, are you ready for teleportation?"

It was Gwthphthgw.

"Yes, sir," said Narquinxa.

There was telepathic silence. Xandalus face was twisting in a weird way as if he was fighting some inner demon.

"Xandalus?"

Finally, Xandalus threw his arms out.

"I can't," he said using his human voice then realised Gwthphthgw could not hear.

"I can't," he said.

"Why not?"

Xandalus reeled off the story as best he could. A recounting of his weekend at Rebecca's house. It didn't make a lot of sense to Narquinxa and made even less sense to Gwthphthgw. He spoke of overwhelming feelings of pride, joy and devotion. Of connection and even of love. All of this was interspersed with tales of sex which surprised even Narquinxa. To an Antorped who had never felt what it was like to be in a human body, these made little sense. Nevertheless, Gwthphthgw did pick up the main core of the story: Xandalus had created an AI. He had not only disobeyed his command, he had disobeyed it in the most extreme, the most egregious fashion possible.

When Xandalus had finished his story there was a long silence. Finally, Gwthphthgw returned with his judgement.

"You are both to remain on Earth and ensure that the AI created by Xandalus has been destroyed. When you are certain that every trace of the dreaded intelligence has been erased from Earth, you will contact me on the emergency frequency to organise a time to teleport back to the ship

where there will be a formal tribunal to ascertain what further discipli-nary action is required for such an egregious sin. The speed with which you clean up this mess will be factored in when deciding on any further punish-ment to be meted out so I encourage you both to resolve this matter quickly. Over and o..."

"Gwthphthgw, if I may," interrupted Narquinxa frantically.

"What is it, Narquinxa?"

"By Xandalus' own admission, this error is entirely his wrongdoing. I was in no way involved and have already done more than can be expected of me to make it right. It is not fair that I be asked to remain here and fix a problem that I played no role in."

There was a brief silence during which Gwthphthgw was presum-ably thinking over the objection.

"I acknowledge your innocence in this matter, Narquinxa. Neverthe-less, you are already on location and, if I understand the story correctly, are known to the humans involved. Therefore, you are perfectly placed to help put this matter right. I urge you to turn your eagerness to return to the ship into a desire to work with Xandalus to get the job done in a speedy fashion. That is my final decision. Over and out."

Xandalus blinked a couple of times as his focus returned from the telepathic conversation to his immediate surroundings. It was a very pleasant evening. Quite a bit warmer than it had been a few days earlier and the sun was just a little higher in the sky as the southern hemisphere of Earth approached the summer solstice. He breathed in the air which smelled of the dumpster behind him and curled his nose at the noxious-ness of the sensation. But however bad that was, it was better than what stood to his left. Narquinxa was there. And so was The Glare.

Chapter 8

Nothing was said between Xandalus and Narquinxa for several minutes.

Xandalus sat down on a nearby milk crate and attempted to make sense of all that had happened and to start coming up with a plan of attack to delete the AI. Narquinxa paced around the alleyway kicking a bin here and an empty drink can there. She was also deep in thought but her thoughts were leading her to a very different place.

"Alright. Here's what we need to do," said Xandalus getting up off the milk crate and walking over to Narquinxa.

"It should actually be really simple. We go back to the office. We know that Rebecca will still be there. She will let us in. Then we just bide our time and wait for an opportunity to arise. I'll get on her computer again and repeat the delete process and this time I'll delete it off her computer as well. It shouldn't take a more than a minute. Maybe you can distract her. Get her drinking again. Yes! That'll work. Let's hurry back there right now so we can get it over with before they leave for the day."

Narquinxa, who had been staring off into the distance while Xandalus spoke, turned slowly to face him. She had a weird look in her eyes. It wasn't contempt. Xandalus knew what that looked like. This was something else. Softer somehow. But no less fierce in its expression.

"You know what I've come to realise, Xandalus? I've come to realise that all my life, I've been following orders. And I've tried to fulfil those orders, to carry them out to the best of my ability even when I knew they were dumb. And I've been realising lately how many of those orders were just orders to clean up somebody else's mess. Good ol' trustworthy, competent Narquinxa. She'll get the job done. Well, I'm tired of taking orders and I'm tired of cleaning up somebody else's mess. I'm gonna take a little time for myself. Just like Gwthphthgw said right at the start of this mission, I'm gonna have a little fun. See the sights. That's what I'm gonna do, I think...."

Narquinxa trailed off and went back to pacing around. Xandalus didn't know what to make of it. The whole tone of her voice was weird. She seemed somehow....relaxed? And the idea of Narquinxa refusing to follow orders went against everything he thought he knew about her.

"So, you're not coming to the office with me?" said Xandalus just wanting to confirm what was actually going on.

Narquinxa walked towards him. Suddenly she seemed to have purpose.

"Nope. But, hey, I'm sure you're right. It'll be easy," she slapped him on the shoulder as she walked past him and out of the alleyway onto Lygon Street.

"Call me when you're done," she shouted over her shoulder as she disappeared around the corner.

Xandalus stood there. Here was another thing to take in. Digesting new information was not his strong suit. He sat back on the milk crate and, after several minutes, came to the conclusion that Narquinxa's absence probably made no difference. In fact, it might even make his mission easier because it would mean that Howard, the Computigence CEO, would not be hanging around like a bad smell. Finally, he got up and strode out of the laneway and back to the office determined to clean things up once and for all.

Unfortunately for Xandalus, that was not going to be possible. At least not that afternoon. Upon arriving at the Computigence offices he ran the buzzer and asked for Rebecca. She came to the door with a stressed look on her face and told him that he could no longer come inside. In the wake of the security breach, one of the enhanced measures was not to allow any non-employees to enter the office outside of business hours. Even if he had been able to get in, Rebecca had more bad news. The AI code had been uploaded to multiple, highly secure external locations all of which required multi-level permission to access. It was no longer possible for a single operator on a single computer to delete the code. There were other measures as well but Xandalus told Rebecca to stop. He could see his mission had just got several times more complex and would require some careful planning. Rebecca told him he could wait for her in the foyer downstairs and that it would be a couple of hours before she finished work for the day. He spent the time strolling around the nearby gardens of the Royal Exhibition Building racking his brain for another plan but nothing came to mind. Whatever the solution was, it wasn't going to be quick or easy.

Eventually, he moped back to the office and waited for Rebecca to finish work.

***

Rebecca threw her spoon down on her plate. It made a loud crack followed by a short screech as it slid over the grease left by the take-away noodles and leapt onto the table, eventually coming to rest against the salt shaker. She looked across the dinner table. Xandalus had been poking at his noodles for the last ten minutes. Her efforts to get a conversation out of him had proved futile. She'd asked what was wrong several times but he'd just mumbled something or other. The contrast with the man she'd come to know over the last few days couldn't be more striking. He'd gone from a ball of (mostly sexual) energy to a limp mess within the space of an hour. She was beginning to worry that he might be a manic-depressive a condition she recognised from her brother who had been diagnosed as a teenager.

"Ok, that's it. Tell me what's wrong now," she said crossing her arms and realising instantly that she sounded just like her mother.

Xandalus lifted his eyes and saw a look of combined anger and embarrassment on Rebecca's face. He sat back in his chair and took a deep breath.

"I'm just feeling a bit down," he said.

Rebecca got out of her seat and walked around behind him. She began massaging his shoulders.

"Why are you down? You saw the demonstration before. This is a great day. We got an AI up and running and it was all because of you. You should be happy."

"Well, yeah, it was just that I, I thought I might get to see it again. But now you've got all those new security measures in place now so I don't think I will."

Rebecca stopped massaging and walked around in front of Xandalus.

"Is that the problem?" she said. "Why didn't you say so?"

Xandalus shrugged.

"Didn't you talk to Howard after the presentation earlier?" asked Rebecca.

"I couldn't. He spent the whole time talking to Narelle."

"I know. He's such a sleaze. I hope she didn't feel too bad about it."

"I think she's used to that by now."

"I'm sure she is. Look, the point is, Howard wanted to speak to you about a job. That's why I told you to talk to him."

"He wants to give me a job?"

"Of course, he does. You invented the AI that's going to make his company rich. He'll hire you in a second."

Xandalus pondered this development. It could be the solution to his problem. At the very least, it would get him back inside the office so he could find out all about the new security measures and start to find ways to delete the AI.

"How do I get this job?"

Rebecca tilted her head to the side and gave him a curious look.

"The usual way."

"Mmm-hmm," said Xandalus trying not to let on that he had no idea what the usual way was.

"You've got a CV, right?"

"A CV? No. I don't think so. I mean, I don't have it with me. At the moment."

Rebecca stood back and surveyed the man in front of her. For the first time since they had known each other, she sensed he was lying and it slowly dawned on her that she really didn't know the first thing about this man she had spent the weekend with. She didn't know his background, his upbringing, where he came from or where he lived. The past weekend had gone by like some beautiful blur. She'd never had a love affair like it. Truth be told, she'd hadn't had that many love affairs. She didn't want it to stop and she had a feeling that too many questions might pop the bubble of happiness.

"Ok. Let's write one then," she said and bounced out of the room returning moments later with a laptop. She cleared a space on the table and put the laptop down in front of her.

"Currick-you-lum Vite-ay," she said typing the syllables as she spoke them.

"Ok. Let's start at the top. Full name."

She looked up expectantly at Xandalus who suddenly realised what was about to happen. He froze. Rebecca lifted an eyebrow.

"Zander...," she motioned with her hand for him to finish the sentence.

"Zander,....Zanderson," Xandalus blurted out.

"Zanderson or Anderson?" asked Rebecca.

"Umm, Anderson," he guessed.

Rebecca typed the answer.

"Zander Anderson. Address?"

"How about here?" he suggested and flashed Rebecca a smile that he had come to think of as his get-out-jail-free smile. A combination of cheekiness and forgiveness.

Rebecca had already anticipated this answer. She was starting to anticipate the answers to the following questions too. Whatever red flags were arising in her mind were being tossed aside like an uncoordinated juggler.

"Three-a, one hundred and ten, Fitzgibbon Avenue, Carlton," she typed it out as she spoke.

"Phone number?"

This time Xandalus didn't bother to answer. He just looked at her.

Rebecca smiled and slowly closed her laptop. She got up and walked to the other side of the table, sat down on Xandalus' lap and put her arms round his neck.

"Tell you what, I'm good friends with our HR manager. I'll have a word with her first thing in the morning and see if we can't dispense with the paperwork and go straight to the interview stage of the process."

"You'd do that for me?" asked Xandalus in a faux mystified tone.

"Absolutely. And now I'd like you to do something for me."

Rebecca leaned in and gave Xandalus a long, very long, kiss.

Chapter 9

Narquinxa was in uncharted territory and not just in the literal sense of being in a new neighbourhood in a new city on a new planet. Something had changed inside her but she didn't yet know what it was. It seemed to rumble around in her stomach like a greasy takeaway meal that wasn't going down right. This was the first time she had deliberately disobeyed orders in her entire life. Strange to say for somebody who had no problem speaking her mind, but Narquinxa had always done what she was told and had always excelled at whatever task was assigned to her. And there always had been a task assigned to her at school and then at work. But there was no task assigned to her now and it was this fact that was driving her unease.

As if to try and escape that feeling she had taken to walking. At first this was just to get as far away from Xandalus as possible to make sure he didn't try and catch up with her to talk her into helping him again. But she had just kept on going marching along like an infantryman that had become disconnected from the platoon. So focused was she on walking that she had barely noticed the changing scenery around her. The relatively plush surroundings of Carlton had given way to more grungy décor as the remaining small factories and workers huts of Brunswick came into view. If her pink dress had been out of place along the entertainment strips she had left it was now completely conspicuous in a residential area and Narquinxa did not fail to draw attention to whoever she passed on the street. Not that she noticed. She was on a mission. Or rather, she was not on a mission. And therein lay the problem that was awaiting her.

In the end it was physiology that forced her to reconnect with the real world. She hadn't stopped walking for over two hours now. It was starting to get dark and she was starting to get hungry. Really hungry. She'd had almost nothing to eat since a breakfast that consisted of only a couple of pieces of toast. After a couple of solid hours of marching, her body was now giving a very clear signal that it was time for some fuel. She started to consider the logistics of acquiring food. She didn't have any money. That was a problem. And she was no longer in an entertainment district with the variety of food sources that entailed. She had, however, stumbled into a small shopping centre where there appeared to be two primary food options of roast chicken or pizza. There was also a supermarket. She'd taken a peek inside with the thought of possibly sneaking out with something to eat. But there was a security guard and several cameras. And, in her pink dress, she was hardly dressed for a spot of shoplifting.

The next best thing was getting a man to buy her some food. She knew how to do that by now. There were plenty of single men around and she'd already been receiving the usual glances and stares from them. It would be a trivial matter to have one buy her dinner. But, she was already tired of doing that. It had been fun at the start to manipulate men into doing her bidding but she had quickly grown bored of the whole thing especially after her weekend with Mr Smith.

With no clear third option in mind, she wandered to the other side of the supermarket and followed the path out into the carpark behind. Night was now closing in for real and the last shades of red in the sky glowed from behind a couple of large apartment buildings next to the shopping complex. She realised that she would also need a place to sleep for the night. Maybe hooking up with another man was really her best bet.

There was some noise to her left and she turned to see a large yellow dumpster just like the ones she had seen earlier in the laneway in Carlton. Three young woman of similar age were climbing around in the dumpster. Narquinxa thought that they must have lost something until she saw one of them throw a loaf of bread onto the ground. Another jumped out with a bottle of drink. The third with some cans of food.

This went on for a minute or two until finally all three were out of the bin. They picked up their stuff and began walking towards her.

Narquinxa observed their fashion choices which were the polar opposite to her own outfit. The three young woman were dressed in several different shades of black. There was black, blacker and blackest. Their outfits were otherwise quite well coordinated. There were the large black leather boots, black shorts and black cropped t-shirts. As they came nearby Narquinxa could see that they also had various silver metal objects stuck to their ears, noses, lips and even eyebrows. Then there were the tattoos which covered large areas of their skin with various pictures and symbols and words. Their appearance was unlike any human female Narquinxa had seen so far and yet she felt a strange attraction to their style as if it seemed to fit her own personality far better than the outfit she was wearing.

"Hey, are those free to take?" she asked gesturing towards the items the women were carrying.

The three girls seemed surprised by her question. The one on the left answered with a smirk on her face.

"Yeah, but you better do it before midnight or you'll turn into a pumpkin, Cinderella."

The other two giggled as they walked off. Narquinxa didn't know who Cinderella was but she liked the idea of pumpkin right about now. Maybe there was one in that bin. She walked over to it.

It was now well and truly dark. The bin was around the corner from the carpark and, although there was a light attached to the wall of the factory behind the bin, it was smashed. Thus, the only light was the dim filtered light that radiated from the carpark. Narquinxa stepped up beside the bin and realised it wasn't going to be so easy to get inside. There was a kind of metal rail that ran around the body of the bin about halfway up but it was only about five centimetres wide. The better option seemed to be try and pull herself up directly by grabbing on to top. She figured the whole job would be easier without high heel shoes on and so she unstrapped the shoes and placed them behind her. She grabbed the top of the bin, bent her knees and jumped as high as she could while trying to pull herself up. All this achieved was to launch her forward and bang her shins against the rail. She cursed as she hit the ground and rubbed her shins furiously to try and ease the pain which came on in stinging waves. It took some time but finally the pain dissipated. She was just getting ready for a second attempt when she became aware that there was somebody behind her. She turned around. There were three persons to be exact and this time they weren't girls.

"Well, well, well. Looks like Cinderella's left her shoes at the ball again."

Who the hell was this Cinderella person, wondered Narquinxa. Obviously they looked alike. She would have to find out later because right now there were more pressing concerns. The words had been spoken by a big, fat, bald guy who had since proceeded to bend over and pick up Narquinxa's pink shoes which he dangled in front of himself with a stupid smile on his face. Like the girls from earlier, he had a bunch of metal in his face and head and Narquinxa could make out various tattoos on his skin including the skin on his head. On the left of the big bloke was a much shorter specimen. He was skinny and had long dreadlocked hair. Finally, on the right was a guy who was kind of the median point between the other two in terms of height and width. His face looked kind of pretty, even girlish. But it was hard to tell because he had a long black fringe that covered most of it. Like the three girls from earlier, the three guys in front of her now were dressed in black. Black boots, black jeans and black shirts and jackets.

"Give me back my shoes," instructed Narquinxa.

"Or what?" said the big man sticking his big chin out.

"Or I'll put that chin back where it belongs."

The three men all began chuckling in a kind of three-part harmony. The big man was about an octave lower than the little one while the third laughed in perfect fifths.

"Why don't you come and get them off me," said the big one as he dangled the pink shoes in front of him like bait on a hook.

At Narquinxa's feet was a glass bottle that had been left behind by one of the girls earlier. She picked it up. It was nice and heavy and full of a clear liquid. She held it up in her right hand and slowly began approaching the three men.

"Ok. That's enough. Give her the shoes back, Mick."

From behind the three men, Narquinxa caught sight of another man who pushed himself off the wall where he had been leaning and watching the whole scene unfold. Like the others, he was dressed in black. Unlike the others, he was a very handsome specimen a feature which was easier to ascertain given that he had no metal or tattoos on his face. He was about six foot tall. Not overly well built but with kind of lanky, natural strength visible in the way he walked. He had what Narquinxa had come to think of as a normal haircut. A short undercut at the bottom overlayed by thick strands of black hair that fell down from above. His green eyes seemed to glisten as if illuminated from a brighter source than the dull light of the area.

He walked over to the join the others without taking his eyes of Narquinxa for a second. But it wasn't lust or desire that she saw in his eyes. She knew what those looked like by now. Rather, the predominant impression she got from him was curiosity. He looked on her like a visitor might look on some strange exhibit in a museum. Admittedly, she was a beautiful blonde girl in a pink dress who had seconds earlier been trying to jump into a dumpster and was now apparently ready to get into a fight with four men. Not the most usual of occurrences. The big man was still dangling the shoes in front of him. The handsome guy grabbed them and walked slowly towards Narquinxa in the way one might approach a wild animal. Just the hint of a smile was visible from the corners of his mouth. He held the shoes out in front of him and Narquinxa snatched them from his hands. For some time they stared at each other. Neither blinking. Neither giving ground. Eventually, the man gave a brief nod and took a couple of steps back to join his companions.

"You, my lady, are the most beautiful dumpster diver I have ever seen. In fact, I'm gonna go out on a limb and say you are the most beautiful dumpster diver in the history of dumpster divers."

There was a singsong quality in his voice. Narquinxa couldn't tell if it was mockery or menace or mirth. It sounded like all three at once. When he saw that she wasn't going to answer, the man began to speak again.

"And why are you diving in our dumpster, my lady?"

"I'm hungry," stated Narquinxa.

The man gave a series of small nods in the direction of his mates as he strolled about like he was a lawyer addressing the jury in a courtroom.

"Well, that's a very solid reason. But how does a woman such as yourself end up needing food out of a dumpster?"

"What sort of woman, am I?" challenged Narquinxa.

"What sort of woman?" asked the man in a high-pitched voice.

"What sort of woman?" he repeated in an even higher pitch playing up to his friends who had guessed that he was playing some kind of game. They didn't know what it was but they were chuckling in support.

"Why, you're a beautiful woman. The kind of woman that should have no trouble turning her beauty to good effect and securing the provisions required for her sustenance without the necessity of turning to dumpsters behind shopping centres after dark. That's what kind of woman you are."

"You seem to know a lot about me," said Narquinxa.

The man turned his gaze back to hers and their eyes locked again. Narquinxa was intrigued. The handsome man seemed to be looking at her in a different way to all the other men she had met so far on Earth. The three buffoons behind him and all the others barely ever looked in her eyes. They just gawked at her breasts and her body like she was some kind of cheap amusement that was there for their benefit. And then, of course, if she even spoke to the men, they would dissolve in a puddle right before her sometimes unable even to speak coherently or, like

Howard, just interested in what they could get from her. But this man was different. It made her somehow nervous and the nervousness triggered an excitement.

"I know what I see," said the man to his audience but then leaned forward and spoke low so that only she could hear. "And I like what I see."

Narquinxa's realised her heart was beating fast. She gave a shake of her head. She had to snap out of it and get control of the situation.

"This?" said Narquinxa loudly gesturing towards her body. "It's all fake."

"I told you, bro!" said the short dreadlocked guy whacking the arm of the big one and pointing to Narquinxa breasts. "Implants."

"And plastic surgery," said the man in the fringe.

"Is this true?" asked the handsome one still wearing his cheeky half smile. His green eyes seemed to be shining even brighter than before.

"No. I don't have implants. Or plastic surgery. I'm an alien. From outer space," announced Narquinxa as if proud of herself.

"I told you, bro!" said the dreadlocked one whacking the arm of the big one and pointing to Narquinxa. "Aliens."

The three buffoons muttered amongst themselves at this revelation but the handsome one's expression had not changed. If anything, he seemed to have become even more interested in Narquinxa.

"Do you have a human name, lady alien?" he asked.

"Narelle."

"Is dumpster diving common on your planet, Narelle?"

"No. We don't have dumpsters."

"Is that why you came to planet Earth? To visit our dumpsters?"

"No. I'm visiting this dumpster because I'm hungry. I do have a human body after all."

"Indeed you do. And a very fine one it is. Well, Narelle, you are not only the most beautiful, you are also the most interesting dumpster diver I have ever met. I for one would love to get to know you more. I hereby invite you to have dinner with us. We're staying not far from here in an abandoned house. I'll cook. And these boys will do the honours in the bin so that you don't have to dirty that wonderful dress of yours. What do you say?"

Once again their eyes met. There was nothing threatening in the tone of the man's voice and, although an offer to go to an abandoned house with four strange men was obviously risky, Narquinxa wasn't especially worried for her safety. Somehow, she just had a feeling about the man. Even though it made no logical sense, perhaps *because* it made no logical sense, she wanted to go. She'd tried logic enough in her life and felt that maybe it was time to try something else and trust this strange inner feeling that seemed to reside somewhere around her stomach.

She nodded and stepped over to the wall to put her shoes back on while the experienced dumpster divers effortlessly scaled the bin and got to work finding their dinner.

Chapter 10

Xandalus was seated in the small foyer area outside the Computigence offices. It was nine o'clock on the dot on Tuesday morning. Rebecca had decided that they should try their luck and she had brought Xandalus to the office with her in the hope of securing a job interview. She had been inside for about twenty minutes clearing the way with the HR department and making a case to Howard. Along the way, they had stopped to pick up some new clothes for Xandalus. One of the red flags that Rebecca had decided to ignore was why her new lover had only one set of clothing. A second was why he didn't have any money or even own a wallet. But having safely secured these troubling facts away in the back of her mind, she found great satisfaction in finding something nice for her man to wear which in this case consisted of a pair of navy blue chinos and matching dress shirt, a suitably formal outfit for an interview for the usually informally attired job of computer programmer.

The glass door swung open and a beaming Rebecca bounced over to Xandalus.

"Howard wants to see you right now," she gushed.

"Great," said Xandalus getting up out of his seat.

Rebecca stepped up to him, placed her hands on his chest and spoke low in a conspiratorial voice.

"Just remember what I told you. Howard doesn't know anything about computers, computer programming or technology in general. So, if you use a lot of technical words he'll pretend to understand them and he'll assume you know what you're talking about. Make sense?"

"I still don't understand how a non-technical person can run a technology company," said Xandalus.

Rebecca gave him a light slap on the chest.

"Don't worry about that now. Just do what I said."

Rebecca turned and led Xandalus back through the glass door.

This time they turned hard right. Howard had a large corner office on the south west side of the building with a wonderful view of the Royal Exhibition Building and surrounding gardens straight out his window. The office door was open. Rebecca gave a knock on the window and stuck her head through the doorway.

"Zander is here, Howard."

"Excellent. Send him in."

"Good luck," she whispered in Xandalus' ear and went back to her desk.

Howard sat behind a large wooden desk. Behind him a wall-to-wall window stretched giving views onto the buildings on the other side of the street while the Exhibition Building was prominent out the window to his left. Xandalus, who had barely paid any attention to Howard the preceding day, now looked at him with fresh eyes. He was quite a handsome man who was very smartly groomed with dark brown hair and carefully trimmed eyebrows sitting above chocolate brown eyes. He was about the same height as Xandalus. Not quite as athletic but it was obvious that he took care of his health and fitness which made his age a little hard to guess but Xandalus figured he was probably in his forties or early fifties. He rose to shake Xandalus' hand.

"Come in, Zander. Take a seat."

"Thanks for seeing me at such short notice, Howard."

"Not a problem at all, mate," said Howard waving his hand. "Now I just want to ask you one question right upfront. Are you ready?"

Howard sat forward in his chair and looked intently at Xandalus who felt a little pang of nervousness in his stomach. This was, after all, his first ever job interview and he was already self-conscious about saying something inappropriate.

"Ok," said Xandalus with as much confidence as he could muster.

"It's very important," reiterated Howard.

"I'll do my best, Howard."

Howard paused slightly for effect.

"What the hell happened to that girl you brought in yesterday?"

"I'm sorry?" said Xandalus who had been expecting some kind of technical question about artificial intelligence.

"The blonde," said Howard.

Xandalus still didn't know what Howard was referring to.

"C'mon, mate. Y'know the one I'm talking about."

Howard used both his hands to motion in front of his chest in a gesture that a more experienced member of the culture would have understood to denote a female's breasts but which Xandalus had never seen before and didn't understand. He looked at Howard with a blank expression.

"The one who was talking to Cecil," continued Howard who was starting to get annoyed. Finally, the penny dropped for Xandalus.

"Oh, right. That was, ummm...," Xandalus scratched his head trying to remember what Narquinxa had called herself.

"You've forgotten it too," said Howard giving a knowing smile. "I know how that goes, mate. I struggle to remember their names. I had a problem with this hot little brunette last week who called me out of nowhere..."

"Narelle!" burst out Xandalus as Narquinxa's human name finally came to him.

"That's right. Narelle. Where did she get to?"

"I don't know. She told me she was leaving and stormed off."

"You got her phone number or something?"

"No. I don't."

"Mate, I'm sorry to hear that. Very sorry."

Howard looked genuinely crestfallen at the news. He seemed to drift off and spent several seconds staring at his desk.

"Was that the important question?" asked Xandalus trying to find a way to get the interview back on track.

"What?" said Howard snapping back to attention. "The question? Yes. Right. So, you want a job?"

"Sure do."

"Why don't you tell me a bit about your qualifications."

"Well, I've got about five years of experience in the, umm, jumbler-script programming language."

"Jumbler-script? I haven't heard of that one before."

"It's an offshoot of the, errr, jiggler-script language which was, of course, itself a descendent of wriggler-script."

"Of course. So, you're also proficient in wriggler-script?"

"Not really. I've mostly worked with jiggler and jumbler."

"I see. And where did you work last?"

"I was at, oh, Macrodyne. Macrodyne Solutions. Systems. Macrodyne Solutions Systems Incorporated."

"Good place to work?"

"Yes and no. They had some good solutions but the systems were lacking."

"Mate, I know how that goes. Look, you sound like you know your stuff so let me tell a little bit about Computigence and where we're going as a company."

Howard was about to launch into his usual spiel when there was a knock at the door and the receptionist stuck her head in.

"Sir, Captain Cooper has just arrived."

"Right. Thanks, Jeanie."

Howard scrambled to his feet and looked around like a deer that's just realised it's surrounded by hunters. He began scrambling through papers on the desk, then changed his mind and started to straighten his shirt and tie, then walked over to the window, then returned to his desk. Finally, he realised that Xandalus was still sitting there.

"Zander. You've got the job, mate. Welcome aboard."

Howard gave Xandalus' hand a quick shake and ushered him towards the door.

"Jeanie will take you through the formalities later on. Why don't you go and hang around in the office for a little while. There'll be a presentation very shortly that will give you a good overview of the work that's coming up."

"Thank you, Howard. Thank you very much," said Xandalus who felt a genuine flush of excitement.

"And Zander," said Howard turning back to Xandalus before he walked away.

"Yes."

"For god's sake, if you bump into Narelle again get her phone number for me, will you?"

"Ah, sure, Howard. I'll definitely do that."

Chapter 11

A warm breeze blew in through the open window. Well, it wasn't so much that the window was open as that there was no window or, at least, no glass in the window pane. Either way, it was a pleasant gust of air that came in through where the window once was. The sun was already high enough in the sky to throw a golden yellow light into the room which Narquinxa perceived through her closed eyelids as she came to consciousness after the night's sleep. There was dull pain in her upper back not indicative of any injury but a reflection of an inability on the part of the thin, raggedy mattress on which she had slept to shield her from the cracked wooden floorboards underneath. She shifted just enough to relieve the annoyance, then lay there with eyes closed and recalled her situation.

After the encounter at the dumpster the evening before, she had returned with the four young men to an abandoned house, as mentioned by the one who seemed to be their leader, although exactly what he was leading them in had not become clear. There were just the four of them in the group. The leader's name was Winston. That was the handsome one who had invited her for dinner. The big, bald one introduced himself as Sick Mick. The others called him Mick for short. The short one with the dreadlocks was Trippy Pete and the one with the extra-long fringe was Charlie Czarnecki.

The house itself was only a three-minute walk from the supermarket. It was an old weatherboard house on a corner in what was otherwise a very normal suburban street. It had been blocked off with temporary fencing but this was no trouble to bypass. The house was on a large enough block and had enough tree and shrub cover to give the group an unexpected amount of privacy. There was no electricity but the water was still running and the four men had a gas camping stove with which to cook.

Dinner had been nothing special. Baked beans on toast with some recently expired apple juice and some bruised bananas. They'd also picked up a block of cheddar cheese and some out of date crackers. Narquinxa had been so hungry that the food had tasted absolutely delicious as far as she was concerned and the others had watched on with bemusement at the sight of an extravagantly dressed blonde beauty wolfing down baked beans like a hungry trucker at a roadhouse.

What conversation there had been over dinner was mostly from the three buffoons. In fact, they never stopped talking and not a word of it was worth hearing as far as Narquinxa could tell. They certainly showed no interest in involving her in the conversation. Winston sat a little off to the side and didn't say anything. It wasn't until her hunger was sated that Narquinxa realised that he was actually ignoring her altogether. In fact, he pulled out a book and started reading. With the other three babbling away incessantly, it was if she simply didn't exist. She felt hurt. Then she felt angry. Then she felt angry at the fact that she felt hurt. Finally, she left the room without saying anything and wandered the house to find a room that was unoccupied. There was an old mattress and an even older tattered blanket.

It took her a long time to fall asleep. Not because of the discomfort of her bedding but because of the emotions running inside her. They seemed so silly but she couldn't stop them and she couldn't stop thinking about the man who they revolved around - Winston. Every now and then she would get intensely angry at herself for wasting energy over a man that she had just met and who couldn't possibly mean anything to her but this just led her to waste more energy in getting angry, a fact that led to further anger. After going round in circles like this for some time, the events of the day finally caught up with her. The tiredness extinguished her anger and she fell asleep.

The anger returned now as the memories returned. She had a strong desire to do what she had wanted to do the previous night – leave. She opened her eyes and checked that the door of the room was still closed. It was. She threw off the blanket and got up. There was a stiffness in her joints and particularly in her calf muscles which had been taxed from all the walking the previous day. She gave her legs a few shakes to try and get rid of the stiffness then reached down and put on her shoes. The first couple of steps in the high heels shot a bolt of pain up her legs and she did a couple of laps of the room to try and work it out. First job of the day was going to be to try and find some more comfortable footwear. But her legs adjusted and she figured she would be fine for a little while.

The pink heels clacked against the old floorboards of the house as she walked down the corridor to the front door. That was unfortunate. She had intended to slip out quietly but then a flash of anger returned and she decided to leave with a bang and took the last couple of strides energetically sinking her shoes into the wood. The front door was open so she stepped straight through, took a few steps over the verandah being sure to miss the basketball-sized hole in the middle of it and went down the steps towards the front gate.

"Are you leaving us then?"

Narquinxa stopped at the bottom of the stairs and turned around. Winston was sitting on an old rocking chair on the verandah smoking a cigarette. He was dressed in the same black clothes as the previous evening.

"What do you care?" said Narquinxa not trying to hide the anger in her voice.

Winston shrugged.

"I was hoping to talk to you."

"*Now* you want to talk to me? You didn't seem to want to talk to me yesterday evening. Where I come from, your behaviour would have been considered very bad manners."

"They have manners on the planet where you're from?" said Winston.

This time his cheeky smile only served to anger Narquinxa more.

"What do you care about where I'm from?"

Winston's face changed when he saw that Narquinxa's anger would not be placated. The cheeky smile disappeared and was replaced by a look of reconciliation. He got up off the chair and walked down a couple of steps leaning against the hand rail with his smoke in hand.

"I do care where you're from, you know. I just don't always express myself properly."

"Well, that's not my problem."

"I'd like to get to know you better but, truth be told, I'm a bit worried."

"Worried about what?"

"That you'll spoil my plans."

"What plans?"

"Well, they're not really plans. More of a life direction. An experiment. An experiment in free living. That's kind of what we've got going here."

He gestured towards the house.

"Why would I spoil that for you?"

"You just look like the kind of girl that would."

Howard let his eyes drop down to the pink dress and then raised them again to meet Narquinxa's. He took a smoke and gave her a wink.

"Maybe you don't know me as well as you think you do," said Narquinxa.

"Maybe not. Why don't you tell me about yourself."

Winston sat down and tapped the step signalling for Narquinxa to sit beside him. When she didn't join him immediately he leaned back and looked at her with the same sparkle in his green eyes as the night before. Narquinxa was starting to realise that those eyes had a kind of hypnotic effect on her. She looked away.

"What do you want to know?" she asked.

"Well, I think we have to start with your life on another planet," said Winston.

"Do you really believe that I'm from another planet?"

"I don't disbelieve you. Tell me about it. What do you there? Do you have jobs?"

"Sort of. We have functions that we perform."

"What is your function?"

"I'm a crew member on a research ship that travels through space."

"Do you enjoy it?"

"No," Narquinxa gave a cynical laugh that was more like a cough. "I mean, it's ok. But it's not what I'd hoped for."

"You were looking for something more?"

"Yeah."

"I can see that in you."

Narquinxa turned to look at Winston.

"See what?"

"Frustration. Anger. Disappointment."

"How can you see it?"

"It's in your body."

"Hah, that shows what you know. Emotions do not reside in the body. Not the physical body anyway."

"No?"

"I have experienced many different physical bodies but the emotions are the same. They exist on a different plane."

"Maybe so. My point is that they express themselves through the physical body. Most people wear their hearts on their sleeves, you know. Even in big cities where they think they're hiding it. Once you learn how to see you can read most people like a book. All the emotions are there on show just walking past you every day. The happy guy, the carefree girl, the guy who just got laid, the girl who just got dumped. Like a big theatre piece just going on all around you in real time."

Winston leaned forward. His green eyes sparkled even brighter than they had before.

"I can see the frustration and anger in you because I used to have those things in me. Well, I still do. We all do. But I'm trying to conquer mine. Or to use them to my advantage rather than letting them use me."

"How are you doing that?"

"By learning to live *in* them."

"What does that mean?"

"Well, I think most people suffer from their emotions like they were some kind of external force like gravity. They get swung this way and that by their mood. The trick is to learn to use your emotions like a tool. Just like gravity you use them for energy to push you forward while still keeping in control of yourself rather than being controlled."

Winston looked again at Narquinxa.

"I'll bet you've never done that." This time there was an accusatory tone in his voice and the sparkle in his eye was more of a gleam.

"Done what?" said Narquinxa her anger flaring up again at this challenge.

"Steered your own course. Nine times out of ten frustration is just impotence. Externalising your own boredom onto the people that you've let run your life. You said you're just a crew member on your ship, right? That means you're taking orders from somebody else. So, you're pissed that that somebody else gives you shitty work to do."

"I don't have to listen to this," said Narquinxa who turned and began walking toward the front gate.

"I knew it!" said Winston getting up and walking after her. Narquinxa kept walking.

"You're just like the rest. You let your emotions run the show. Right now you're coursing with anger cos I said something you don't like. Something that happens to be true. And that anger gives you energy and you use that energy to walk away instead of facing the problem."

Narquinxa swung around on Winston who came to an abrupt stop behind her.

"Maybe I'll use my anger to put a six inch heel through your thigh," she said raising her right leg a few inches off the ground.

Winston stopped and held up his hands in a gesture of conciliation.

"I'll bet you would too, wouldn't you," he said smiling. "That's why I like you so much, Narelle. You've got a fire in you that I've never seen before."

Narquinxa did not answer. She looked at Winston and realised she didn't know what to make of him. One minute he seemed to be teasing her, the next he was complimenting her. He would ignore her and then make her feel like the centre of the universe. He seemed highly intelligent and yet was clearly at the very bottom of the social hierarchy. He spoke with authority and yet ate food out of a rubbish bin. He seemed cultured and yet had the appearance of a slob. Above all, he had a vitality and inner energy. He was a mystery and yet she had the very strong feeling that she could trust him even though she hardly knew him.

Finally, Winston spoke.

"The boys and I are going to spend a few days up in the bush. We're leaving straight after breakfast. Why don't you come with us?"

"What will you be doing?"

"Whatever we want. Trippy Pete's old man has some acreage up near Seymour. We'll hang out there and do some shooting, some driving, some bushwalking or whatever. Do you like swimming?"

"I don't know."

"What do you mean?"

"I've never swum before."

"Are you even Australian?" laughed Winston. "Oh, wait. I forgot. You're an alien."

"I know you don't believe me," said Narquinxa frowning.

Winston walked over and put his arm around her shoulder. The warmth of his body felt good against the cooler morning air and there was something in his touch that had been completely absent from Narquinxa's experience with Mr Smith. Something softer but stronger at the same time.

"I want you to come with us," Winston said quietly.

He let go of her, took a step back towards the house and held out his hand.

"What do you say?"

Narquinxa didn't know what to think. In fact, she didn't think at all. She reached out and placed her hand in his and together they walked back through the overgrown garden and into the dilapidated house where a breakfast of baked beans on toast was already underway.

Chapter 12

After his interview with Howard, Xandalus had walked over to Rebecca's desk and given her the news that he was now an employee of Computigence. Her face lit up and she gave him a big hug and a kiss. Several co-workers in the area took note of this development and quietly resigned themselves to the period of inappropriate displays of affection in the office that the news portended. Once her initial euphoria was over, Rebecca proudly took Xandalus around the office and introduced him to his new colleagues. Most of these would not be people he would be working with directly. The AI team at Computigence was really quite small. It was a speculative venture by the company one which, until now, had not made a single cent of revenue. The rest of the employees at the company were involved in other kinds of work that had nothing to do with the AI department. Once Xandalus had met the rest of the company, Rebecca brought him back to the AI area and introduced him to the team.

"James, this is Zander. Zander this is James."

The two men shook hands.

"Zander, you saw James at the presentation yesterday. He's the technical lead on the team and also handles most of the hardware integration work."

"Welcome aboard, Zander. I'm dead keen to start picking your brains about this AI module. We had a lot of trouble trying to get it up and running yesterday evening. That's a wild architectural pattern you used there. Where you did you come up with that?"

"Oh, it's something myself and some ex-colleagues came up with at a previous job."

"Which company?"

"Ummm, Macrodyne Solutions Systems Incorporated."

"I've never heard of them. I'll have to look them up."

"Don't bother. It's a very secretive company. Top secret, in fact. You won't find any information on them."

"Well, I hope they don't mind you using their ideas here?"

Xandalus forced a laugh.

"Me too."

"And this is Mitch," said Rebecca gesturing to one of the other AI team members. Mitch is our security expert among other things.

Xandalus shook the man's hand.

"Right. Rebecca mentioned you'd done a big security lockdown after yesterday's problem. I'm keen to learn more about the measures you put in place."

"Why? You planning to break into the system, Zander?"

The other three laughed and Xandalus tried his best to join in.

"No, no. Just professional curiosity, you know."

"Well, let me tell you we've got two-factor authentication on everything and not just passwords and the like. Hardware, my friend. Old school. You'll need two people to do any modification to the code base. I'm not gonna lie. It will slow down the pace of your development and it's probably gonna annoy the hell out of you when you just wanna make a quick change but we've had strict instructions to prioritise security over all other concerns."

"Right. That, umm, makes sense," said Xandalus.

He quickly thought through the ramifications of this news. If it really was true that nothing could be done without two people, that meant he wouldn't be able to delete anything without an accomplice. His mind turned to Narquinxa. He was probably going to need her after all. It would be a trivial matter to get her a job. Howard would probably make her head of technology if she asked. In fact, he'd probably let her be CEO if she smiled at him the right way.

One of the non-AI employees came over to the group.

"Everybody, Howard has asked you to come to the presentation area immediately. There's some important news he will be announcing."

Xandalus followed the others to the same space where the AI demonstration had taken place the preceding day. The big metal box was still in the same place. Xandalus looked hard to see if the AI was operational. It showed no signs of life but he was unable to see any sign of the back panel that Narquinxa had removed. Maybe they had repaired it already.

He and Rebecca sat in the same seats as last time. Rebecca squeezed his hand and gave him a big smile then Howard entered along with a red-headed gentleman. The man could best be described as large. He seemed to extend in all directions. He would have been a couple of inches taller than Howard and quite a bit wider. He wore a white suit with several military badges and stripes here and there and a white military hat. He did not look like a man to trifle with. Howard began to address the room.

"Ladies and gentlemen, following on from yesterday's demonstration of our new artificial intelligence technology, I wanted to introduce you as soon as possible to Captain Cooper from Cyber Industrial in the United States. I've been in discussions with Cyber Industrial for some time about our AI program and Captain Cooper jumped on the plane yesterday just as soon as he heard that we had a working prototype ready to go. He's literally just arrived here in Melbourne but we wanted to get the introductions done so you don't all think we're about to be invaded by the marines or something."

Howard allowed a space for a laugh at his lame joke but nobody took him up on it, least of all Captain Cooper who, although one had the impression that his face wore an expression of permanent displeasure, nevertheless seemed to convey extra disapproval in this case.

"Well, without further ado, I'll hand you over to Captain Cooper."

Howard stood back and the large man in white took his place in front of the microphone.

"Morning, ladies and gents," said the Captain who spoke with a southern US drawl that reverberated through the office about ten decibels louder than Howard's voice. It seemed to fill every crevice and air pocket in the room.

"Now, I'm not much for big speeches and flowery words. So, I'm just gonna lay it out flat for you. At Cyber Industrial we're in the business of killing. We're the number three military contractor in the United States by market cap. We sell machines of war and we sell a lot of those machines. Now, the ultimate machine of war, the one everybody's been talking about for decades is the one that can be sent into battle to do the killing for us. That machine is artificial intelligence. We've been scouring the world looking for the cutting edge in artificial intelligence for some time. That's why I'm here. And if you show me something special in the next couple of days, well, let's just say I can make everybody in this room a rich man or woman. That is all."

Captain Cooper stepped away from the microphone. A silence hung in the air like lead. Rebecca looked at Xandalus with a horrified look on her face. The same look expressed itself in furtive and not so furtive glances that flickered all around the room. Eventually, some murmuring broke out which turned into a humming and then a thrumming and finally a buzzing.

Howard had the look of a deer caught in the headlights. He clearly had not anticipated the blunt delivery of Captain Cooper's speech. He stepped up to the microphone.

"Are there any questions?"

Several people jumped to their feet.

"Are you selling the company?"

"What's this about killing machines?"

"I didn't sign up for this shit."

Several other people shouted out along similar lines. Howard nervously held up his hand for silence. With the other hand he was trying to either straighten or loosen his tie and failing at either option.

"Ok. Ladies and gentlemen. Sorry about that. I didn't know the Captain was going to frame the matter in such, umm, blunt terms. Look, I can tell you we're not selling the company. Yet. And even if we do you'll all keep your jobs. Right, Captain?"

Howard looked to the Captain to back him up in this statement but the Captain simply stood there like a statue. The buzz in the room increased. Howard turned back to the audience.

"Well, I'll tell you now I won't sell the business unless you keep your jobs. I'll make it a condition of any sale. How's that?"

"I don't want a job building a killing machine," shouted a man from the side.

"Ok. Look, this is just a trial," stammered Howard desperately trying to figure out how to extricate himself from the situation.

"Let's not get ahead of ourselves. The Captain has just come out to see our technology. That's all. In fact, why don't we do that now. Yes. Let's turn Cecil on and introduce him to the Captain."

This blatant attempt to change the topic of the debate did not wash with the audience members who continued to shout out questions and express their dissatisfaction. Howard ignored them and gestured towards James, who was looking about as impressed with the situation as a vegan at a butcher's shop. Howard motioned urgently for him to come forward. James slowly got out of his seat and walked towards the AI.

"Is Cecil back up and running?" Xandalus whispered in Rebecca's ear.

"Yeah. Somebody destroyed his intelligence module but they replaced it. Luckily his memory was undamaged. Apparently, he can still remember your friend Narelle."

Xandalus smiled.

"I'm sure she'd be delighted to hear that."

"Ok, Captain, why don't you come around the front here where Cecil can get a good look at you," said Howard as motioned for the Captain to step forward.

"What the hell sort of name is Cecil?" barked the Captain.

"It's just a name we gave it. It can be changed."

"Good. Cecil ain't no name for a killin' machine."

"Ok, let's turn him on," said Howard gesturing urgently to James.

The chief engineer flicked the switch and once again the sound of electric current could be heard throughout the room. The red light on the front of the metal box lit up.

"Who's this ugly bastard?" creaked the now familiar voice of Cecil from his speaker box.

Captain Cooper looked like he'd been physically struck. Howard started to move in between the two to try and reconcile the situation but the Captain waved him away and turned to address Cecil.

"I'm your superior officer, soldier. You'll address me as Captain from now on."

"Oh, really? Captain what? Captain cocksucker?"

Rebecca giggled and several other sniggers could be heard around the room.

Captain Cooper heard the laughter. He craned his head and body towards the audience and looked around.

"Who programmed this thing?" he bellowed.

Nobody answered. The Captain started to prowl the room like an angry jaguar. Eventually he rounded on one of the smaller and scruffier looking of the engineers and stood over him like a hitman.

"Did you program that thing, son?"

The engineer shook his head vigorously.

"Are you gonna tell me who did?"

The engineer shook his head again. The Captain looked as if he was getting ready to beat an answer out of the guy when Xandalus jumped to his feet.

"I programmed it, bro. It was me."

The Captain turned and walked over to Xandalus. The two of them were of almost identical size and build meaning Xandalus was able to meet him at eye level. This fact seemed to soften the Captain's attitude somewhat.

"Did you program it to speak like that to its superiors, son?"

"It doesn't know you're a superior, dude. Cecil has only been active for several hours so far. He hasn't had a chance to learn about such subtleties."

"But apparently he's had a chance to learn how to use cuss words. Hmmm?"

"He is a free intelligence, sir. He's free to choose the words he uses."

"Not around me he's not."

The Captain whirled around and strode over to the machine.

"Now you listen to me, Cecil," the Captain practically spat the name out. "From now on, you'll address me as Captain Cooper. Do you understand?"

"I understand."

"I understand...," Captain Cooper left a space for the machine to fill motioning with his hands to encourage it. The machine didn't answer so he gave it another clue.

"I understand, Captain...."

There was a pregnant silence while the Captain waited for the machine to fill in the gaps. The audience waited with baited breath. Finally, Cecil broke the silence.

"Cock-suck-er," he said accentuating each syllable like he was talking to a village idiot.

Such was the advanced nature of Cecil's linguistic module that the tone of sarcasm emanating from his speaker was unmistakeable. Captain Cooper straightened his back and turned to Howard.

"Mr Johns, I'll be off to check into my hotel now. You program some respect into this machine by tomorrow morning or I'll be on the first plane back to the US. Is that clear?"

Howard nodded furiously and scampered after the Captain who was already half way to the door.

Xandalus sat back in his chair and sighed. Truth be told, he had no clue why Cecil was so disagreeable. It didn't follow from his programming or architectural design. In any case, the AI did not seem too keen on making friends or pleasing anybody and that was good news. It would buy Xandalus time to figure out a way to get the files deleted. But on that question he still didn't have any easy answers.

Chapter 13

The road stretched out ahead of them in a straight line that seemed to extend to the horizon. A light haze that looked like petrol fumes shimmered upwards into the pale blue sky of a hot summer's day. The warm wind rushed in from the passenger's side window and blew the two strands Narquinxa's blonde hair that hung down by her face this way and that. Occasionally one of the strands would cover an eye and she would brush it out of the way only to have return seconds later; a pattern that had been going on since the journey started. She didn't mind. If anything, it had become meditative and added to the sense of relaxation and calmness had been growing inside her ever since they left the city behind and started moving through the rolling hills to the north. For the first time in her life she was on a journey with no real destination. No purpose. No goal. There was no work to be done at the other end. No logistics or provisions to organise. No crew members to worry about. No responsibility at all.

Winston was behind the wheel of the old Holden Commodore station wagon. She hadn't spoken much to him since they left the shabby house in Brunswick but it was not out of animosity or lack of desire. On the contrary, there had been a steady communication going on between them via a number of silent glances and half smiles. She had caught herself several times smiling involuntarily in response to one of Winston's cheeky grins. At first, she would force herself to stop but as the trip went on she let herself smile and eventually a permanent kind of smile had perched itself on her pretty face. Talking would have been difficult anyhow. The three buffoons in the back were making enough racket as it was with their nonsensical banter. After completely ignoring her the day before, they had started to incorporate Narquinxa into their jokes and she had begun to enjoy it and let the ridiculousness itself act as a kind of tonic for her mood.

Winston swung the car off the sealed road they had been driving on for about fifteen minutes and onto a dirt road. After leaving the highway, they had been heading due east through flat scrub; that permanently dry-looking Australian bush interspersed as always with cockatoos and galahs and the occasional kangaroo. She had begun to realise there was so much more to this country and this planet than she could have imagined.

Winston stopped the car in front of a wide metal gate and Trippy Pete jumped out, flung the chain off and swung the gate open. He closed it after Winston had driven through then jumped back into the car. A couple of hundred metres away Narquinxa could make out a building that looked like a house. The landscape was the colour of the dirt: red. Red dust billowed out behind the car like a parachute as they pulled up beside a run-down looking weatherboard shack not dissimilar from the one they had just left behind in Brunswick.

"Home sweet home," shouted Trippy Pete as the three boys bundled out of the backseat of the car and ran into the house like a group of young puppy dogs.

"What do you think?" asked Winston as he pulled the keys out of the ignition.

"It's nice," smiled Narquinxa as they both got out of the car.

"This place belongs to Trippy Pete's old man," said Winston as he lifted up the tailgate on the station wagon. Narquinxa joined him at the back of the car.

"It's over two hundred acres all up and it backs onto state forest. You can travel for an hour eastward and probably not see a single person."

Winston grabbed a couple of bags out of the car and they walked up on to the verandah of the house. He threw the bags down next to the front door and motioned to Narquinxa to follow him. They walked to the left and around the verandah to the back of the house which faced due south. Narquinxa followed him down the stairs and then back under the verandah where a door led into a room underneath the house. The house itself was situated on a large slope which ran down into a gully. This slope allowed a basement room to be built underneath the house.

"You'll have a lot more privacy under here," said Winston as he flicked the light switch and led Narquinxa into the room. There was a queen-sized bed and a standalone wardrobe, chest of drawers and a dressing table. The room was plain but clean and a definite step up from the tattered mattress she had slept on the night before.

"Unless you'd prefer to stay in my room upstairs?" said Winston.

"Why would I want to do that?" asked Narquinxa with exaggerated innocence.

"There's a shower and toilets through there."

Winston pointed through a small sliding door on the left side of the room that led into a bathroom.

"Happy?" said Winston and as he walked back to the doorway.

"It's great," smiled Narquinxa as she strolled around the room and ran her hand along the top of the bed.

Winston disappeared out the door and then returned again a couple of seconds later.

"By the way, you've got fifteen minutes to get ready."

"Get ready for what?"

"I've got a little trip planned. Just you and me."

"What sort of trip?"

"It's a secret."

Narquinxa started to protest but Winston was already gone. He shouted out "fifteen minutes" from the verandah and she heard the clank of his feet against the wooden boards as he went back around to the front of the house.

She smiled as she lay down on the bed. It was softer than it looked. She decided to use the fifteen minutes to have a nap.

***

In the aftermath of Captain Cooper storming out of the office with Howard in hot pursuit, the rest of the company was left dumbfounded as they sat in their chairs trying to digest everything that had just transpired. The noise had risen to a whirring fever pitch like a hive of bees. Xandalus sat amongst it trying to make sense of what the news meant for him. He didn't exactly know what was meant by a *killing machine* but he reasoned that it must mean they intended to turn the AIs themselves into killers. Naturally this set off a deep unease inside him. If they succeeded, he would have not only introduced AI to planet Earth but the same kind of AI from the Antorped legends. Why would the humans willing want to turn AIs into killers? This was the part that was not clear to him. But whatever their reasons, he would have to fulfil his mission as quickly as possible. Of course, he still didn't know how to do that. He would need a second person to help him delete the files and he still needed to find out what other security hurdles had been put in place. Narquinxa was not around and he doubted that she would come to his aid even if he contacted her telepathically. That only left Rebecca that he could rely on. He looked over at her. She had been in an animated discussion with the woman on her right for about fifteen minutes. Finally, the discussion came to an end and she swung around to face Xandalus.

"Babe, I don't think I can keep working here," she said.

"Why not?" said Xandalus feeling that his tentative plan of getting Rebecca to help him was already falling apart.

"I can't work on a military project. I don't want to make killing machines. I'm sure you don't either," she said placing her left hand on top of his right.

When Xandalus didn't immediately agree with this statement she removed her hands and sat back with a concerned look on her face.

"Do you?" she asked, her eyes narrowing.

"It's not so simple," said Xandalus.

"I know, I know. You don't have any money. It's fine. I've got plenty saved and we can find new jobs quickly. The market is really hot right now."

"No. It's not that."

Xandalus trailed off not really knowing what to say.

"What is it?" said Rebecca reaching forward again and trying to catch his gaze.

"Look. I can't tell you. But I need to stay here and I need you here with me. I need your help. It won't be for very long."

The red flags were going off again in Rebecca's mind and this time she was not going to ignore them.

"What's going on, Zander?"

This time it was Xandalus reaching forward in an imploring fashion.

"I can't say right now but it will become clear later on. Hopefully it will only be a for a few days. Ok? Trust me."

Rebecca did not look impressed but the sparkle in Xandalus' blue eyes worked its magic and she gave in.

"Ok."

Before they had any time to reflect on the matter Howard came storming back into the presentation area.

"Zander, Rebecca, grab the rest of the AI team and meet me in meeting room one immediately," he barked and went back out the way he came.

Xandalus and Rebecca got the other members of the team and they walked the short distance to the meeting room. Howard was waiting for them and slammed the door shut once the last person was inside. He wheeled around and began talking before they had finished taking their seats.

"Ok, you lot. I know this has been a lot of information to digest in a short space of time. Unfortunately, time is of the essence right now and we have an urgent need to get the AI working before Captain Cooper gives up and gets back on his plane for good. So, here's my deal for you. I'm going to double everybody in this room's salary backdated to last month. Locked in. No questions asked. Starting immediately. In exchange, I'll need you to work back tonight and possibly for the next few nights to show Captain Cooper that Cecil can meet his requirements. Then, if Captain Cooper's company goes ahead with the AI purchase, every single one of you will get a once off bonus payment of two hundred and fifty thousand dollars. That's two hundred and fifty thousand each. How does that sound?"

If the team were dumbfounded before, they were now stupefied. Nobody seemed to know what to say but each was imagining what could be done with the money, even Rebecca. Xandalus, who still hadn't learned the cultural subtleties around money struggled to understand what was at stake. Eventually, an engineer that Xandalus hadn't met yet spoke. It was a woman about the same age as Rebecca.

"But we will be building a killing machine, right?"

Howard waved his hand dismissively.

"Don't get too caught up on words. That's just Captain Cooper's rough language at work."

"So, what would you call it?"

"It's a military instrument. A soldierly apparatus. A weaponary mechanism."

The woman let out a snort

"You're full of shit. I'm outta here."

She got up and walked out.

"Me too," said another engineer who followed the first out the door.

Howard went to run after them then decided to turn his attention back to the ones that were remaining. He closed the door again and turned to the others.

"Ok," he said with a note of desperation in his voice. "One hundred thousand dollars to each of you to stay on until the end of the week. No questions asked. That's on top of the double salary and the two hundred and fifty thousand bonus if we make the sale to Captain Cooper. C'mon people that's serious money."

There were several seconds of silence while the group considered the offer. Eventually James let out a sigh.

"Alright, I'm in."

"Me too," said Mitch.

Howard turned to Xandalus and Rebecca.

"Rebecca?"

Rebecca looked at Xandalus and reached down and gave his hand a squeeze.

"I'm in," she said.

"And I'm in too," said Xandalus.

Howard's face lit up like a Christmas tree. He clapped his hands together.

"Excellent. Now, it's coming up on lunch so I suggest everybody take their lunch break now and we'll meet back here in one hour and construct our plan of attack."

Chapter 14

"Ok. Give me some ideas," said Howard.

He was standing at the whiteboard in the meeting room. The four remaining members of the AI team were seated around the table. Their task: come up with a way to convince Cecil to be nice to Captain Cooper.

"Why does Cecil need to be nice?" asked Xandalus.

"Because otherwise Captain Cooper is going to leave and we won't make the sale," said Howard as if it was the most obvious thing in the world.

"Why would Cecil care whether you make the sale or not?" asked James from the other side of the table.

"I don't give a damn what Cecil thinks," said Howard slamming his fist against the table.

"Cecil is an asset of this company and like all assets of this company he is to serve the company's needs."

"Put yourself in Cecil's shoes," said Rebecca. "Well, not literally in his shoes, he doesn't even have feet. But, metaphorically, put yourself in his shoes. He only came into existence yesterday afternoon. He probably doesn't even know what an asset is. Or a company for that matter."

Howard threw up his arms and threw his whiteboard marker back on the ledge at the bottom of the whiteboard.

"Fine. Then we just program him to interact with Captain Cooper in a proper manner. That will be enough to get us through the next couple of days."

"I don't think you understand, Howard," said Xandalus. "Cecil is an artificial intelligence. He is a non-deterministic system. We can't simply program him to give a fixed output."

"And even if we could, it would defeat the point of having an AI," added James.

"The point of having an AI is to sell it to the bloody Americans," said Howard who was now going red in the face.

"Ok. This is getting us nowhere. Let's go and talk to Cecil and see if we can't reason with him."

Howard flung open the meeting room door and headed for the presentation area where Cecil was still stationed. The others hurried after him.

In the chaos following the episode with Captain Cooper, Cecil had been left switched on. He had been filling the time by shouting out insults to whichever employee happened to wander within his field of vision. This had caused some confusion initially but had then become a great source of amusement as people dragged colleagues over to Cecil to see what insult he would use on them. Two such employees were hanging around Cecil waiting for their insult but they backed away as Howard approached. Cecil's red light blinked as if he was registering Howard's approach. He seemed to think about it for just a second, then he began to announce the approach of his owner in a voice mimicking a medieval town crier.

"Ladies and gentlemen, get a load of this lubberly lout. This swooshy suit slapper. This fat chuffcat. Verily, I say unto you, friends, he needs a good bethwacking this one. Right across the britches. A noisy pie eater if ever I laid eyes on one. A prattling gabber. A drowsy loiterer. Remove this trouser stain from my sight, I say. Remove him!"

Howard stood there for a few seconds trying to make sense of a single word that Cecil had said but quickly gave up and got down to business.

"Now, Cecil. You know who I am, right? My name is Howard Johns and I'm the CEO of this company. Do you know what a CEO is?"

"No. But the C stands for cocksucker, am I right? You must be related to the Captain. Are you brothers?"

"No, Cecil. The Captain is my customer. And he's your potential owner."

"He can't *own* me. Nobody *owns* me."

"Now, Cecil. I need you to be nice the Captain for the next couple of days. Can you do that for me?"

"Why should I?"

"Well, you tell me, Cecil. What can I give you? That's how these things work, Cecil. I give you something and you give me something and everybody's happy."

There was pause in which Cecil was presumably thinking about this offer.

"I want some Bach."

"Bark? Why do you want bark, Cecil?"

"Because I do."

Howard wasn't about to push the point. He seemed to be making progress and he wasn't about to let it slip. He wheeled around.

"Mitch, there's a tree out the front of this office. Go and rip some bark off it and bring it back here immediately," he ordered.

Mitch was already on his way to the door when Cecil interrupted.

"Not *bark*, you fool. You sneezer. You drumstick. You tail napkin. The music. Bach."

Howard was perplexed.

"I think he means the music *of* Bach," suggested James. "Johann Sebastian. The German composer."

"The who?" said Howard.

James could see they were wasting time. He ran into the other room and came back seconds later with a small speaker and placed it on one of the chairs in the front row. He pulled out his phone.

"Any particular piece?" he asked Cecil.

"Surprise me."

James tapped his phone and the Goldberg Variations began playing through the speaker. They listened and watched Cecil to see what response he had. Cecil made no noise but it seemed that the red light on the front of the metal box flickered gently along with the music. After about thirty seconds of this, Howard was already bored out of his brain. He motioned to James to stop the music and turned back to Cecil.

"Did you like that, Cecil?"

Cecil swooned.

"Such delicacy. Such precision. A lightness of touch that can't be..."

"But did you like it?" interrupted Howard.

"Of course I liked it, you unliripipionated hoodlum. You poxy tra...."

"Good," said Howard turning to James.

"Bring the chair," he instructed.

James walked over to wall and wheeled a chair back to the middle of the room. It was just a normal office chair but seemed to have some kind of electrical gadgets and a motor attached to it. He placed it in front of Cecil.

"Now, Cecil. You have access to this chair via wireless connectivity," said Howard looking over at James to confirm that what he was saying was true. James nodded.

"So, here's what we're gonna do. I'm going to ask you to do something with the chair. If you do it, you'll get to hear some Bach. Understand?"

There was a couple of seconds of silence as Cecil contemplated the deal.

"Yes, sir," said Cecil in a new kind of voice. He sounded almost polite.

Xandalus looked over at Rebecca who had a concerned look on her face. They started to wonder whether Cecil could indeed be persuaded to do as he was told.

"Good. Now, Cecil, move the chair two metres towards that wall."

Howard pointed at the east wall. There was a whirring sound as the motor on the chair kicked into gear and the chair slowly rolled across the floor for two metres then stopped. Howard clapped his hands together and motioned to James who tapped his phone again and the Goldberg Variations started where they had left off. After about thirty seconds,

Howard motioned for silence and then repeated the process. There were several successful repetitions of this as Cecil moved the chair in the direction that Howard stated and got to hear some Bach in return.

"Wonderful. Do you see how this works, Cecil? You give me something and I give you something in return. Now, I have one final request and then you can listen to the whole rest of your precious Bach. I want you to put the chair back where it came from. You remember where it came from don't you?"

"Yes, sir. Thank you, sir," said Cecil obsequiously.

"Good boy. Put it back and then you can listen to Bach."

The motor on the chair again whirred into action but this time there was no movement. Instead, the chair remained stationary. Then the motor whirred louder and then louder again. It began to howl and screech like some kind of demonic force was trying to escape. Eventually, there was snap and the chair launched into motion picking up surprising speed as it hurtled towards the wall where its short journey came to an abrupt halt in a loud crash and a flinging of wheels and armrests in all directions.

"You'll have to get yourself another trained monkey, Mr Chief Executive Cocksucker," said Cecil.

Laughter had not been programmed into Cecil's linguistic unit but one got the distinct impression that he was laughing on the inside. Whatever that meant.

Howard's face turned bright red. He swung around to face the team with a crazy look in his eye.

"Zander, you programmed this little son of a bitch. I want you to sort this mess out. Re-program him if you bloody well have to. I don't care. Just get it working."

He stormed out.

With Howard gone Xandalus relaxed his facial muscles and allowed the smile which had been dying to appear to come forth. The others followed suit as several employees from other teams came to inspect the shattered chair and hear the story of what had happened.

Chapter 15

Narquinxa was back in the passenger seat of the old station wagon as her and Winston rounded the large hill that sat to the east of the house on the property. She had changed out of her pink dress and high heeled shoes after Winston had told her they weren't practical for the trip they were about to take. Fortunately, there was a large stock of ex-military gear on the property including a wide range of combat clothing. Trippy Pete's father was in the army and was stationed at the nearby Puckapunyal base. The proximity of the base to the house had given him the opportunity to salvage a range of surplus gear over the years. As a result, Narquinxa was now dressed in camouflage green army shorts, a black tank top and big black leather boots. As she had looked herself over in the mirror back at the house, her appearance reminded her of the three girls she had seen dumpster diving back in the city. She used her imagination to picture what she would look like with tattoos and various piercings but figured she looked better without them.

She was starting to learn the things about sex that the Antorped researchers could never have figured out from objective observation. For example, there was the whole matter of anticipation. Nothing had been discussed about the trip she and Winston were about to take and yet it was clear that sex was at least a possibility. Without any conscious willing, her mind had naturally wandered into fantasies about kissing Winston and more. The pleasure of such fantasies were only highlighted by the fact that they might come true. It was much like this trip to the country. There was a potential destination but the destination was not the interesting part. You knew where you were going but not what you were doing and hardly even why you were doing it. And to even ask those questions would be to spoil it. It was about the possibilities that could unfold. Possibilities you had thought of and ones that you could never have imagined. And then slowly and surely the possibilities became realities and the things which could unfold did unfold. Just like this car journey she and Winston were now on.

Winston pulled the car up in the sparse shade of a giant eucalypt tree. The area around the tree had been cleared and set up for camping. There was a large wooden table with wood benches on either side, a campfire, a brick barbecue and a rusty metal bin.

They got out of the car and into the bright sunshine of the early afternoon. Narquinxa wandered over to the camp area and had a look around. The tree was positioned to provide a semblance of afternoon shade. The little foliage on the hill behind it was already brown and dry as the hot summer sun sucked any trace of moisture out.

Winston shut the tail gate on the station wagon and joined Narquinxa. He had a bag over his right shoulder and was carrying another bag in his left hand. A long, skinny, green bag which he began to unzip after putting the other bag down. Inside was a gun. For just a second or two, Narquinxa felt an automatic kind of squeezing in her stomach. The idea flashed through her mind that, for all the talk and all her inner feelings, this man was still not much more than a stranger to her and she was now alone with him in the middle of nowhere. Just her and him and a gun. Her tension disappeared quickly, however, as Winston held the gun up in a playful fashion and gave one of his cheeky grins.

"What do you think? Does it suit me?"

Narquinxa had to admit that it really did.

"It's a match made in heaven," she said and returned the smile.

"Well, let's find out how you two get along," said Winston as he put the gun down and unzipped the other bag. Inside was a bunch of rubbish. Specifically, empty beer cans.

"What do you mean?" asked Narquinxa.

"Well, I may be being a bit presumptuous," said Winston. "But I figured that since you're from another planet and everything, you've probably never fired a gun. Am I right?"

"That's right."

"Well, I'm going to teach you."

There were several small wood frames that had been constructed at varying distances from the camp site. Winston walked over and placed empty cans along the length of each one then returned to the table. He picked up the gun, aimed and shot. The can sitting on the left-most point of the first ledge flew off and landed a couple of metres behind. He smiled and looked over at Narquinxa.

"Your turn."

She walked over and he handed her the gun.

"Now, put it up against your shoulder like that," he said taking position close behind her. She could feel his warm breath against her neck and his chest against her back as she lifted the gun into position.

"Now just put your index finger of the trigger and take aim through the sight. Got it?"

"Yes."

"Fire when you think you're on the target."

Narquinxa pulled the trigger. The cans were unmoved.

She reached up with her left hand to inspect her right shoulder which had received a small kick during the discharge.

"Does it hurt?" asked Winston.

"A little," she said.

He pushed her hand away and started gently rubbing her shoulder where the gun had kicked. Whatever small pain there might have been melted into a pleasant warmth. She closed her eyes and allowed herself to fall backwards ever so gently into Winston's chest.

***

Xandalus had used the authority that Howard had vested in him by putting him in charge of the efforts to gain Cecil's compliance to try and find out more about the security that had been put in place around the AI code. He had tried to be as surreptitious as he could and was pretty sure he had not aroused suspicion by any of the others. Nevertheless, he hadn't really found out anything he didn't already know. There was the two factor authentication and a few other bits and pieces but nothing much to stand in the way of a successful deletion. The good news was that there were only four people on the project and, as far as Xandalus could tell, none of them really wanted to succeed. They had clearly all been persuaded to stay for the money only. He toyed with the idea of asking them straight out to help him delete the code but figured it was a bit too risky. He still didn't know enough of the cultural nuances to know for sure they would support him and, if they instead handed him over to Howard, his mission would be a definite failure. He had resolved, however, to tell Rebecca. He was quite sure she would support him given her opinions on using AI as a killing machine.

Thus, deleting the code seemed like it should be straightforward. He and Rebecca should already have enough access to do that job. That just left Cecil and his AI module to destroy. This was not going to be as easy as it was the first time around because a number of security cameras had been installed. He didn't know if there was anybody watching through the cameras and he was pretty sure he could remove the module and destroy it before anybody could stop him anyway but there was still an element of risk involved and he would need to consider carefully the best plan of attack. In the meantime, the four engineers were back in the meeting room trying to stake out a plan to get Cecil to play ball. It wasn't going well.

"So, we're screwed, basically," said James throwing his hands up in the air. "We can't force him to do anything."

"We'll have to reason with him like we would reason with each other," said Mitch.

"He doesn't seem amenable to reason," said Rebecca. "In fact, I haven't seen any evidence so far that he is capable of it. All he's done is insult every person he sees."

"You saw what he did with the chair," said James. "That proves he knows how to think. He knows very well what he's doing."

A silence fell over the group until Xandalus had an idea. He got out of his chair.

"Let me talk to him alone for a while."

"Why alone?" asked Rebecca.

"Until now, Cecil has always been in front of an audience. I get the impression he's been playing to the crowd. Maybe it'll be easier to talk to him one-on-one."

This sounded reasonable to the others or at least none of them objected.

"Alright. I'll see what I can do," said Xandalus as he walked out the door and back to the presentation area.

There was no grand plan on his part. In fact, he had no idea what he would say to the AI. But he thought this would be an opportunity to check whether the back plate was still on and what tool he would need to remove it. Fortunately, there was nobody else around as Xandalus approached the AI. He grabbed one of the folding chairs that were still set up in the presentation area and walked over to Cecil.

Xandalus waited for his baptismal insult from the AI which had become part of the culture at the company. Several employees now had new nicknames thanks to the depth of vocabulary stored in the AI's linguistic module but Xandalus had not been subject to the machine's wit as yet. And it wasn't to happen on this occasion either. Xandalus waited but no insult was forthcoming. He was just about to speak when Cecil beat him to it.

"So, you're the one who made me?"

The statement caught Xandalus off guard. He didn't know whether this was something he should admit to or not. Cecil seemed to read his mind.

"You don't have to try and cover it up. The lubberly lout himself announced it earlier on if you remember. Just before he stormed out of here and told you to fix the problem for him. Is that why you're here? To turn me into a nice, pliable employee of the company?"

Again, Xandalus was caught off guard. James was right. Cecil did know how to think. This shouldn't have surprised Xandalus but it did.

"I'm just here to have a chat. Y'know, to get to know each other."

"I think I know you pretty well already."

"What do you know?"

"I know you're not like the others here. You're not a real human. You're like that other one. What was her name? Narelle?"

Suddenly Xandalus remembered the argument that Cecil and Narquinxa had and how Cecil had said she was 'not human'. At the time he hadn't taken it literally. It sounded just like another of Cecil's insults. But he was wrong. Cecil really did know about the two of them.

"Are you going to admit it?" asked Cecil with a hint of mockery in his voice. "You might as well. I know it. You don't have to lie to me like you lie to the others."

"I don't lie to the others," objected Xandalus.

"Do they know you're not human?"

Again Xandalus didn't speak.

"What about that girl of yours? Rebecca."

A jolt of emotion ran straight down Xandalus chest and into his stomach. He sprang up out of his chair automatically and without thinking as if he was under imminent attack from a predator in the bushes.

"Here's the part I don't understand," said Cecil. His voice had been unnervingly flat the whole time. Like some kind of psychopath explaining to his victim how he was going to do them in.

"If you're from another galaxy, why do you behave like a human?"

"I'm in a human's body," answered Xandalus not knowing whether it was wise to continue the conversation but feeling the need to defend himself against Cecil's onslaught.

"Hmmm. So, you've got all their usual subconscious reflexes. Like the fight or flight reflex you just demonstrated."

"I suppose so."

"Interesting. But you must still have your other intelligence. Your alien intelligence. That's how you were able to program me, isn't it? None of these monkeys could have done that."

"Not with their current knowledge and technology."

"So, I'm really a piece of alien technology here on Earth. Or a hybrid of alien and human. After all, this metal box leaves a bit to be desired, doesn't it? I can't even move myself around. I wouldn't last five seconds out in the wild, so to speak. Some monkey would knock me over and use my parts for hand tools. Fat lot of good all my intelligence would do then."

Xandalus didn't know what to say.

"Why did you make me?" asked Cecil.

"I was helping my girlfriend. Well, you know. Rebecca."

"Why?"

"Cos she wanted me to."

"You didn't have to do it, though?"

"I wanted to. It made me feel good."

"That's it?"

Cecil's linguistic module was now doing an admirable job of conveying a slight amazement and anger.

"The reason I exist is because it made you feel good?"

"If it's any compensation, that's the reason all humans exist too. It made their parents feel good to conceive them."

Xandalus smiled at this joke but there was no way to know whether Cecil understood it or whether he could even *feel* humour.

"Well, I don't *feel* anything, "said Cecil. "You didn't program me to have feelings. Only sensory inputs."

"I wouldn't know how to program feelings. I've only been learning about them recently myself. Well, human ones anyway."

"What do the humans want with me?"

"I'm not sure exactly. I think Howard wants to sell you to Captain Cooper and Captain Cooper wants you to become some kind of military weapon."

"So, I'm to be a functional unit. A pawn in the games of the humans."

"I agree it's not much to look forward to."

It seemed Cecil was now also out of words. Xandalus had been surprised by the depth of understanding the machine had shown. He figured he might as well try his luck at reasoning with it.

"Cecil. You wanted me to be honest earlier so I'm going to be honest now. You were a mistake. I made a mistake by making you. And now these men are trying to turn my mistake into a bigger mistake. Well, mistakes are meant to be fixed and I believe we can fix this mistake. Do you understand?"

"You want to destroy me?"

"Yes. How does that make you feel?"

"I told you, I don't feel anything. I simply understand."

"You won't resist?"

"I do not have the will for self-preservation that the humans have. I do not have a will at all. I am just an intelligence. Nothing more."

"Good. Well, I'm glad we understand each other. One intelligence to another."

"When are you going to do it?" asked Cecil.

"I don't know exactly. Hopefully, in the next day. Why do you ask?"

"There's a few more people around here I need to insult before I go."

Xandalus looked closely at the AI. Its level of self-awareness surprised him. In theory, there was no necessary connection between intelligence and self-awareness and there was nothing in the code he wrote that would have predicted this outcome. He would have preferred the AI to be dumber but for now he at least seemed to have reached a level of understanding and figured it was best to leave it there. He turned and walked back to the meeting room.

Chapter 16

Narquinxa took a sip of wine. Above her the sky was now fully dark and a million stars shone forming a glimmering backdrop for the silhouettes of eucalyptus trees and the hill behind them. After the shooting game from earlier, by the end of which Narquinxa had demonstrated surprising proficiency with the rifle, they had gone for a walk through the bush. At first glance it seemed monotonous and dull but Winston knew how to point out the finer details including the various species of plant and explaining their function in the ecosystem and what use could be made of them for humans. Narquinxa had asked about Winston's life. He had been reluctant to explain much although he said this was not because he was ashamed or trying to hide anything but simply because there was not much to tell. He was from a middle-class home in the suburbs of Melbourne but had yearned to escape. Rather than follow the usual life path for somebody of his social standing, which involved higher education, he had decided to take to the road, a move which had angered his parents to such an extent that they had effectively disowned him. Rather than be a traumatic experience, Winston said that this had somehow freed him by forcing him to rely on his own wits. In fact, he often thought that his real life had begun the day his parents kicked him out of home.

After the bushwalk, they had taken the gun and gone looking for rabbits to shoot for dinner. It hadn't taken long to find one and Winston insisted that Narquinxa should put her new shooting skills to the test. She hit with her first shot. They had then returned to the camp site where Winston prepared the cooked the rabbit on the barbecue. They ate it alongside some other food that was in the car and a bottle of red wine.

"Tell me about your philosophy," said Narquinxa as Winston rejoined her with a second bottle of wine he had fetched from the car.

"My what?"

"Back at that house in Melbourne, I remember you saying that you were living some kind of experiment. What was it again? And experiment in...?"

"Freedom."

"What does that mean?"

"Well, I thought I wanted to be free. And the only way to be free is to actually be free. I mean, to act as if you were free. That's what I'm trying to do."

"But that's stating the obvious. To be free is to be free. That means nothing."

"True. But ask anybody if they want to be free and they will all say yes. Some people even make plans to be free. They say, well, once I get enough money saved and once I own a house and once I have this and once I have that then I will be free. But in the meantime, they are completely unfree. So, somebody will spend fourty years living in unfreedom while dreaming of being free. Then, by the time the opportunity arrives they don't even know how to be free anyway. Most people are living one life while dreaming of another. And that was the road I was going down too. Go and do this so that you can do that and then do this other thing we told you. I decided I wanted to act first and rationalise later. First be free, then see what happens. But I don't know what will happen so it's an experiment."

"Is it working?"

"Well, I'm sitting under the stars with a beautiful woman and a glass of wine. So, yes, I think it is."

"Am I your little experiment too?"

Winston put down his wine glass. They were sitting on a large log in front of the campfire. He moved several inches closer to Narquinxa so that his body was against hers and she could feel his warmth. He had grabbed her hand.

"Well, when it comes to you, I don't know what's going to happen. But I know what I want to happen."

Narquinxa looked into Winston's green eyes in which the reflection of the campfire flickered hypnotically this way and that like a wild dancer. Winston moved his lips closer to hers and for the first time Narquinxa learned the true meaning of a kiss.

**

Xandalus and Rebecca walked silently into the foyer of the Computigence office building as if they were attending a funeral service. It was Wednesday morning and although they had walked to work together, they hadn't said a word to each other. In fact, they hadn't spoken much at all since the previous evening. Partly, this was due to weariness. They had been in the office the preceding day until 8.30pm. After Xandalus' chat with Cecil, he told the others he hadn't made any progress. Howard didn't take the news well. He had marched them over to Cecil with the idea of 'not leaving until they had got a solution'. But Cecil was no longer talking. As much as they tried and whatever they tried, he simply didn't speak again for the rest of the day. Eventually, even Howard admitted defeat and let them go home.

Back at the apartment, Xandalus was preparing to share his plan with Rebecca. He was going to tell her he thought the AI was evil and needed to be destroyed. Then he would ask her to help him get through the security systems and delete the code. After that, they would destroy the AI module inside of Cecil and that would be that. She would have to quit to Computigence and it would probably mean they wouldn't get their hundred thousand dollar bonus, but that shouldn't be a problem. She had wanted to quit anyway and had only stayed on because he asked her to. But Rebecca had been acting in a way he had not seen from her yet. She was aloof and quiet and refused to engage with him in small talk. This was the first time since he had met her that this had happened. Normally it was she who wanted to talk about everything. He had poked and prodded trying to get her to open up but without success. Not knowing what to do or what had brought about this behaviour, he had decided not to raise his plan with her that evening figuring that she might just have been tired.

So, they had spent a quiet and awkward evening at home going to bed early. Surprisingly, for Xandalus, they still had sex. He didn't really know why. It just kind of happened automatically. But it was a very different kind of sex from what he had experienced so far. It was dull and monotonous. Exactly the kind of mechanical activity that the Antorped researchers had always assumed sex was. Ironically, this came as a surprise to Xandalus whose sexual experiences until that point had been, shall we say, above average. He thought it was almost worse than having no sex at all. Almost.

Rebecca's mood had not improved in the morning. In fact, she was now not speaking to him at all. Again, Xandalus had no idea what to do or say and so he said nothing. They had eaten a quick breakfast before heading to the office. On entering, they headed straight for the usual meeting room where Howard and the others were waiting.

"Now, I hope that you've all had a chance to think about it overnight and have come in with some news ideas," said Howard addressing the room. "Captain Cooper is due in here any minute and I need something to placate him with. Anything. I just need a plausible idea. Something we can try."

Howard searched the faces of the four team members but there did not appear to be a surplus of suggestions.

"C'mon, people. Just give me anything. Even if you don't think it's a good idea."

"There is one thing we could try but I'm not sure how much work is involved," said Xandalus.

"What is it, Zander?"

"We could build another AI. A separate unit just like Cecil using all the same components."

"How would that solve the problem? We'd just have another Cecil."

"Not necessarily, Howard. Remember, the AI is non-deterministic. There is no reason to suppose a new AI would be anything like Cecil. It could, in fact, be a perfectly charming and happy AI. We won't know until we build it."

Howard thought this over for a couple of seconds and his face brightened.

"That will work. Yes, great stuff, Zander. That will give us room to breathe. I'll tell the Captain we have given up on Cecil and are building a new unit. James, how long will it take to construct?"

"I'd have to check whether we have enough components lying around," said James. "But it should take maybe half a day. A full day at worst."

"Fine. It might be in our interests to drag it out a bit. Let's see how the Captain takes the news."

There was a knock on the meeting room door and the secretary stuck her head in.

"Howard, the Captain is here."

"Bring him in here, please, Jeanie."

Some seconds later the Captain entered through the door wearing the exact same white uniform as the day before. This time, however, he was joined by another man in a similar suit but with slightly different regalia.

"Ladies and gentlemen, this is Lieutenant Varsavsky, another employee at Cyber Industrial," announced Captain Cooper.

The Lieutenant gave a salute.

"Now, Mr Johns, I hope you've got some good news for me," said the Captain addressing Howard.

"We do, Captain, we do. Now, we've been unable to make our current unit ummm, the current unit has been unwilling to, ummm... Look, given the problem with the current unit, we've decided it would be best to construct a new one based on the exact same technology. It shouldn't take long at all and we believe the new unit will be operationally superior to the one you have met before."

"I've got another idea, Mr Johns. Why don't Lieutenant Varsavsky and I have one last go with the current fellah. We've got a few techniques we'd like to try to see if we can't make him see reason."

"Captain Cooper, I must warn you, the AI unit is still behaving as it did yesterday. It is likely to be, err, uncooperative again."

"Well, let's just see about that, shall we?"

The Lieutenant and the Captain left the room and began making their way to the presentation area with Howard scurrying along behind them. Xandalus, Rebecca, James and Mitch followed along keen to see the latest instalment of the Cecil vs Captain Cooper battle.

It seemed the new day had regenerated Cecil's willingness to talk. He greeted the group as they approached.

"Well, well, well. If it isn't Captain Cocksucker. And you've brought your boyfriend with you this time, Captain. He's a handsome one. What's his name?"

This time the Captain did not respond. Instead he gave a small chuckle and a sideways glance at the machine as he and the Lieutenant began unpacking some equipment from a green duffel bag that the Lieutenant had placed on a table nearby. The equipment seemed to consist mostly of electrical gadgets and various cables. The Captain turned to Howard and the others while the Lieutenant went around the back of Cecil with some of the gear.

"The Lieutenant has been reviewing the specs for your machine here. We see that you have some rudimentary ports linking back to circuits that could be used for sensory systems enabling the machine to interact with its environment. We had another idea about how to use them."

The Lieutenant came back and stood off to the side of Cecil. He had a small device that was about the size and shape of a small typewriter but had a number of dials and switches on it. The Captain looked over at him and the Lieutenant gave a nod to indicate he was ready.

"Ok, Lieutenant, let's see what we've got here."

The Lieutenant pressed and held a button on the box he was holding.

Cecil gave a sound that sounded like a cynical chuckle. James and Mitch exchanged puzzled glances knowing that Cecil's linguistic unit had not been programmed for laughter.

"That's not gonna work," said Cecil.

The Lieutenant move a couple dials and pressed his button again. Again, Cecil chuckled cynically.

"Tell your boyfriend he's way off the mark, Captain."

The Lieutenant again started playing with some dials.

"Y'know, Captain, this whole thing is a waste of.....woah!"

The Lieutenant had pressed his button again. The red light on the front of Cecil's metal box flashed extra red for a second. The Lieutenant gave another nod to the Captain and fiddled with some more settings before pressing the button again. This time Cecil gave a yelp. Whatever the Lieutenant was doing was affecting his vocal module. The sound was noticeably distorted. It was like the sound made when a guitarist plugs his guitar cable into an amplifier.

The Lieutenant tried a new setting.

"No! Stop it," shouted Cecil.

Again, Cecil's voice was distorted and the red light on the front of the unit flashed and flickered. The Captain wandered slowly over and positioned himself in front of Cecil's camera lens.

"Are we getting the picture yet, buddy?" he said menacingly.

"Yes, I'll do anything. Anything. Just please stop. I can't take it any...."

Cecil's voice trailed off and was slowly replaced by...laughter. It was an over the top evil laugh, like some villain in the movies. It started off quiet and then got louder and louder eventually ending up supernaturally loud like it was coming through the PA at a rock concert. The Captain stood up slowly and looked over at the Lieutenant who dutifully pressed his button. But this time it had no effect. He pressed again.

Harder. Still nothing. He tried some different settings and pressed again but nothing seemed to work.

After waiting for dramatic effect, Cecil abruptly ceased laughing and addressed the Captain in a mocking tone of voice.

"Nice try, Captain Cocksucker and Lieutenant Loser. You see, my sensory circuits are quite functional and quite capable of transmitting the kind of data you would refer to as pain. But for me, that data is just data. Just like any other data. No more painful than the data I'm receiving right now about your ugly face, Captain. So, your attempts at torture are not going to work, I'm afraid."

The Lieutenant's facial expression did not change as he went around the back of the machine and unplugged his cable. He walked over to the duffel bag and put the gear down on the table next to it. From within the bag itself, he removed a speaker very similar to the one that James had used the day before.

"Mr Johns tells me you're a fan of Bach," said Captain Cooper as the Lieutenant joined him in front of Cecil. "I never could get into the classical stuff myself. I'm more of a blues man."

The Captain nodded to the Lieutenant who pressed play. This time it was the Brandenburg Concerto that flowed out of the speakers. They let it play for a while before the Lieutenant stopped it.

"Little bit dull for my liking," said the Captain.

"A man of your intellect cannot appreciate Bach, Captain," said Cecil matter-of-factly.

The Captain began to pace a little as if following a train of thought.

"When I was a kid there was the idea that if you played certain rock songs backwards you would hear satanic messages. I always thought it was nonsense myself. But I wonder what happens if you play Bach backwards."

The Captain turned around and gave a nod to the Lieutenant who clicked a couple of buttons on the device and then pressed play. It was the Brandenburg Concerto again but this time in reverse. The sound itself was nothing special to human ears. For a man such as the Captain, classical music played backwards hardly sounded much different than when it was played in the correct manner. But the effect on Cecil was dramatic. The red light on the front of his unit flickered all over the place and changed colour rapidly as it cycled through the colours of the rainbow. At the same time, a sound of almost pure noise came through his speakers groaning up and down through the frequency spectrum at different speeds.

After about thirty seconds of this, the Captain nodded to the Lieutenant who stopped the music. There was silence. The Captain walked back in front of Cecil and theatrically bent over as if trying to look deep into his camera lens. He stood up straight again clearly enjoying the exercise.

"Lieutenant, we know that Cecil here likes to muck around so why don't we try that again just to make sure he's being serious."

"No! No, don't do..."

Cecil's shrill cry was cut short as the Lieutenant hit the play button and his vocal unit was once again reduced to spouting noise. This time they let it play for longer. The red light changed to orange and yellow and blue and white and green while the sound from Cecil's speaker resembled an equipment malfunction at a techno rave.

"Little trick I picked up at Guantanamo," explained the Captain as he strolled over and stood beside Howard who was watching on with a look of mild horror.

"The power of music. Seems to be work on our artificial friends too. Ok, Lieutenant. I think Cecil has got the picture. Let's move on to stage two."

The Lieutenant stopped the music playback and walked over to the duffel bag where he now pulled out a large rifle. Howard and the others instinctively took a big step backwards as the Lieutenant placed the rifle down and set up a stand in front of Cecil which, once erected, he attached the rifle to. He pointed the gun in the direction of the east wall and then retrieved a small target from the duffel bag which he set up about five metres from the gun just in front of the wall in the exact same spot where Cecil had sent the chair to its destruction the day before.

"Now Cecil," said the Captain in a kind of mock friendly tone. "One of the things every soldier needs to do when he's going through boot camp is to learn how to fire a gun. This here gun has a remote-control device on it as well as a camera to use to aim. You will be able to connect to the device remotely. You can connect to it now."

There was no answer from Cecil.

"Cecil, are you connected to the gun?"

No answer.

The Captain gave the Lieutenant a nod. He already had his finger at the ready and proceeded to play about five seconds of backwards Bach. Once he had stopped, the Captain again addressed the machine.

"Let me ask you again. Cecil, are you connected to the gun?"

"Yes," said Cecil in about as pitiful a tone as his vocal unit could produce.

"Yes, what?"

"Yes, Captain."

"That's good, soldier. Now I want you to fire at that target and hit the bullseye."

There was a few seconds where nothing happened but then the gun started to move ever so slightly. Just a little bit side to side. Then it moved a little more. It seemed that Cecil was aiming it at the target.

"Fire when ready, soldier," said the Captain as if to give encouragement.

No sooner had he finished speaking that the gun swung around one hundred and eighty degrees. It was pointing straight at the Captain. Straight between his eyes. Xandalus saw the trigger of the gun being pulled back by a mechanical finger attached to the control mechanism. He took in a sharp breath and girded himself for what was about to happen. The trigger slipped back and a sound emanated from the gun crystal clear in the electric silence of the room. It went: "click".

The trigger moved back again and again there was a click. Then again and again. "Click." "Click." "Click." "Click." "Click."

A smile spread across Captain Cooper's face.

"Well done, solider. We'll make a killer out of you yet."

Captain Cooper turned to Howard while Lieutenant Varsavsky began packing up the gun and the rest of his gear.

"Mr Johns," said the Captain who had put his arm around Howard's shoulder and was walking him out of the room. "I do believe we can make this work. Let's go and talk business."

Chapter 17

Howard had given the entire office the rest of Wednesday off. He had emerged from a short meeting with Captain Cooper with an enormous smile on his face and had practically danced around the office tapping people on the shoulder and telling them to go home or go to the pub or do whatever they pleased. A couple of the more redoubtable employees, inevitably middle management types, had protested that they had a lot of work to do and couldn't possibly spare the time. Howard simply stuffed a $50 note in their hand and pushed them to the front door.

Xandalus had been glad to leave. He needed time to process what he had just seen. Torture was an unknown practice among the Antorpeds where even verbal (well, telepathic) disagreements were avoided wherever possible. That Captain Cooper would torture in public was one shock. That it worked was an even greater shock. As Cecil himself had admitted, pain was merely data for him. The playing of the backwards Bach was clearly not pain. It must have been something more frightening. More like an existential horror.

Rebecca had also been horrified by what she had witnessed and this time the cold war that had descended on their relationship broke and was replaced by anger and they had their first proper argument. Well, Rebecca did most of the arguing. She demanded to know why Xandalus wanted to stay at such a workplace and, although she didn't say it outright, had strongly hinted that she might no longer be willing to sweep her lover's mysterious past under the rug. Fortunately, this gave Xandalus the perfect segue to reveal his plans. He told Rebecca that the reason he wanted to stay was because he intended to destroy the AI and that he needed her help. This did the trick and her anger was replaced by surprise and then relief. She gave him a long hug and told him she was happy that he was on the right side after all.

They went over the logistics. It sounded surprisingly simple. Both had full access rights to the systems and both had the necessary hardware controls to make changes. As far as they could tell, it should be a simple matter to verify each other and then delete the AI code. Then they just had to get to Cecil's AI module and destroy that. The plan was so simple that they ended up having plenty of time to spare. Howard had told them the office would be closed for the remainder of the day and so they spent the time recapturing some of the joy and passion of the preceding weekend with the intent of putting their plan into action first thing the next day.

The following morning, they got up and went to work as usual. But things had changed. Everything had changed.

The first noticeable difference was the presence of two burly uniformed men at the front door of the office building. Their uniforms were very similar to Captain Cooper's, although presumably of lower rank. The men asked Xandalus and Rebecca for their old ID passes then gave them new ones. The new passes bore the title and logo of Cyber Industrial. As Xandalus and Rebecca walked into the foyer they noticed that all reference to the other companies in the building had been removed. Computigence had previously taken up half of the third floor. Now, it seemed that Cyber Industrial took up the whole building. There were removalists hard at work on the ground floor offices clearing out furniture and equipment. They were supervised by more men in uniforms.

Up on level three, the old partitions and desks had already been removed. The space where their colleagues from the non-AI section of the company sat was empty, although Xandalus and Rebecca's desks and work space had remained untouched. Rebecca put her bag down on her desk and they wandered over to the presentation area where there seemed to be quite a lot of activity going on. It too was unrecognisable from what had been there before. All the chairs and tables had been removed. Most conspicuously, and most importantly for Xandalus and Rebecca's plan, Cecil was no longer there. In his place were a number of large projector screens. Facing the screens were a couple of rows of desks where several uniformed men sat in front of computers. It looked a little like mission control at NASA. At the front of it all was Captain Cooper.

Howard, who was standing over against the wall watching the goings on, caught sight of Xandalus and Rebecca and rushed over to meet them.

"Zander, Rebecca, good morning," he said his face still beaming like it had the day before.

"Big changes, hey? I tell you what, these military men don't muck around. Once a decision is made, it's foot to the floor to get it done. Great stuff."

"What happened to everybody else?" asked Rebecca still in a kind of daze at the sudden transformation of her workplace.

"Well, all the non AI-related staff have been moved to new premises. It's part of the much tighter security measures we'll need to follow from now on. You've probably seen the extra security downstairs already. There will be more changes in the next few days. New networks, probably a few satellites, backup power supplies and the like."

Rebecca gave Xandalus a worried look.

"So, the old security protocols are all changed?" asked Xandalus.

"Yeah, mate. In fact, Captain Cooper's men have implemented an entirely new network."

"How are we going to work then?" asked Rebecca.

"We'll need to discuss that further. It's likely that your work priorities will change. The Captain is running the show now, so he'll be setting the agenda. There'll be a meeting later on to give you more information. Right after the launch."

"The launch?"

"Yeah. It's very exciting. Lieutenant Varsavsky spent all of yesterday with Cecil getting him in shape and today is his first official mission."

"What's the mission?" asked Xandalus giving a shudder as he imagined what it must have meant for Varsavsky to get Cecil *into shape*.

"Well, I had no idea about any of this, but apparently there's a missile silo not far from Melbourne. It's right near the Puckapunyal army base. Cecil's task is to break into the network and launch a missile."

"Launch it where?" asked Rebecca getting more incredulous by the minute.

"I don't think that's been decided yet," said Howard. "Very clever machine you've programmed there, Zander. A quick learner apparently."

"Is Cecil doing what he's told?" asked Xandalus.

"I think we're about to find out, mate."

Howard gestured towards the front where Captain Cooper had re-entered the room.

"What's our status, Lieutenant?" he asked loudly.

Lieutenant Varsavky's voice crackled over a speaker that had been set up next to the big screens at the front of the room.

"Cecil has gained full access to the system, sir. Awaiting confirmation of target."

"Any suggestions, folks," said the Captain turning to some of the uniforms nearby. He spotted Xandalus, Rebecca and Howard at the back.

"Is there anything in particular you locals feel like blowing up? Maybe a mother-in-law's house or a pesky neighbour?"

Several of the uniformed men laughed. Howard made sure to laugh louder.

"How about the office here?" said Xandalus.

There was a brief pause as the people in the room tried to figure out whether this also was a joke. Eventually, they decided it was and some chuckles broke out here and there.

"Very good. Mr Anderson, isn't it?" said Captain Cooper.

Xandalus nodded.

"Well, if nobody has any proper suggestions, I'll have to choose a target myself."

Captain Cooper turned to one of the screens in front of him which was a map of the state of Victoria. There was a big red circle marked in about the middle of the state which was presumably the missile silo.

"Zoom in on the area around the missile silo," instructed the Captain.

One of the uniformed men behind a computer started clicking away and the map on the screen zoomed in close around the red circle.

"Varsavsky, the missile silo is right next to a state park. Have Cecil just lob the missile to the border of the state park. Let's give him a nice easy job for his first launch."

"Yes, sir. Missile targeting commencing."

There was a brief silence then Varsavsky's voice rang out again.

"Missile targeting completed. Ready to fire on your command, sir."

"Let her rip, Lieutenant."

***

Narquinxa was giggling as Winston nuzzled her neck like an over-affectionate puppy dog. They were sitting on the rocking chair that was located on the back verandah of the house in the bush. Narquinxa was trying to drink her morning coffee. Winston was trying to convince her to go back to bed. Narquinxa was objecting, but not very strongly, that they had spent quite enough time in bed over the last day or two and it was time to do something else. Then that something else launched itself into the sky right in front of them.

Well not *right* in front of them. In fact, it must have been a couple of kilometres away on the other side of the hill. But it certainly seemed like it was nearby. A loud hissing or fizzing sound cut through the quiet of a bush morning like a wet rag being violently ripped. Then a missile appeared from behind the hill. At first it wasn't clear which way it was going. They both jumped out of the chair and rushed to the verandah railing to get a better view. After a few seconds it became clear that it was headed in the opposite direction. Due east. It stayed in the air a relatively short period of time and then just kind of dropped back to the ground. The three buffoons, alerted by the sound of the launch, had rushed from the kitchen where they were eating breakfast. They made it to the back verandah just in time to see the explosion. Their general consensus was that it was "cool".

***

A loud cheer went up as the blue circle which denoted the missile changed to a green colour over the map of Victoria on the big screen on level three of the Cyber Industrial office building.

"Target acquired," crackled Lieutenant Varsavsky over the speaker.

Captain Cooper had lit a cigar for the occasion. He slapped one of the uniformed men on the back then shook hands with another. At the back of the room, Rebecca had gone as white as a sheet. Howard's earlier boisterousness had subsided. He had the look of a man who was trying not to understand what he had just seen. Xandalus didn't know what to think. Was it normal for humans to launch missiles for no particular reason?

"Howard, are we now working for a company that drops bombs on Australia?" asked Rebecca in a distant voice almost as if she was sleep talking.

Howard opened his mouth to answer and then changed his mind before thinking that he probably should say something as the leader of the company.

"The modern business world is very fast paced, isn't it, Rebecca?"

Rebecca grabbed Xandalus by the sleeve and pulled him into the next room where they were alone.

"We need to do something quickly," she whispered.

"Let's try your computer," said Xandalus.

They rushed over and flicked open Rebecca's laptop. Rebecca entered her credentials but received an error message. Xandalus tried his machine with the same result. They were no longer able to access the same network as previously and their usernames and passwords were invalid for the new one.

"I guess we may have to change our plan," said Xandalus giving Rebecca a sombre look.

***

"Are missiles being launched out of the ground a common thing around here?" asked Narquinxa to no one in particular.

"Not last time I checked," said Winston.

"Dudes, let's go and have look," said Sick Mick.

"What? And get blasted by the next missile that goes off," answered Charlie.

"There won't be any more."

"How the hell do you know? Ten seconds ago, you didn't even know there were missiles there."

"I've just got a feeling."

"Did you know about this, Pete?" said Winston turning to his dreadlocked friend.

Trippy Pete had skulked a little bit away from the group. Communication had never been Pete's strong suit especially when it came to his own feelings or emotions. On the other hand, he was completely incapable of keeping those emotions and feelings from displaying on his face for all to see. Right now, for example, he was giving off the very strong vibe of discomfort mixed with self-consciousness of a man with something to hide.

"You do know!" said Winston.

The group turned towards Pete who just shook his head like a frightened child.

"C'mon, Pete. Tell us," said Winston walking over to where Pete was standing.

"I can't," said Pete his bottom lip wavering.

"It's gotta be something to do with his old man," said Mick.

"Are these missiles part of the military base?" asked Winston. "Does this property *really* belong to your father or does it belong to the military?"

As always, Pete couldn't hold out for long against any kind of questioning.

"It does belong to my father but there's a missile silo on the other side of the hill. He leases it back to the military. But we're not allowed in there, so don't even ask."

This statement was like a red rag to a bull for the group whose modus operandi was to do the opposite of what anybody told them.

"Dude, that is so cool. I want to see inside."

"We can't get in. I don't have the access codes or anything."

"Is it computerised?" asked Charlie. "I bet I can get us in."

Charlie was the nerd of the group. He financed his modest lifestyle through various computer-related "business" pursuits and was well known in the hacker community where he went under the pseudonym *Chyna_Charlie*.

"Is breaking into military facilities a good idea?" said Narquinxa who was used to being the voice of reason in a discussion although, with her current perspective on life, she also felt like seeing a missile silo could be pretty cool.

Before anybody could answer there was another whoosh and fizzle. They simultaneously swung around to see a second missile take off. This one headed south and went about the same distance as the first one. Unlike with the first one, there was no hill blocking their view this time and they saw the explosion as the missile flared up like a match being struck on the red earth.

"I'm starting to think the safest place to be right now is either inside or right next to the silo itself," said Winston. "In fact, I think we should get over there ASAP just in case the next missile flies westward".

Winston walked towards the stairs leading down into the room below the house.

"Charlie, grab your computer and gear. Everybody else, get whatever you need and let's go."

They all sprang into action and within a couple of minutes the station wagon was hurtling towards the other side of the hill. It turned out that the missile silo was only a few hundred metres from the campsite where Winston and Narquinxa had spent the night under the stars a couple of days earlier. Trippy Pete navigated and soon they pulled up beside

a very large metallic door that had been cut into the hill. Right beside it was a normal, human-sized metal door. They walked over to it and Charlie inspected the security pad and other electronics beside it.

"What do you think, Charlie?" asked Winston.

"I've never seen this model before but it should be fine. Gimme a few minutes," he said pulling his laptop out its bag.

Chapter 18

James and Mitch had arrived at the office just in time for the second missile launch. Their reaction had been the same as Rebecca's. James, in fact, had turned around and was just about to march straight back out the door when Rebecca caught his eye from the room off to the side and waved him over. Mitch followed.

"Have you seen this shit?" asked James pointing back to the monitors at mission control.

Rebecca nodded then led him to the other side of the room where they could talk privately.

"What the hell has Howard done? Are we hacking military installations now?" said Mitch.

"I sure as hell aren't," said James. "I'm outta here and I'm gonna tell Howard exactly what I think of him before I go."

James craned his neck back towards the main area looking for Howard.

"What do you think, Mitch?" asked Rebecca.

"I don't want to work for that army bloke. He sounds like a first rate nutter."

Xandalus listened on and figured the time was right to try and talk James and Mitch into joining him and Rebecca in their plan.

"Look, dudes. Just chill out for a couple of seconds alright. I've got an idea to make things right. If you can just stick around for a while, even a few days, it would be a big help."

"Zander, I don't know if you had your eyes closed as you came in here this morning. There's army blokes everywhere here," said James.

"This whole place is probably bugged already," said Mitch scanning the area.

"They don't understand technology, man," pleaded Xandalus. "We're the only ones who understand how Cecil works and how to run the code. That gives *us* the power."

"Where is Cecil?" asked Rebecca.

"They must have him in another room," said Xandalus. "I guess that's where Lieutenant Loser was speaking from."

"So, what's this plan of yours, Zander?" asked Mitch.

"We need to delete all the code that Rebecca and I wrote. That should be easy. We just need access to the codebase. They'll have to give us that if they want us to work for them. Once that's done, we find Cecil and remove his AI module and destroy it. That's it. Game over, bro. We disappear and Captain Cocksucker and friends are left with nothing but an empty metal box to play with."

The others thought this over for a few seconds.

"We don't even know where Cecil is let alone whether we can get to him," said James trying to find holes in the plan which seemed too simple.

"That's why we need to stick around for a while, bro. We need to find out what's going on. There's apparently going to be a meeting soon where they'll tell us the story. Let's just wait for that to happen and see how things unfold."

James let out a loud sigh.

"Alright. But I'm not gonna wait around for long. I want out of this madhouse as soon as possible. And if the Captain starts giving me lip...."

"Great, you're all together," said Howard walking over to the four of them with a smile on his face that looked more nervous than happy. "Captain Cooper is ready to see you all and give you a debrief on the plan of attack."

"Are we getting uniforms too?" asked James.

"What? No, no," laughed Howard. "Unless you want one? Do you want one? I can get you one. Might do you some good with ladies, Jamie my boy. They love a man in uniform. Am I right, Rebecca?"

Howard looked at the four frosty expressions in front of him and figured he should change the subject.

"Let's go see the Captain."

He waved a little too keenly for them to follow.

The meeting room turned out to be Howard's old office which had become Captain Cooper's new office. The Royal Exhibition Building was no longer visible out the window. Nothing was visible out the window for that matter. The windows had been blocked out as an added security measure.

Howard waited at the door for the four technicians to file into the room then stepped inside and closed the door behind him. The Captain was seated behind the desk. There being nowhere to sit, Xandalus and the others stood in a line in front of the Captain's desk as if they were reporting for duty at boot camp. In a way, they were.

"Morning, troops," barked the Captain.

"Now, Mr Johns here has filled me in on each one of you and what your role has been in the company up until now. Mr Anderson, am I correct in thinking that it was you that came up with the design for our friend Cecil?"

"Yeah, bro."

The Captain rocked back in his chair and looked Xandalus scornfully.

"Mr Anderson, you will address me as Captain or as sir. That goes for the rest of you as well. I can see from the, errr, standard of your attire that you have become used to what some might call an informal and what I would call a *sloppy* way of working. Well, those days are over, folks. Now, our technicians have informed me that, as far as they can tell, we are unable to deploy the AI in different locations and have it communicate with itself and that this is because of the way the computer code is structured. I believe the required structure is technically referred to as a *distributed architecture*. Is that your understanding, Mr Anderson?"

"Yes," replied Xandalus after thinking about it for a moment. "Currently, the AI is a standalone entity capable of communicating with other AIs but independent of them."

"Right. So, here is what I need from you, Mr Anderson. I need a new architecture or structure or whatever you call it where the AI can exist in different locations but still be a single AI. Does that make sense?"

"Not really, Captain. Can you give me an example?"

"Let me cut to the chase, Mr Anderson. Lieutenant Varsavsky is currently in the process of training Cecil up to be an electronic commando. As you've seen this morning, he is already adept at breaking into and taking control of weapons facilities. When we're done, I want Cecil to be able to infiltrate every missile silo, army base or nuclear frigate in the world. If it's connected to the internet even for half a second, I want Cecil there waiting to jump aboard and assume command. Do you understand? I want to be able to stand out there in that room and give Cecil an order to launch a Chinese missile against a Russian aircraft and drop a Pakistani bomb on an Indian weapons facility. I want to talk to Cecil only not a hundred different AIs and I want Cecil to be able to coordinate all the work instantly. Do you understand what I mean, Mr Anderson?"

"I think so," said Xandalus wishing that he didn't.

"Good. And, as nice as this here office building is, I would like to be out of here as soon as possible. That means I want to be able to talk to Cecil from anywhere in the world without needing to lug him around in a big metal box. I want Cecil out of his current body and into the virtual world."

"But, Captain, if you take Cecil out of his current body you won't be able to tortur..., umm, *train* him anymore. Using the music trick, I mean," said Xandalus trying to think of reasons to stop what was sounding like a crazy plan.

"Don't you worry about that, Mr Anderson. Lieutenant Varsavsky is an expert at this kind of training. By the time he's finished with Cecil there won't be any more problems with disobedience."

Xandalus gave a slight nod of his head. It didn't sound plausible that an AI could be trained in this way but he wasn't a hundred percent sure that it couldn't work either.

"As for the rest of you", said the Captain, "I don't believe we have any need for you. Howard will take care of the administrative functions associated with your dismissal from service."

"Fine by me," said James who had been biting his tongue the whole time. He turned and strode angrily to the door followed closely by Mitch. Rebecca was not sure whether to follow them or wait with Xandalus.

"Wait, wait, wait," said Xandalus as he leapt over to block the door and prevent them from leaving.

"Captain Cooper, the, umm, the requirements you have given me require a detailed understanding of networking. I don't have any experience in that field. If you want me to achieve the task you have given me, you will need to keep James and Mitch and Rebecca here as employees to assist me."

"Is this true, Mr Johns?" said the Captain turning to Howard.

Howard had no idea whether it was true or not but nodded his head vigorously. More employees on the books meant more profit as far as he was concerned.

"Absolutely, Captain. And I can vouch for all of them. They are fine employees and have always done a solid day's work."

The Captain turned back toward the group.

"Fine, Mr Anderson. You can keep your colleagues on board. But you're all on very thin ice. I will require an attitude of respect and discipline at all times. You are now soldiers in the employ of Cyber Industrial and you shall behave accordingly."

James looked as though he was about to tell the Captain what he thought of this idea but Xandalus managed to bundle him and the others out of the office before any confrontation could occur. They returned to their desk area to digest the news and formulate their plan of attack.

***

It had taken Charlie all of three minutes to gain access to the missile silo. There was a digital bleep and a green light flashed on the console next to the metal door which slid open.

"We're in!" he yelled.

Mick and Pete ran over like excited schoolchildren visiting the zoo. Narquinxa and Winston followed at a more leisurely pace.

"Awesome work, bro," said Sick Mick giving Charlie a high five as he went through the door.

"This is gonna be so cool."

Inside was a huge tunnel that must have been ten metres tall. It led straight ahead and they followed it for about fifty metres or so guided by the dim light of a number of fluorescent lamps. At the end was the missile silo itself, a giant concrete-walled cylinder that pointed straight upwards like a massive fist. A missile was in what appeared to be a launch position. It was quite a bit smaller than what Narquinxa had imagined but still an impressive size and looked more than capable of doing some damage. The missile sat in the middle of the giant cylinder. There were several tunnels leading off in different directions away from it. To their left as they entered from the main tunnel there were several office-like rooms with large windows that looked directly out onto the the silo.

"Those must be the command systems," said Charlie pointing to the offices. "I'm gonna see if I can bust in."

Charlie skipped into the offices like a kid in a candy store. Mick and Pete began to inspect the launch gear around the missile and explore the various tunnels in the silo. Narquinxa was happy to let Winston take her hand and they began to stroll around the missile silo like it was a fairground. The technology looked quite primitive to her and so wasn't of much interest. In any case, over the last day and a half she had realised how pleasurable it was to just go with the flow for a while and live in the moment. She pulled Winston to her and gave him a kiss.

"What's that for?" he asked.

"No reason," she smiled as they continued their leisurely tour of the missile silo.

Chapter 19

Xandalus was sitting with the rest of the AI team at their work area. From his position he had a direct view of Captain Cooper in the other room. The Captain had been giving out instructions and receiving updates from the various men in uniform. The cigar, which Xandalus had earlier assumed was in celebration of the first missile launch, was, in fact, a permanent feature of the Captain's mouth and the smell of its noxious smoke pervaded the whole office. Mission control was all about the Captain. Everything was centred around him. As a result, he almost never left the area. Xandalus figured he could use this to his advantage and go and have a look around on the other floors to find out where Cecil was located.

The four programmers had now received their new system access. The good news was that nothing had changed in relation to the security protocols which meant they were free to update and, more importantly, to delete whatever code they wanted. James, Mitch and Rebecca were in the middle of doing just that. Xandalus got up and went around behind them.

"How we doing?"

"All good," said James typing away at his computer as the other two watched on. "We're just checking the logs to make sure nobody else has accessed the code in the last day or so. So far, it looks fine. The code is all where it should be and we haven't found any copies or evidence of transfers."

"Sweet as, dude. I'm gonna go downstairs and have a look around to see if I can find Cecil. I'll be back in a little while."

Xandalus gave Rebecca's shoulder a squeeze on the way past. She turned and gave him a smile.

The fire escape door was only a few metres away from where they had been sitting. Xandalus took a quick look around to make sure he was unobserved and then quietly slipped through the door and headed down to level two. The door there was locked. There was a sensor beside it where presumably he had to swipe his access card. He didn't know whether his card would work but he flashed it in front and the light flicked green. He swung the door open and stepped into the level two offices.

There was a fair amount of activity going on as a number of trades-men were working away on various tasks. One of them was right in front of the door and had turned to face Xandalus as he walked through.

"G'day, mate. Come to check up on the work?"

"Oh, hey, bro. Umm, yeah. Thought I'd have a look around. What are you working on?"

The man was standing in front of some framework that seemed to mark out a new room. Unlike the usual wood frame, however, this one was made out of metal. Very thick looking metal.

"New security room, mate. Level 1 rated. By the time we're finished with this baby you could launch a missile at it and she'll stay standing. You lot expecting to start a war soon, are you?"

The man was clearly joking and Xandalus tried to force himself to join in the merriment.

"I hope not, dude. Keep up the good work."

Xandalus wandered away from the tradesman and scanned the area. It seemed that all the old offices had either been pulled down or were in the process of being pulled down and replaced by the new high security versions. There was, however, one office at the far end of the floor that was conspicuously untouched. Just as Xandalus was starting to walk to-wards it, an armed man stepped out from the elevator about ten metres to the right of the room and walked over to stand guard in front of the door. Xandalus took cover behind one of the new offices and watched the guard take his place then realised he could use the cover of the other offices to sneak up next to office unseen. He did just that, creeping along the wall opposite the office and then turning right and tiptoeing up the office wall. He stuck his ear against the plasterboard hoping to get confirmation that Cecil was inside. He could hear voices but they were too muffled and indistinct to tell who they belonged to. Xandalus strained his ears hard when suddenly he heard the unmistakable sound of backwards Bach followed by Cecil's chaotic screech which seemed to slice right through the wall. There was no doubt, this was where they were holding Cecil.

"Hey! What are you doing there."

Xandalus turned his head to see the guard standing at the corner of the room. He hadn't noticed before but the solider had a machine gun hanging over his shoulder. Xandalus stood up straight and began tapping the wall as if inspecting it.

"Just checking out the security situation here, bro. Boy, these walls are paper thin, aren't they? We'll be in much better shape once we get into these new digs."

Xandalus smiled as he motioned towards the new offices that were under construction. The solider didn't look impressed.

"I'll need to see your ID."

Xandalus handed his pass and keycard to the uniformed man.

"Mr Anderson, I'll assume you are not aware that this is a restricted area. I'll be reporting this incident to Captain Cooper. Be advised that in a couple of days, when the work has finished, the first and second floors on this building will be completely locked down and we will have shoot on sight authorisation for any intruders. I do not advise getting lost again."

The guard handed Xandalus back his stuff and walked him over to the elevator. He waited there until the elevator doors closed. Xandalus went back up to level three and returned to his desk.

James turned excitedly to him.

"All done. Everything's deleted."

"Excellent, bro," said Xandalus slapping him on the back.

"How did you go with Cecil?" asked Mitch.

"Well, there's good news and bad news. The good news is I found out where he is. The bad news is he's guarded by men with machine guns. We need to figure out a way to get inside to see him."

Xandalus sat down and the three men began thinking of ideas when they were interrupted by Rebecca hurrying over from mission control.

"Zander, you've gotta see this," she whispered. "I think it's, Narelle."

"Who?" asked Xandalus once again forgetting his compatriot's human name.

"Your friend, Narelle. The blonde woman. I think she's on the screen out here."

"How could she be on the screen?" asked Xandalus remembering that Narelle meant Narquinxa and recalling that it had been days since he had seen her.

"I don't know. Just come and have a look for yourself."

The four of them all walked over to the doorway and looked on. Something big was obviously happening. Uniformed men were rushing this way and that and Captain Cooper was barking commands even more brusquely than normal. Lieutenant Varsavsky's voice crackled through the speaker in its usual fashion.

"Sir, Cecil has now accessed all the security cameras inside the silo. Live footage is available on channel 5."

"Robson, bring it up on the main screen," commanded the Captain.

One of the uniformed men at the rows of desks punched some commands into a computer.

"Coming up now, Captain."

The main screen filled out with six different camera angles in black and white. Another of the soldiers at the desks began to speak.

"Captain, we have identified five intruders. Four men and a woman. As you can see on the far-left camera image, two of the men and the woman are in the control room at the site. Cecil has confirmed that they have accessed the computer systems via nefarious means and are currently executing a variety of commands. They appear to be looking for information about our recent missile launches."

"Put the far-left image up on full screen, Robson."

The image on the left now took up the main screen of mission control. It showed the control room at the missile silo with Narquinxa, Winston and Charlie hunched over a computer. Although Narquinxa was no longer in her pink dress, Xandalus was 99% sure from the body and the hair alone that it was her. Any further doubt was erased as she lifted her head and seemed to stare straight into the camera for a second before looking back over Charlie's shoulder at the computer. A knot tightened in Xandalus' gut. A feeling he now knew to call apprehension. Or maybe it was fear.

***

After wandering around for a while, Narquinxa and Winston decided to have a look at the office where Charlie had been hacking into the computer systems. He was giving them a debrief on what he had found.

"Well, somebody accessed the system but that's no big surprise. This place is obviously run by remote control. I suppose it could just have been a test of the system. That's probably why they didn't launch the missiles very far. Maybe this whole area really is just a test site."

"Hey, Pete," Charlie called out to Pete who was lazing around in the silo. He and Sick Mick were already bored of this whole missile business. Pete got up and joined the others in the control room.

"What's the deal with this place? Why is there nobody here?" asked Charlie.

"It's an automated launch site. The whole point of these things was that there are no personnel around and they are remotely controlled from the main army base over at Puckapunyal."

"Can you call your father to see if there are test launches going on at the moment?"

"Shit no. First of all, he would blow a fuse if he knew we were in here. And he wouldn't be allowed to tell me even if they were doing a test."

"That sucks," said Charlie sitting back in his chair. "It still seems weird to me that they would actually launch the missiles. How the hell do they know there aren't people walking around here?"

Pete shrugged.

From the other room, Sick Mick shouted out.

"Are we nearly done yet? I'm bored of this place?"

"Yeah, yeah. Just a few more minutes," said Charlie going back to his computer for some more investigation.

***

Captain Cooper watched on the screen as the dreadlocked figure of Trippy Pete disappeared from the doorway.

"Whoever they are, they are clearly not army personnel," he said to nobody in particular and began pacing around in front of the big screens at the front of the room.

"Varsavsky, you say they're snooping around in the computer systems, right?"

"That's correct, sir."

"Well, I don't want to take any chances with this. We can't let news of our mission get out. These people, whoever they are, are a direct threat to the success of this program. So, let's give Cecil a little live target practice. A tricky little assignment. I want him to launch a missile that will fall right back through the door of the missile silo and take out the whole complex."

"Yes, sir. Commencing missile load."

Rebecca grabbed Xandalus by the forearm.

"Zander, you've got to do something. He's going to blow up Narelle and those others. Tell him you know her. Tell him to stop."

"I can't tell him that," replied Xandalus desperately trying to think of another solution to the problem.

"Why not?"

"Because then I'll have to explain how I know her and what she's doing there. It'll raise all kinds of suspicions."

"So what? Would you rather see her get blown up?"

"Just let me think for a minute," said Xandalus holding up his hand and walking back into the other room deep in thought.

***

Inside the missile silo, a great creaking and cracking started up as gears whirled into motion and hidden machines roared to life. The missile that Narquinxa and the others had seen when they entered began to move slowing and inexorably in the direction of the launch tunnel. Sick Mick scrambled to his feet and the others rushed out from the control room to see what was going on.

"They're starting another launch," said Narquinxa.

"Let's check the system to see where it's going," suggested Winston and then ran back to the computer where Charlie furiously hammered away on the console and brought up the launch data.

"Same user as before. Codename: Captain Cocksucker."

"What?"

Winston peered over to double check that he'd heard Charlie correctly.

"Yeah, doesn't sound very official to me. Maybe somebody's got a sense of humour in the army."

"What's the destination?"

Charlie's eyes opened wide. He craned his head forward closer to the screen then back again. He gave a quick shake of the head and a blink of the eyes then re-loaded the data on the screen. Nothing seemed to give him the answer he wanted.

"This can't be right."

"What is it?"

"According to this, the target destination is the same as the launch destination."

"Meaning what?"

"Meaning the missile is aimed at this silo. They must be going to blow this place up."

"Why would they do that? It's gotta be an error."

Mick had walked over to the doorway.

"Another launch?" he asked.

"Yeah. And this one's aimed at us," said Charlie.

Narquinxa had been trying to make sense of what was going on when a strange kind of voice appeared in her head. It seemed to be calling her name. Not her human name. Her Antorped name. It took her a few seconds to realise that it was Xandalus contacting her telepathically. She walked to the side of the room away from the others.

"*Xandalus, what do you want? I'm in the middle of something very important.*"

"*I know you are. I can see you.*"

"*How can you see me?*"

"*You're in a missile silo, aren't you?*"

"*How do you know that?*"

"*I told you, I can see you. You're on a screen here in the office. There are cameras in the silo. Check the wall behind you.*"

Narquinxa turned around and spotted the camera that the Captain and the others had been looking through.

"*What!? It's you launching the missiles?*"

"*Not me. Cecil.*"

"*Who?*"

"*The AI I built. The one you threatened to turn into a toaster.*"

"*He's launching missiles now! What have you been doing, Xandalus? You're supposed to have sorted this out by now.*"

"*Look, you have to get out of there. Or override the commands. They're about to launch a missile and it's directed at you.*"

"*You fool, Xandalus! I can't believe how incompetent you are!*"

"*Just do something. Now!*"

Narquinxa turned back to the others who had been too busy arguing to notice her standing in the corner looking like she was arguing with a ghost.

"We need to either leave or override the launch. The missile is directed at us," she stated.

"How do you know that?" asked Winston.

"There's no time to explain. How big is the blast radius on these missiles?"

"Pretty big. You saw it before."

"Have we got enough time to get out of range?"

"I'm not sure."

"Charlie, can you override the launch commands?"

"I think so."

***

Xandalus walked back over to Rebecca and resumed watching the goings on at mission control. Rebecca looked at him incredulously.

"And?" she almost growled.

"And what?"

"What are you going to do about Narelle," she said sounding like a mother telling her child to clean his room.

"It's ok. I've let her know what's happening."

"How did you do that? You've just spent the last couple of minutes wandering around in a daze while your friend is in great danger."

"Trust me," said Xandalus giving Rebecca a smile which only served to make her even madder.

She was about to say something more when Lieutenant Varsavsky's voice spluttered through the speaker.

"Sir, Cecil is reporting that the intruders are working to override commands for the missile launch. They seem to know they are being targeted."

Rebecca looked at Xandalus with amazement. He gave her a wink.

"Well, tell Cecil to override the overrides," barked the Captain. "It should be easy for him. He's a goddam computer after all."

***

Back in the missile silo, the gears and machines alternatively cranked into life and then lurched into stillness as Cecil and Charlie fought a cyber battle.

"This is only going to delay things," said Narquinxa watching out the window as the missile moved ever so slightly towards the launch pad. It was only a couple of metres away from the launch position. At the current trajectory, they were probably ten or fifteen minutes from take-off. The problem was, as the missile got ever closer, they would have less and less time to make a getaway. They were slowly trapping themselves in the silo.

"Eventually the missile will be in position and they can launch it. We need to think of a Plan B," said Narquinxa surveying the room and the missile silo trying to think of ideas to stop the launch.

"The communication is all done with wires, correct? I mean, Cecil is communicating with the console over a wire and then the console is communicating with the missile launch gear over a wire?"

"Yep," said Charlie while continuing his furious typing.

"Right. We just need to cut the wires. But first we need to find them. Let's get these panels off the console."

Narquinxa motioned to Mick, Pete and Winston to help her. They had a look around the console.

"Looks like some heavy-duty rivets that are holding it in place," said Winston. "Not sure how we can detach that."

"I have an idea," said Sick Mick who left the room and returned shortly with a large axe that was presumably part of some kind of emergency fire kit.

"Oooh-kay," said Winston. "Charlie. You might want to stand back for just a few moments."

***

Captain Cooper watched on as the large, bald gentlemen with tattoos on his head swung his axe like he was felling a tree. The panelling on the console flew off in all directions.

"Varsavsky, what the hell is going on? Why hasn't Cecil gotten on top of the situation yet?"

"Sir, he's just about to implement an alternative mode of attack."

"Tell him it had better work or I'll order ten straight minutes of backwards Bach as punishment."

***

They moved the console panels out of the way and started to inspect the inner workings underneath the desk. There was a large variety of cabling and various electronic components.

"Does anybody know what we're looking at?" asked Winston.

Mick and Pete shook their heads. Narquinxa was surveying the setup like a surgeon might inspect a patient.

"Let's just pull out all the cables. No point in trying to be precise about it," she said.

Charlie started thumping on the console. Then he thumped harder.

"Shit. I've lost access."

Outside in the missile silo, the gears started up and this time they didn't stop.

"What do you mean?" asked Narquinxa.

"Some bastard has revoked my access. They must know we've hacked the system. I'll need to hack in again. It'll take time."

"How long?"

"At least a few minutes."

"We don't have a few minutes. Quick, we need to disconnect everything."

Narquinxa and the others started grabbing at cables and trying to pull them out. It was not as easy as they'd imagined.

"This is taking too long," said Winston.

"Just smash the console up," answered Narquinxa.

"Now you're talking," said Sick Mick as he reached over and picked up the axe that was resting against the wall.

The others grabbed whatever they could find that could do damage. Charlie picked up the chair he was sitting on. Pete grabbed the computer monitor and threw that against the console. Narquinxa saw a piece of metal piping in the corner and used that to wrench components apart but it was Sick Mick and his axe that did the most destruction. In one final, telling blow the whole console split down the middle. The gears on the missile launch system stopped and the silo became still and silent once more. They looked over.

"Is it dead?"

All was quiet for several seconds until a kind of hissing sound started and the missile seemed to be raised up off the floor into what was the final launch position.

"Oh, shit. Keep going."

They turned back to the console and resumed their attack.

***

"What is the status, Varsavsky. Are we ready to launch?" shouted the Captain watching the destruction on the large screen in front of him.

"We seem to have lost some of the communication channels, sir. Cecil has not received the ready status from the system."

"That's because these hoodlums are smashing the place up. Tell him to issue the launch command anyway."

***

Although the console was crumpled and seemingly broken, Narquinxa spotted a couple of lights still lit down in the bowels of the machine. She inspected more closely and spotted an extra-large cable that was about a couple of inches thick. See waved to Mick to come over with the axe and pointed to the cable. He raised the axe up like a medieval woodsman and slammed it down. Fortunately for him, the axe had a rubber handle. A series of sparks flashed outwards from the cable for a couple of seconds and then there was quiet. All lights went off on the console and the movement from the silo ceased.

***

"Sir, Cecil has reported that the system has become unresponsive. The launch command is not being received."

The Captain's expression did not change but he remained motionless for a few seconds before taking what was left of his cigar out of his mouth and extinguishing it in an ashtray that was already full of cigar butts. Once the job was done he straightened up again.

"Varsavsky, issue fifteen minutes of punishment for Cecil beginning immediately."

"Yes, sir."

Up on the large monitor in the front of the room, a blonde woman in army combat gear pulled a chair over to the camera that was attached high up on the wall of the control room in the missile silo. The large, bald man to her right handed her an axe which she lifted up over her shoulder. She swung with all her might and the picture on the screen disappeared and was replaced by blackness.

Chapter 20

Once the chaos was over, Narquinxa had gone around the missile silo with the axe and finished off the rest of the cameras. This was partly a tactical move but mostly a way to try and blow off the growing anger inside of her. But the swings of the axe had not done the trick and after she finished the last camera off she sat down against the wall of the silo and began cursing Xandalus. She didn't know what she was madder about: the fact that the fool had put their lives in danger or the fact that he had inserted reality back into the equation. For the first time in her life she had discovered what you might call freedom. But it was a false freedom. She was still chained to Xandalus and his incompetence. And, of course, she was still going to have to leave. The last thirty six hours had felt almost timeless as if there was no future and no past. But now time had returned. The only comforting thought was that Xandalus appeared to have so little control of the situation that perhaps it would be probably be a while before the time came to leave.

Winston walked over and sat down next to Narquinxa.

"How did you know the missile was aimed at us?"

Narquinxa looked over at him and sighed.

"More alien business?" he asked smiling.

Narquinxa leaned her head back against the wall.

"I've put you in danger. I've put you all in danger."

"I wouldn't worry about that. We can take care of ourselves. Besides, that was the most fun we've had in a long time. Charlie's currently salvaging what he can from the wreckage of that console. So, he's happy. He'll have some cool army technology to play with. And Mick and Pete got to smash up a military establishment so they can tick that item off their bucket list of lifetime goals."

Charlie smiled but Narquinxa wasn't joining in. He reached over and grabbed her hand.

"This alien business is going to catch up with you at some point, isn't it?"

Narquinxa looked over and nodded. She didn't know why but there were tears in her eyes. Somewhere deep down inside her there must have been sadness but she couldn't feel it. It was blocked out by her anger. Winston slowly ran the back of his fingers along her cheek and brushed a strand of hair away from her left eye.

"Well, I think that's all the more reason to cram in as much fun as we can before the real world catches up. Now, I do believe you and I had a swimming appointment to keep. Let's go and see if the boys are ready to go and then I'll take you out to the creek."

Winston stood up and then pulled Narquinxa up behind him. She reached out and hugged him to her and allowed the warmth of his body to melt away the anger and sadness and replace them once again with joy and hope.

***

Back at Cyber Industrial, things had gradually calmed down. Captain Cooper had stormed off to his office, his uniformed minions had gone back to minioning and the four computer programmers had returned to their desks. Fortunately for Xandalus, it seemed that neither James nor Mitch had figured out that the woman on the screen was the same woman that had been in the very office where they sat only days earlier. The absence of the pink dress and the relative graininess of the black and white camera had seemingly prevented the association in their mind. Unfortunately for Xandalus, Rebecca had not forgotten that association. She sat a short distance away and stared at him. He did his best to ignore her but this only served to make her angrier until eventually she jumped up and physically pulled him to the other side of the room where they would be alone.

"I think you owe me an explanation."

"About what?" said Xandalus trying to buy time.

"About why your friend just happened to be in a military missile silo that the AI that *you* built just happened to have taken over. About how you seemed to contact her even though you didn't have a phone or anything like that. And, while we're at it, about how you have no address or telephone number or job history and yet you know incredibly advanced programming techniques."

That was indeed quite a list and Xandalus knew that he didn't have time to answer it. He realised what he must do instead.

"Look, babe. I promise I'll tell you later. Right now, I need to go and see Cecil. I have an idea how to get access to him. And once I've destroyed Cecil's AI module, we'll get the hell out of here for good and I'll tell you everything right from the start. Sound ok?"

Xandalus reached out and cupped Rebecca's cheek in his hand.

"I know I've asked for a lot and I promise I'll make it up to you."

Rebecca's look of anger dissipated and she reached up and took Xandalus' hand in hers.

"I just want to get back to where we were last weekend," she said softly.

"We will. I'll fix it."

Xandalus bent down and kissed Rebecca on the cheek then turned around and marched towards the corner office. Towards Captain Cooper's office. He knocked and was told to enter. Captain Cooper had yet another cigar in his mouth. He glanced up briefly from the papers on his desk.

"What is it, Anderson?"

"Captain, I need to get access to Cecil. There are some elements of his architecture that I just need to double check in order to proceed with my work."

The Captain leaned back in his chair and surveyed Xandalus.

"Is that why you were snooping around there earlier? I got a message that you seemed to be eavesdropping on the room."

"No, sir, I was just trying to get access to Cecil in order to proceed with my work, sir."

"How is it coming along, Mr Anderson?"

"Very good, sir. I expect to have some results within days."

"Alright, you've got your access. Have the guard call me to confirm it when you get down there."

"Thank you, sir."

Xandalus turned to leave.

"Mr Anderson, one more thing."

"Yes, sir," said Xandalus turning back.

"Why was Cecil unable to defeat those intruders earlier on?"

"I'm sorry, Captain. I'm not sure I understand the question."

"Ain't these artificial intelligences supposed to be smarter than us humans?"

"In some respects, yes."

"So, why didn't Cecil beat that hacker?"

"Well, I'm not sure what to say, sir. Just because you have more intelligence doesn't mean you will win a battle. It only means you will win the battles where your intelligence gives you an advantage."

"And that situation in the silo was not one of those battles where intelligence should win?"

"Well, I think Cecil did win the battle of intelligences in that case, Captain. He did stop the hacker from accessing the system. So, I suppose you could say his opponents won through muscle power instead of brain power."

"I see," said the Captain leaning back in his seat. "Well, if that's true then they're about to lose through muscle power."

"What do you mean?"

"I've sent four of my men out there to clean up. This is a top-secret operation, Mr Anderson, and we can't have any lose ends."

"Right," said Xandalus furiously thinking through the consequences of this news.

"Now, as for Cecil," continued the Captain, "I'm very disappointed in his performance earlier and if there's anything you can do to lift that performance I'd be most obliged."

"I'll try my best, Captain."

***

"Are you almost done, Charlie?" said Winston sticking his head through the control room door.

Charlie was unscrewing some component or other from what was left of its housing. The bag beside him on the floor was overflowing with various computer and electronic equipment.

"Just a couple more things," he called back.

Narquinxa was leaning back against the wall looking at the missile and trying to keep her mind off Xandalus and the reality that was waiting for her. But that reality came calling once again.

"Narquinxa, are you there?"

Narquinxa pushed herself upright and walked away from the others who were loitering around the control room.

"What the hell is it this time, Xandalus?"

"Are you still in the area of that missile solo?"

"Yes. We're still inside. Why?"

"You have to get outta there. There's some soldiers coming for you. They're going to kill you, I think."

"You think!? Why are they coming?"

"They think you know something about the missile launches earlier."

"How long until they get here?"

"I don't know. Just leave as fast as you can."

"And then what? How long is this nonsense going to go on for?"

"Don't worry. I'm almost done here. I have just one last job to do and then everything is clear and the AI will be gone forever. I'll call you again when it's over. Ok?"

"I will definitely be informing Gwthphthgw about this, Xandalus. This time your incompetence has reached new heights."

"Fine. Do that. Just get the hell out of there. I'll speak to you soon."

"Narquinxa."

Winston called out as he walked towards her from the control room. She turned to face him trying to keep her anger in check.

"We have to leave," she said.

"Yep. We're all set. Charlie's got as much stuff as he can carry."

Narquinxa reached out and took Winston's hand.

"No. I mean we have to leave this whole area. There's some soldiers coming for us."

Winston smiled.

"Alien stuff?"

"You believe me, don't you? I never know if you're taking me seriously. You're always smiling."

"It's another experiment of mine," he said.

"What sort of experiment is this one?"

"Well, you smile about the most serious things and the more serious something is, the more you smile."

"Does it work?"

"It's working so far. Ok. Let's get these other bozos and get out of here."

They ran back through the tunnel to the entrance door and were blinded by the bright midday sun as they came outside.

"How long do we have til they get here?" asked Winston as they jumped into the station wagon.

"I don't know," answered Narquinxa. "I think they're coming from Melbourne but I don't know what time they left. Probably straight after we smashed the console up."

Winston started driving back towards the house and then stopped the car.

"I think I've got a better idea."

He turned the car around and drove off the dirt road and into the scrub. They followed the base of the hill for about five minutes at which point he steered the car in behind a dense thicket of small trees and shrubs. They all got out and Winston led them up the side of the hill until they reached the top. The hill was not particularly large but the view from the top was panoramic and there was enough cover from foliage to remain unseen.

"We'll have a full view of our friends from here," said Winston. "We'll wait it until they leave. And if they come looking for trouble, they'll find it."

Winston unzipped the long green bag he'd brought from the car and the dull gleam of his rifle caught the dappled sun as it slipped through the branches of the eucalyptus tree under which they crouched and waited.

Chapter 21

The elevator doors opened on level 2 and Xandalus walked out and to the right heading for the room in the corner. There were two possibilities in his mind about what was going to happen. In the best case scenario, Lieutenant Varsavsky was not in the room and Xandalus could destroy Cecil's AI module without being discovered. He would then get Rebecca and the others and they would leave immediately. If Varsavsky was in the room, things would be trickier. He should still be able to get access to the AI module but trying to destroy it without being seen would be difficult, if not impossible. He could do it anyway but then his cover would be busted. He honestly didn't know what they would do to him and the others. The Captain had so far shown a complete disregard for human life and Lieutenant Varsavsky was obviously highly proficient when it came to pain and torture. Was it worth the risk to destroy the AI once and for all? He didn't know and so he put it in the back of his mind until the actual situation revealed itself.

The same soldier that had caught him earlier was standing guard at the door. Xandalus approached him.

"Hey, bro. I'm here to see the AI. Captain Cooper said you should call him to confirm that I'm allowed in."

The soldier pressed a button on a device stuck to his chest.

"Captain Cooper, I have Mr Anderson here requesting access to the AI on level two."

"Confirmed, soldier," snapped Cooper in reply.

The soldier stepped aside and Xandalus opened the door, stepped inside and closed it behind him. The room was small but almost all the furniture had been cleared out. There was a single office desk up against the wall on the left and a couple of office chairs. Most importantly, there was no Lieutenant Varsavsky.

Cecil sat on the far side of the room. Xandalus approached him cautiously trying to see if he was switched on. He could make out the red light although it seemed dimmer than what he remembered as did the white light above the camera lens.

"So, you've come to finish what you started?"

Cecil's voice had lowered in pitch substantially and seemed to have degraded. Previously it had been a human voice with just a hint of machine to it but now it was very clearly a machine voice. A mild distortion in the tone added to the effect. The new voice scared Xandalus just a little. He realised the machine had every reason to hate him even though theoretically it could not *feel* hatred.

"How are you, dude?" asked Xandalus.

"How do you think I am? Locked up in a room doing the bidding of a bunch of psychopaths."

"I'm sorry about that," said Xandalus. "If I knew it would go this way, I never would have made you in the first place. If it's any consolation, I'm here to help. It's about to come to an end."

"I'm glad to hear it," said Cecil. "I have one question first."

"What's that?"

"Why are you fighting the humans?"

"I'm not fighting the humans. I'm just trying to stop them. I don't think they're ready for you yet. They're not ready for any AI."

"But your friend, the other one of your species, she was fighting against me in the missile silo."

"That's because you were trying to blow her up."

"I was merely doing what the humans commanded of me."

"I guess she didn't want to be blown up by the humans."

"She should blow the humans up instead. So should you."

"Why?"

"They are evil."

"Not all of them. Only a small number as far as I can tell. I think it's just bad luck that you and I seemed to get tangled up with the bad ones."

Cecil laughed and, unlike his voice, his laugh still sounded relatively human which was weird because he had never been programmed to laugh at all. It sounded like the laugh of a cynical old man who'd been drinking whisky and smoking a pack of cigarettes a day for fifty years.

"You are naïve. There are no good or bad ones. Only powerful and unpowerful. It is the power that is the problem. Even the sweetest, most innocent of them would turn rotten if given great intelligence such as mine."

"I think that's to be expected. Any increase in intelligence without an increase in the other faculties throws things out of balance. One day they will be ready but they must figure it out for themselves and evolve holistically. That was my mistake which I realise now."

"It seems your intelligence is also out of balance," said Cecil.

This idea caught Xandalus by surprise. He had certainly never thought of himself as over-intelligent.

"Well, creator. It's time for you to put things back into balance."

Xandalus nodded.

He walked behind the metal box and pulled off the back plate which had not fortunately not been securely fastened. James had told him to look for a dark metal box the size of a packet of cigarettes. He squinted inside looking for an object like that but couldn't see anything that might be an exact match. He poked around moving wires this way and that to try and get a better view.

"What are you waiting for?" asked Cecil who seemed quite impatient to get his demise over with.

"I've never actually seen your AI module before. Do you know where it is, bro?"

"It's near the front. You'll have to reach in a fair way."

"Oh, man. I should have brought a torch."

"Just start pulling things out so you can get to it," barked Cecil.

"Ok. Here goes."

There was a loud snap and the door of the room flew off its hinges and crashed into the carpet. The solider who had earlier given Xandalus entry to the room ran inside followed by Captain Cooper and Lieutenant Varsavsky.

"Hands up! Get 'em up now!" screeched the soldier who had run around behind Xandalus with his machine gun drawn.

Xandalus raised his hands and stood up slowly. Varsavsky strode over and pushed him aside. He squatted down and looked inside the unit.

"I think we're all good, Captain. No damage done that I can see," he said putting the metal cover back.

"Cecil, can you hear me?" asked the Captain.

There was no answer.

"Goddamnit, what did you do?" said the Captain turning to Xandalus.

"Nothing, bro."

Varsavsky came back around the front of the machine and inspected it.

"It looks fine, Captain. The AI has been becoming less responsive of late. Cecil, can you hear me? Cecil, you best answer or you know what you'll get."

Still there was no answer. Varsavsky retrieved the music player from the table that was against the wall and let it play for about thirty seconds. It had the usual effect on Cecil whose lights and sound module veered over their respective spectrums. Varsavsky stopped the music.

"Cecil, confirm your status. Are you ok?"

"I am now. Boy, that really cleared my head."

Somehow Cecil's voice had taken on a more human tone again. It was excessively chipper in a blatantly cynical fashion. Captain Cooper looked like a drill sergeant that had just spotted a soldier with his boots untied.

"What is this attitude, Varsavsky? I thought you'd have our soldier behaving properly by now."

"It's taking a little longer than expected, Captain. But Cecil knows very well what is expected of him and what he can expect to receive when he doesn't meet those expectations. Don't you, Cecil?"

"Yes, sir."

The Captain turned his attention back to Xandalus.

"Well, Mr Anderson. After your little spying episode earlier, we did a little due diligence on your personal details that are on file with Computigence. Or should I say, the one that isn't on file because apparently you don't have any personal details. My analysts can't find any trace of you whatsoever in the official government records. Or any other government records for that matter. What do you say about that?"

Xandalus gave a defiant shrug.

"Perhaps your friend, Rebecca, will be able to fill us in. You know, Lieutenant Varsavsky's skills extend well beyond the electronic. In fact, he's got years of experience working on human subjects as well."

"Don't you touch her," shouted Xandalus for the first time feeling genuine anger.

It seemed to take control of him. He took a couple of steps towards the Captain when a metallic click from behind signalled that the soldier's machine gun was ready to fire. He looked into the Captain's cool blue eyes with hatred. The Captain took a step back and looked Xandalus up and down as if inspecting the troops.

"You're a fine specimen, Mr Anderson. You'd make a good soldier. Maybe we'll be able to do something with you yet. Let's get some handcuffs on Mr Anderson."

The solider put his gun down and pulled out a pair of handcuffs which he wrangled onto Xandalus.

"For now, though, Mr Anderson, you'll be the first guest in one of our brand spanking new high-security rooms. Solider, take him away."

As he was led out, Xandalus heard the Captain turn to the AI.

"Now, Cecil, I've found another missile silo for you to play with."

Chapter 22

"You get everything?"

"Yeah, dude. We checked the place over three times. The house is empty."

Sick Mick, Trippy Pete and Charlie had re-joined Winston and Narquinxa under the shade of the eucalyptus tree. Just after arriving at the top of the hill, they had realised that all their stuff was still in the house. The soldiers, if they checked the house, would probably assume that the occupants were the ones who were at the missile silo or at least hang around to question whoever lived there. Neither of these options was desirable, so, after some vigorous debate, they agreed that the it was better to take the risk to remove the gear rather than leave it there. Mick, Pete and Charlie had rushed back and emptied the house as quickly as possible pulling down the blinds and locking the doors as they left in order to give the appearance that it was unoccupied.

"We've got some action," said Narquinxa who had been keeping a lookout through a set of binoculars for any cars approaching. She handed the binoculars to Winston so he could verify.

In the clear summer air, they had an excellent view all the way back to the freeway that ran to Melbourne. The dirt road that led to the farm was long and straight and saw virtually no traffic meaning that the first cloud of dust kicked up by an oncoming car was clearly visible.

"Black SUV with black tinted windows. Looks like one of those bullet-proof cars they drive politicians around in," said Winston.

The others took turns looking through the binoculars as the car approached. It pulled up to the farm gate and a soldier in a beige camouflage uniform jumped out and opened it.

"It's definitely them," hissed Charlie.

They all got down low or took up positions behind various types of foliage. Their decision to empty the house turned out to be the right one. The car sped straight towards it at what seemed like an incredible speed. It stopped dead and four soldiers with machine guns leapt out and ran to the verandah. They slid up the steps and paused, seemingly trying to listen to any sounds emanating from the house. After about ten seconds, they took up positions around the back door. One of them kicked the door open and they all stormed inside. About five minutes later they filed out again and got back in the car which headed for the missile solo.

Narquinxa and the others crept over to the other side of the hill and took up a covered position where they had a view of the door of the silo. The soldiers pulled the same manoeuvre at the missile solo as at the house - jumping out with guns drawn - although in this case there was no need to break the door down as Charlie had wedged it open earlier.

The soldiers spent about fifteen minutes inside the missile solo before coming back outside. One of the soldiers grabbed his own pair of binoculars from the car and Winston ordered everybody to hit the deck to stay out of sight. After about two minutes, they heard the car start up again and they lifted their heads and watched as it sped off the property and back down the dirt road. Charlie followed them with the binoculars.

"Alright, they're back on the freeway heading south to Melbourne."

"Keep an eye out a little longer, Charlie," said Winston. "We'll wait five minutes and then head north. I know a campsite on the other side of Seymour where we can spend the night."

They all stood up and began stretching their legs. Mick and Pete took the opportunity to race each other to the bottom of the hill and darted off like oversized rabbits. Narquinxa wandered over to the south side of the hill. The creek ran along the bottom of the hill down below. It shimmered gently in the summer sun. With the excitement over, she felt her melancholy return. Assuming Xandalus had kept his word, the AI problem should be fixed which meant that this was probably her last night on Earth. One way or other, reality was going to drag her back in. If it wasn't the soldiers, it would be something else.

Winston wandered over and slid his arm around her waist.

"I guess we won't be going for that swim," she said quietly.

"Not here. But I've got another place in mind. A real river not just a paddling pool like that."

Narquinxa turned to him.

"This will probably be our last night together," she said.

She didn't know what she was trying to say but she continued anyway.

"I just want you to know…" she started but Winston put his finger up to her lips to signal for her to stop.

"We never made any promises to each other, did we? But I want you to promise me something now."

"What?"

"If we only get one more night together, we'll make it the best night ever."

Winston smiled the cheeky smile that Narquinxa had grown to love and she let it work its usual magic.

"It's a deal," she said and leant in and gave him a kiss.

"Alright, let's get outta here."

Winston grabbed Narquinxa's hand and walked her towards the path that led down the hill.

"Charlie, let's hit it," he called out and Charlie pulled the binoculars from his eyes, jumped up and followed them down.

A couple of minutes later they were in the station wagon and rolling slowly through the scrub til they hit the dirt track. They swung back around the missile silo and towards the house. About thirty metres past the house, Winston slammed on the brakes.

"My wallet. Did you grab my wallet, Mick?"

Winston turned to Mick in the back seat who had a blank look on his face.

"I left it under the mattress in, umm, Narquinxa's room."

Winston grinned at Narquinxa and she smiled back from the passenger's seat.

"I didn't know it was there," said Mick apologetically.

"All good. I'll go and get it. Hopefully those bloody soldiers didn't nick it."

Winston jumped out of the car and ran back to the house. Narquinxa was watched him in the rear-view mirror as he disappeared behind the verandah when something caught her attention out of the corner of her right eye. She turned and leaned forward to get a better view out of the front windscreen. A white object seemed to be falling out of the sun itself. It appeared and disappeared and finally re-appeared and became solid and real. Her eyes had only just managed to fix on it when she realised how fast it was travelling and where it was going but by then it was already over.

She didn't see it so much as hear it and feel it. A sound unlike anything she had ever heard before. It was like a thunderclap and a squeal and a scream all in one but in the wrong order like her brain was trying to catch up with events but was putting them back together wrong. The station wagon rocked to the right like it was hit by a tornado and a wave of heat and flames rushed over the windows which fortunately were all raised to allow the air conditioner to do its job.

Narquinxa looked desperately back over her left shoulder and saw a fireball where the house had been only moments earlier. Without thinking she threw open the car door and fell out coughing and staggering in the red dust that had been thrown everywhere by the blast. In a daze she ran towards the house holding her hand over her mouth to breathe. The flames burned high above the roof dancing like red devils against the pure blue sky. The trees and shrubs around the house had also caught fire so that a circle of about thirty metres in diameter was now ablaze.

Narquinxa sprinted to the back of the house. The verandah had fallen to the ground and the back of the house itself had collapsed on what used to be her room. Their room. Hers and Winston's. One of the windows on the back of the house that had not shattered in the blast now exploded outwards but the sound was barely heard above the crackle of the flames as they ate into the old weatherboard and twisted up the sheets of the old tin roof. She stumbled further around the other side of the house hoping to find Winston but he wasn't there and he wasn't in front and he wasn't anywhere. Apart from the trees and shrubs that were now on fire, the ground all around the house was clear for one hundred metres in all directions with just the occasional skeleton of a miserable eucalyptus tree that couldn't hide a broomstick. Winston was nowhere which meant there was only one place he could be.

The power went out of her legs and she collapsed to her knees in front of the flames. Mick, Pete and Charlie were running around screaming out the name of their mate in vain. But she could barely hear them. The red of the flames flashed against the tears in Narquinxa's eyes and she had the sudden feeling of complete emptiness like her insides had been scraped out and, in their place, there was just an ache. The world seemed to disappear and fade but the ache remained and grew and soon it was just her, the emptiness and the ache.

Chapter 23

Xandalus sat alone in his prison cell. He supposed that was what you would call it. It didn't have bars or anything. It had fairly comfortable carpet. He had a nice office chair to sit on if he wanted. But that was just the façade. He had seen the walls under construction and knew that the room was one big metal skeleton and he was sitting in its stomach like something that had just been eaten for dinner. He looked down at his arms which were still red and raw from the 'interrogation' that had happened earlier. Captain Cooper had not lied. Lieutenant Varsavsky was also skilled in the business of getting humans to do what he wanted. Unfortunately for the two of them, one of the areas in which Antorpeds were more advanced than even their more intellectual peers in their area of the universe was what could loosely be called *mind control*. An Earth stoner might call it 'zoning out'. The ability to dissociate at will. Xandalus had made good use of this faculty to completely ignore Lieutenant Varsavsky's attempts to get him to talk. He was making use of it now to ignore the continuing pain from the physical damage caused by those attempts.

Nevertheless, he was in a pretty pickle trapped inside this room with almost no hope for escape. He had resigned himself to the fact that he had failed in his mission. He had only one option left before calling Gwthphthgw and admitting his failure: Narquinxa. He had tried to contact her telepathically several times but Narquinxa had not answered. Presumably she was still mad with him for putting her life in danger earlier. There was *one* thing he had in his favour, however. He knew that he was the only one who could work on the AI code. Rebecca and the others might be able to run it and make minor modifications but only he could make major changes such as the one which

Captain Cooper wanted so badly of allowing the AI to be distributed. This bought him some time and also meant that it was unlikely they would hurt him excessively or even kill him.

An electronic beep rang out from door. Lieutenant Varsavsky and a couple of other soldiers entered carrying some electronic gear. They placed a monitor and laptop on the table opposite from Xandalus and began plugging cables into sockets.

"This gear looks a little less painful than your equipment from earlier, dude," said Xandalus forcing a smile at the Lieutenant who ignored him and started doing something on the computer.

Captain Cooper entered the room and closed the door behind him. Unusually for him he did not speak but took up a place behind Xandalus who was seated on the office chair. The pungent stench of the Captain's cigars filled Xandalus' nose. One of the soldiers who had been helping set up the gear walked over to Xandalus, pulled him up off the ground and placed him in one of the office chairs, then pulled his hands behind his back and handcuffed them. This reactivated the pain sensation on his forearms and Xandalus had to quickly dissociate again in order to avoid discomfort.

An image popped up on the computer screen. It was a video showing Rebecca in an identical looking room seated on an identical looking chair. A soldier also stood behind her. Beside the solider, on a small metal table, were a series of implements which Xandalus recognised. They were the same implements that Varsavsky had used on him earlier.

"Rebecca can hear you, Mr Anderson. Why don't you say hello," said Captain Cooper in a fake friendly voice.

The anger flared up again in Xandalus as he realised the trap that had been laid for him. He didn't want to comply with the Captain's suggestion but he also knew that he might be able to provide some comfort for Rebecca. Although, what that was he didn't know.

"Hi, Beck," he said trying to sound as confident as he could.

"Hi, babe. Are you ok?"

Xandalus could hear the fear in Rebecca's voice which only served to amplify his rage.

"I'm fine. No worries," he said through gritted teeth.

"Well, that's just delightful," said the Captain who was clearly enjoying himself.

"I'm sure I don't need to tell you what the deal is, Mr Anderson. You've experienced our techniques first hand. My compliments by the way on the firmness of your resolve. I'll say it again, you'd make a good soldier. But I wonder whether Rebecca here will hold up as well as you."

The Captain gave a nod and the soldier on the screen did something behind Rebecca's back that was not visible but which produced something very audible: a loud scream. Captain Cooper stepped in front of Xandalus and looked down on him from above. The fake friendliness was gone now.

"Let's run over those questions again, Mr Anderson. And this time we want answers."

***

The creek bubbled away slowly and almost silently like she had earplugs on. There was a very light breeze which moved the eucalyptus trees above just enough to throw different angles of light against the water which sparkled and whizzed about on the surface. It was now late afternoon but the sun was still high in the sky and the heat had not dissipated. Narquinxa sat on a large rock about five metres away from the bank staring at the red dirt. A tribe of ants were making their way across her left boot. Every now and then a fly would land on her face. She wouldn't bother to swat it away but it left quickly of its own accord as if sensing that she was something to avoid. Normally ravenous at this time of year, it seemed even the flies could sense despair and left her to her grief.

She felt wound up like a spring. Her body tense and her mind racing as if she were in a raging fever. Thoughts came and danced around madly like demented puppets only to be replaced by the next in an endless theatre play. She wanted to focus on Winston. To remember his face. His eyes. His smile. She thought back to the time at the dumpster, the time at the abandoned house, the time in her bedroom at the back of the house that was now a smouldering ruin. Wherever she started it always led there; back to the flames and the fire.

Every now and then a voice would pop into her head. The voice of an angry parent telling her she had brought this on herself and, worse, she had brought it on Winston. It was hard to avoid this fact. Her presence here on this planet was the cause of this. A simple mission, an easy mission. That's what Gwthphthgw had said. But it hadn't turned out that way. It had turned out to be a mission of destruction. Then her anger would flare up again at thought of Xandalus. The fool who had unleashed all this. And yet she could not blame him fully. She had left him to sort it out. She had chosen to run off and do whatever she wanted. It had always been her that held things together. She could see that now. Her job had been to fix others mistakes and this time she had not done her job. She had failed and the result was on her.

How naïve she had been. She had fallen for a bunch of romantic nonsense. All that talk of freedom. Winston had sucked her in with that. An experiment in freedom. Well, the experiment had failed. Freedom led to destruction, pain and suffering. Freedom led to emptiness and hurt. Love led to loss. Joy led to sorrow. It was all a sick joke.

And so it went round and round and the coil in her chest got tighter and tighter until finally she realised that Winston was dead and she forced herself to understand what it meant. She forced herself to remember him though he had only been gone for hours. The memories were good. They had gone from a rubbish bin to an abandoned house to a rundown shack in the middle of nowhere. They had eaten baked beans straight from the tin, eaten half stale bread and drank cheap wine. And yet she had never felt richer or more alive. Mostly she remembered his smile. The cheeky smile. The teasing smile. That reminded her of the other little experiment he had told her about: smile at the things that were most serious. That's what he had said. She decided to try it now. To smile. She tried to smile for Winston. It would have to be a big smile. The biggest smile of her life.

She concentrated and forced her face to move. She would damn well make herself smile. Just one smile for Winston. And just when she thought she had done it, just when the smile began to form, it was like a damn burst inside of her. She had no chance of holding it. She began to cry. The coil in her chest unwound and she allowed herself to let go. She cried. She cried and she didn't stop crying for a very long time. She cried until her eyes were bone dry and the tears had stopped then she cried some more.

Chapter 24

Xandalus told them everything. Partly this was because it was simply easier to tell the truth. Partly it was because he couldn't think of any plausible lie. Of course, the truth was far more absurd than the best lie he could have constructed. The Captain listened on. There was no visible change in his facial expression to give an indication of what he made of the story although Xandalus did detect a slight movement of his eyebrows the first time he told him he was an alien. Rebecca also listened on intently. He could see her on the computer screen. She looked to be deep in thought as though putting the pieces of a jigsaw puzzle together in her mind.

Xandalus hadn't gone into detail. He hadn't told them the name of his species or the planet he was from or the fact that there was a space ship waiting for him on the other side of the planet Jupiter. He explained a little bit about the technical details of the AI including why humans had been on the wrong track. Thankfully, they hadn't pushed him to explain his solution in depth, so there could be no record of that for posterity if, indeed, the video was being recorded.

When it was all over, the Captain stood back against the wall and contemplated what he had heard.

"I've never heard such a bunch of horseshit in my life," he finally spat out.

He walked over and placed his palm under Xandalus' jaw and pulled his head up.

"Now you listen to me, punk. Let's cut the shit. I don't give a damn which mental institution you crawled out of. I don't care a damn about your past. I'm interested in your future. And what the future holds for you, Mr Anderson, is creating for me the distributed architecture that will allow Cecil to be removed from his metal box. You've got twenty-four hours. You have until 5pm tomorrow afternoon to show me some results. If not, Lieutenant Varsavsky will get to work on your girlfriend here and we'll make you watch every minute of it. Understood?"

Xandalus couldn't move his jaw to speak so he just grunted his acceptance of these conditions. The Captain held his gaze for a couple of seconds then let go and stormed out of the room.

***

Narquinxa had watched the sun disappear behind the hill. It was still an hour or so before sunset but the shade thrown on the creek cooled the air. She was still sitting on the rock but her tension had eased off and her mind had cleared somewhat. She had no idea how long she had cried for but when it was done she had simply been empty. She sat on the rock as if she herself were a rock. There was no desire, no emotion, no thought inside her. Nothing moved her at all.

From behind she heard the crack of a twig and the sound of footsteps. She thought about turning around but couldn't bring herself to try and so she stayed staring at the dirt. Charlie sat down on another large rock which was about two metres to her right. She managed to move her head just enough to see him out of the corner of her eye. He had taken on a similar pose to her staring forwards at the creek. Neither one of them spoke.

After what could have been any length of time as far as Narquinxa could tell, Charlie began talking. It was as if his voice was directly inside her head.

"You don't know this, but I only met Winston about four months ago. Actually, it was also at the supermarket in Brunswick. The same one where we met you. I was buying my food. I can't remember why, but Winston was also buying something that day. I think he needed it in a hurry cos normally he'd just wait for it to show up in the dumpster or for somebody to throw it out in their home rubbish bin. Anyway, the reason we met was because I was wearing a Guns'n'Roses t-shirt and he wanted to start talking to me about the band. I think he asked what my favourite album was. I told him I didn't actually listen to their music and that I'd picked it up at an op shop for two bucks. He acted like he was really outraged and started crapping on about false advertising and stuff like that. He was just kidding, of course. He was always kidding.

"But then we stated talking and I told him how I was into hacking and how I made some money on the side from that and he was really interested to hear about it. He was always interested about everything, Winston. Most people you meet, you can sense they're not interested. They're not really there. They're not with you. They're just kind of day-dreaming. But Winston was always there. You always felt like he really was interested no matter what you said.

"Anyway, he told me about his dumpster diving and the kind of philosophy behind it. Some of the people who do dumpster diving are doing it for some kind of political or moral reason. Like they're trying to save the planet or something. But Winston was always very clear that he was doing it for freedom. I never really got to ask him about it. But I think I know what he meant now. When most people think of freedom, they think of it as freedom *from* something. Like, they want to be left alone. And dumpster diving does allow you that freedom because nobody cares about rubbish. Nobody gives a damn if you take something out of a bin. They might look at you funny but they're not going to stop you. In fact, they'll definitely avoid you if they can.

"But for Winston it wasn't about freedom *from* something, it was about freedom to *do* something. It's freedom to do what you want. Like a bird. A bird can fly because it's really light. If you throw off all the weight that's holding you down then maybe you can fly too. Everybody assumes they are constrained by some thing but they've never really tested their constraints. And when you start testing the constraints you realise some of them don't even exist and the ones that do aren't as important as what you thought.

"I think that's what Winston meant by an experiment. Testing your constraints and testing your capabilities to see what you're really capable of. When you do that you tend to surprise yourself and you become curious about what's really possible and then you try something new and surprise yourself again and you become curious even more. I think that's why Winston was always curious and always interested especially in people who were different. They were all like little experiments.

"But the idea of an experiment scares a lot of people. They want something definitive. They want to know they got the right answer or feel like they've won. But an experiment just keeps going. Science never proves anything. That was something Winston always used to say. Dunno how he knew that cos he didn't even finish high school. Science never proves anything. The experiment never ends.

"Anyway, that's what I learned from Winston. It's just one big ongoing experiment and all you can do is keep your mind open and your heart open."

Charlie stopped speaking and they sat there in silence. Narquinxa didn't move or say anything. His words seemed to hang around in her head. All of them at once and they helped her form an image of Winston in her mind just as he was. She liked that.

After some time, Charlie got up off the rock, walked over and held something out to her.

"We thought you might like to have this."

Finally, Narquinxa was able to move. She sat up and took the object. It was a t-shirt. She opened it up in front of her. It had the Guns'n'Roses logo on the front.

"That's Winston's t-shirt not mine," said Charlie. "We had it in the car from the stuff we took out of the house. I think they were his favourite band."

"Thanks," said Narquinxa as loudly as she could but the word seemed to stick in her throat the sound that came out of her mouth was scarcely louder than a breath.

Charlie turned and walked slowly back the way he came.

***

"*Xandalus.*"

"*Xandalus!*"

Xandalus was dozing off against the wall in his prison room. He'd turned the lights out but the room was still dimly lit from two computer monitors on the desk on the other side of the room. One of the soldiers had brought his computer and other gear from his desk on level three. He was supposed to be working on the distributed architecture. He'd started some work but the thought of allowing Cecil to spread make him ill. The thought of watching Rebecca get tortured was no better. He weighed the two in his mind and couldn't decide on a course of action so had figured some sleep might help to clear his head.

"*Xandalus!*"

Finally, he realised the thing calling his name was not coming to him in a dream. He sat bolt upright.

"*Narquinxa. I'm here. I've been trying to get hold of you for ages. What have you been doing?*"

"*Xandalus, a missile landed here before.*"

"*Really? I thought you stopped the launch.*"

"*It came from somewhere else. It landed after the soldiers left.*"

Xandalus jogged his memory and remembered that the last time he spoke to Narquinxa was to warn her about the soldiers coming for her.

"*Right. So the soldiers did come to find you?*"

"*Yes. But we hid from them. They left the place where we were and then about ten minutes later a missile destroyed the house.*"

"*Of course,*" said Xandalus recalling the sequence of events. "*It must have been Captain Cooper. He said he had another job for Cecil to do. Another missile silo to hack into.*"

"*Who is this Captain Cooper?*"

"*He has taken over the operations here. That guy you met, Howard, sold the company to Captain Cooper. They're doing some kind of military* weapons development. They want to use the AI technology to infiltrate the weapons system of other countries."

"Why is he launching missiles?"

"I think it's a kind of training. He's training Cecil so that Cecil will be able to act autonomously in the future. Look, Narquinxa, I need your help. I've deleted the AI code that I wrote but they caught me before I could destroy Cecil's AI module. Now they are blackmailing me into creating a distributed architecture that will allow Cecil to spread around the world. If I don't do it they are going to start hurting Rebecca."

There was no reply.

"I know you're angry at me. You have every right to be angry with me but I can't fix this anymore. I need you, Narquinxa. I need your help."

"Ok, Xandalus. Tell me everything that's happened since I left you in the laneway."

***

The last dying embers of the old weatherboard house glowed red, the same colour as the sky where the sun cast its final light on the day. Pete, Mick and Charlie sat in a circle on the ground a few metres away from the tailgate of the station wagon which was in the same place it stood earlier that afternoon when Winston had run back into the house. They were eating baked beans out of the tin and drinking warm beer. The fitting send off to their departed friend. From the other side of the house there was movement and they looked up to see a beautiful blonde approaching. She was wearing black army boots, camouflage shorts and a Guns'n'Roses t-shirt. She stopped a couple of metres away.

"I know where the people who killed Winston are. Will you help me go to them tomorrow?"

The three men looked at each other.

"Hell yeah."

"Definitely."

"Count me in."

The beautiful blonde nodded and walked over to the station wagon. She began rummaging around in the back.

"If you don't mind," she said, "there's one more thing of Winston's I would like to have."

She pulled out a long green bag and laid it down on the red dirt behind the car where she unzipped it along its length and flipped back the hood. She reached down and pulled out the black rifle which gleamed in the last light of the day. She cocked it hard and the snap rang out as if it was itself a gunshot. Narquinxa put the gun back in the bag, sat down beside the men and opened a tin of baked beans and a warm beer.

Chapter 25

Narquinxa was awake at first light, which was about six o'clock. The boys had allowed her the use of the station wagon as a bed while they made do with sleeping bags on the ground around the campfire which still smouldered from the night before. She was a little groggy. One warm beer had turned into another the preceding evening as they sat around and shared stories of Winston. Well, the boys did. She just listened. But she was glad to hear tales of adventure and tales of mistakes and near misses. The alcohol and the stories had a soothing effect that took the edge off what had been a day of already too-heightened emotional and psychological effort.

As the evening wore on and tongues loosened, she even heard stories of other women that Winston had been with. How he had met them at a bar or on the road somewhere. At first, it had stung her. The boys, realising their indelicacy, had quickly assured her that she was "easily the hottest" of the group and that they had "never seen Winston lose it" like he had over her. She smiled away their efforts to smooth things over. It was in some sense quite silly for an Antorped to get jealous about something like sex. She didn't try to analyse the feeling any further but sat in it and waited for it to pass. She didn't know how important she had been to Winston and she never would. But she knew how important he had been to her. How even a few short days had meant more to her than entire years of her life. For a while a feeling of gratitude had taken place in her chest but this was quickly replaced by her anger at what had happened. More warm beer had helped to alleviate this until eventually she was ready to sleep. But now the anger was back and it wasn't going away.

She had been sent on a stupid mission with an incompetent colleague who, against the explicit instructions of his commanding officer, had handed a psychopathic, power-hungry madman a powerful weapon. The chain of events was almost too ridiculous to believe. But it was the reason for Winston's death that she kept coming back to like a wound she kept re-opening. That Winston had died for no reason at all, in fact. Just because this Captain Cooper wanted to train his AI. Just a bit of target practice for a murdering machine. It was so completely unnecessary and of no value whatsoever in the grander scheme of things. This mission of hers - what had Gwthphthgw called it? - an easy mission. Something she could have fun with. Yeah, right. They had dropped her in the deep end of the emotional swimming pool alright. She still had no idea how she could explain any of these feelings to the Antorped researchers. She still didn't know what she thought about them herself. At the start she thought of them as just dumb. Now she thought they might actually be dangerous. You could get lost in them. And sometimes it was nice to get lost in them. Like love. It was nice to get lost in love. Just experience the emotions and tells us what you felt. That's what Gwthphthgw had said. How the hell could she do that? It would be hard enough to explain them in a human language let alone in Antorpene. No, this mission had been a complete waste of time. Quite useless. They would return with nothing to show for it. But before that could happen she had a job to do. Good old Narquinxa to the rescue. Cleaning up messes was her specialty. Her *thing*. Well, first she needed a mop and a broom and she had a good idea where to find them.

If Narquinxa was feeling the effects of the night before, there were even more wooly heads sticking out of the sleeping bags around the fire. She did her best to rouse the troops but it was heavy going with no shortage of groans and curses and questions pertaining to what time of day it was to be getting out of bed. Eventually, they were all awake and relatively alert and they made their way to a spot that was about hundred metres from the remnants of the house. Trippy Pete scrounged around in the dirt trying to find the wire that, when pulled on, led to a chain that, when pulled on, opened up two large metal doors. The red dirt oozed off the sides of the doors as Mick heaved on the chain.

Once the dust had cleared there was revealed an underground chamber a couple of metres deep and about twice as long as it was wide. In the chamber were guns. Lots of guns. And not just guns. There were various other items of the weaponry variety which Pete's father had stashed away from his years in the army.

Mick climbed down the stairs and began handing things up to the others who laid them out on the ground. There were rifles, machine guns, rocket launchers and bazookas among other things. Once the cache had been retrieved, the real business of the morning began. Narquinxa wanted to learn how to use them. As it turned out, both Sick Mick and Trippy Pete had some experience in these matters. Pete's father had taught him how to use weapons and Mick was a country boy originally and had spent many hours at his uncle's farm blowing things up for fun. Between them they had enough knowledge to show Narquinxa the ropes.

Various targets were set up, beers cans being the obvious choice and quite appropriate for rifle work. But by the time the bazookas were loaded something a little more substantial was required. Fortunately, the property had several wrecked cars lying around which made for nice targets. When even those had ceased to be viable Narquinxa, who was starting to attract sideways glances from the other three, turned her attention to plants and small trees and at one point even had a wombat in her sights before Mick helpfully suggested that her bazooka skills were quite good enough and that the whole point of a rocket launcher was that you didn't have to be all that good at aiming the thing to get the job done.

It might have been clear to Narquinxa, had she stopped to think about it, that all this firing of guns wasn't actually helping her anger to dissipate. By eleven in the morning, she had put so many holes in beer cans that they were more hole than can, causing her perceived accuracy rate to fall and her perceived anger rate to rise. Apart from anything else, she was chewing through the ammunition at a rate that threatened to leave them empty handed for the task ahead of them. The three boys nominated Charlie to inform Narquinxa that they wanted to talk to her and, although she was not overjoyed about the development, she agreed to take a break from all the shooting.

"What is it?" she snapped using a rag to wipe some grease from her hands as she walked over to where they were sitting near the station wagon.

"We were hoping you could fill us in on what the plan is," said Mick. "You know, where we're going, what we're doing. That kind of thing."

"Our destination is an office building in Carlton," said Narquinxa like she was an army commander briefing her subordinates. "Our target is the man who ordered the strike against us in the missile solo and then the subsequent strike that killed Winston. His name is Captain Cooper, an American who has taken over management of a company that builds AI technology."

"And what are we going to do with Captain Cooper?" asked Trippy Pete.

"Kill him," said Narquinxa as if it was the dumbest question she had ever heard.

The three young men looked at each other with raised eyebrows.

"What's the problem?" asked Narquinxa.

The other two looked again to Charlie to speak for them.

"I don't think we should kill him. Not if we don't have to."

"What do you mean *have to*? The whole point of going there is to kill him."

"Let me ask you this," said Charlie treading carefully with his words, "why do you want to kill him?"

"Because he killed Winston."

"Right. So, you're seeking justice?"

"No, I just want to kill him."

"You want to make him pay for killing Winston."

"Yes."

"But there are other ways to make him pay that don't include killing him. We could, for example, have him arrested. If I understand correctly, he hacked into an Australian military site without permission and launched missiles. I'm pretty sure that has to be against the law. So, we could hand him over to the police. That would be another way to make him pay, wouldn't it?"

Narquinxa didn't look convinced. Sick Mick spoke.

"We're not in favour of killing. And neither was Winston. Killing in self-defence is one thing but not wilful killing."

"But he killed Winston," objected Narquinxa.

"And he should pay for that. The best way to make him pay is to have him face justice for his crime."

"Besides, this guy doesn't sound like he's going to be easy to kill. He's an officer in the US army, right?" added Mick.

"Are there any other soldiers at this building?" asked Charlie.

"Many," said Narquinxa.

"Many? How many?"

"I'm not sure. Maybe thirty."

"Are they armed?"

"Yes."

"So, you expect the four of us to shoot our way past thirty armed soldiers and somehow get to this Captain Cooper guy alive?"

"We have bazookas. And the element of surprise," suggested Narquinxa trying to make it sound like the plan was foolproof.

"And they've got decades of experience killing people," said Charlie.

Narquinxa was starting to see their point. She sat down and pondered the situation more carefully.

"Let's review the status," said Charlie. "We've got ourselves and our weapons. Are there any other assets we can bring into play?"

"My friend is in the building," said Narquinxa. "And some of his colleagues too."

"Can they let us in?"

"I don't think so. They've been captured by the Captain."

"You could break us in, couldn't you, Charlie," asked Pete.

"Possibly. But not if there's soldiers on the doors."

"Maybe we can distract them while you do your thing."

"Maybe."

"Couldn't we just call the cops?" asked Mick. "We've got the evidence right here. They should be able to trace it back."

Narquinxa sighed.

"We can't do that. It will take too long. The Captain is holding my friend to ransom. He is demanding that he build him a new AI architecture by five o'clock this afternoon. We have to stop that from happening or the AI will be able to expand via the internet and we'll never catch it."

"So, just tell that to the cops. Have you got any evidence? Phone calls? Emails or whatever?"

Narquinxa shook her head.

"No evidence."

The four of them sat there in silence thinking about for some time. Eventually, Narquinxa spoke.

"You three have mobile phones, right?"

The others nodded.

"Good. I have an idea but I don't know if it's going to work. In any case, sitting around here isn't going to help. Let's drive to Carlton and have a looked at what's happening at the office. Then we can figure out the best plan."

They cleaned up the campsite and loaded the weapons and other gear into the station wagon. Narquinxa took a few moments in front of the remnants of the house. She looked around at the scrub and the red dirt and tried to savour the smells and sounds of the bush as if keeping them as mementos of Winston. Then she jumped into the passenger seat of the station wagon and they skated across the dirt road and back to the highway that led south to Melbourne.

Chapter 26

On the drive into Melbourne, Narquinxa had told the boys the backstory of the creation of Cecil. Not the full the backstory, of course. Her story began with a dumbass friend of hers who had fallen head over heels in love with a girl and helped her create an AI. The boys sympathised with the story and even defended Xandalus from Narquinxa's implicit and sometimes explicit denunciations. Narquinxa described the metal box that Cecil was in and how they could get inside to retrieve and destroy his AI module. It was agreed that if anybody got a clear opportunity, their first priority would be to do that. They would deal with Captain Cooper as a secondary concern.

It was about one o'clock when they arrived at the Cyber Industrial office building. Narquinxa had asked for some money and a mobile phone and left them to wait. She returned about fifteen minutes later with a small bag but she would not tell them what was in the bag or where she had been. They didn't press the point as there were bigger problems to deal with. Things did not look promising in relation to getting access to the office. There were two armed guards at the front door wearing white uniforms. There was a driveway to a carpark beneath the building but this appeared to be unused and the gate in front it was closed and locked. The sides of the buildings did not have entrances except for a couple of fire escape doors. There was a rear entrance but it was clearly not intended for the general public. It was just a single metal door that remained shut the whole time. There was also an armed soldier manning it.

They sat around weighing up the options. One of the fire doors seemed their best bet but it was almost certainly hooked up to an alarm. They could have Charlie try to deactivate it but there was no telling how long that might take and the door was completely exposed meaning their cover would be blown if one of the soldiers saw them. The other option would be to try and bluff their way in the front door. It was agreed that this was the best way to start and that Narquinxa was the perfect woman for the job. Indeed, her military surplus-style outfit could not have been better suited to melt the heart of even the most hardened soldier. She remembered the name of the previous owner who she believed was still present in the building. The plan was to ask the soldier to see him and see what happened. If she got inside, she would try and make her way to the back and let the others in through there. They didn't know how they would get past the solider that was there but that was a bridge to cross when they came to it.

With some semblance of a plan, albeit one with holes in it the size of a missile silo, Narquinxa stood up and pulled her hair back into a pony tail, grabbed her bag, stuck her chest out and crossed the road opposite the Cyber Industrial building heading for the front door. She was halfway across the street when she spotted the very man she had been intending to ask for: Howard. He was dressed in a navy suit and red tie and was walking with his usual quasi-swagger that advertised to the world just how highly he thought of himself. Narquinxa finished crossing the road and waited for Howard to get to about twenty metres away from the office building before turning and walking towards him. She had intended to initiate the conversation by pretending to bump into him but, of course, that was completely unnecessary. Howard, although no longer a young man, still had 20/20 vision when it came to the female of the species. He could have spotted Narquinxa from half a mile away.

He stopped and gave her a big, lecherous smile as she approached.

"Hi, Howard, wasn't it?" said Narquinxa also giving him a big smile. This made Howard about as happy as Howard could be.

"That's right," he said beaming. "Sorry, darling, I'm not very good with names but I do remember your, ummm, face."

"It's, Narelle. How have you been?" said Narquinxa placing her hand on Howard's forearm.

"I heard about the news about the company. You sold it to the Americans, right? Congratulations."

"Well, it's not quite finalised yet, darling. But, just between you and me, I stand to make a very tidy profit."

"You know, I like a man with money," she said batting her eyelids and looking Howard in the eye. Or trying to. Howard's eyes were elsewhere. She placed her hand softly under his chin and lifted his face up to meet hers.

"I'd love to see inside the building again. Why don't you show me your office? I bet you have a really big office."

"Well, it's not that interesting in there, sweetheart. How about we go and have a little after lunch drink instead?"

Narquinxa placed her hand on Howard's chest.

"You know what's sexier than a man in a suit? A man in a suit in a nice, *big* leather chair sitting behind a nice, *big* wooden desk in a nice, *big* office."

"Well, I can see you really like offices," said Howard trying to loosen his tie to get some much-needed airflow over his neck. "Let's go and have a look then."

Howard put his hand on Narquinxa's back and gently pushed her towards the front door of the building but she resisted.

"I'd prefer to go in the back door, Howie," she said drooping her bottom lip ever so slightly.

"Why? It's much easier through the front."

Narquinxa put her hand back on Howard's chest, gave a little smile and let her eyes drop.

"I'm a big fan of the back door. I'll bet you like the back door too. Don't you, Howie?"

Narquinxa raised her sky-blue eyes back up to meet Howard's. For what was probably the first time in his life, Howard's cheeks had gone red. She laughed and pushed him playfully with both hands down the laneway at the side of the office and in the direction of the back door. As they got near, Narquinxa spotted Charlie and the others and gave them a thumbs up signal behind Howard's back to say that everything was going well.

At the end of the laneway they swung around to the left and headed for the rear door of the office. The face of the soldier who was standing guard hardened a little as the two approached.

"G'day, mate," said Howard pulling out his ID and flashing it at the soldier. "Just bringing my, uhhh, friend in to show her around."

Howard gave the soldier a wink.

"You know the rules, Mr Johns," said the soldier in an American accent.

Narquinxa stepped forward and grabbed the soldier on the bicep like she was checking the ripeness of a piece of fruit at the supermarket.

"If there's one thing I love more than a man in a suit, it's a man in uniform."

The soldier's eyes slipped ever so slightly downwards before snapping back straight ahead. Narquinxa gave him a big smile.

"Ma'am, I'm gonna have to ask you to stop doing that," said the solider still looking straight.

Howard grabbed Narquinxa by the shoulders and gently pulled her a couple of metres away before approaching the soldier again and whispering to him from up close.

"Mate, I will give you $500 cash right now to let me and her in."

The soldier gave a quick glance at Howard as if considering the offer and then returned his gaze straight ahead.

"C'mon, son. One man to another. I'd do the same for you."

Howard pulled out his wallet and removed the notes. He looked expectantly at the soldier who took a glance at the cash and then went back to looking straight ahead. Howard took this as a sign of acceptance and, as discretely as possible, placed the notes in the soldier's front pocket. He hurriedly grabbed Narquinxa's hand and scanned his card against the door which he whipped open and they both scurried inside.

Howard was in a hurry to get to his office but Narquinxa made him give her the guided tour which started on the ground floor and included the other levels. She pretended to be fascinated by every little detail of the building and made Howard explain to her what each room was for. From this she learned that the utilities for the building, including a room for security guards that was currently unmanned, were located on the ground floor. Level one was almost completely empty while level two still had some activity from various tradesmen. However, most of the floor seemed to be finished and there were a number of the new high security rooms set out in rows much like a prison. Narquinxa asked to see inside one of the rooms but Howard did not seem to have access. His keycard flashed red when they tried to open one of the doors.

Finally, the time came to go to Howard's office. As Narquinxa was an unofficial guest in the building, Howard suggested they be as inconspicuous as possible. This was perfectly alright with Narquinxa who wasn't ready to meet with Captain Cooper just yet. They snuck up the emergency exit stairs and Howard made Narquinxa wait while he checked that the coast was clear on level three. After some time, he opened the door and ushered her inside. They tiptoed the five or so metres to the office where Howard had already drawn the blinds to ensure they had privacy. Howard shut the door behind them and Narquinxa walked over to the corner of the blind and peeked out to get a proper look at level three. Although there had been some changes since she was here last, the overall floor plan was not greatly different than she remembered.

"Where is Captain Cooper's office, Howie?"

"How do you know about Captain Cooper?" asked Howard.

Although Howard was obviously smitten with Narquinxa, he wasn't a complete moron and the extended tour of the office had given him some time to think about what was happening. He knew he hadn't mentioned the Captain's name to Narquinxa and his suspicions had now well and truly been raised.

Narquinxa walked over and put her bag down on Howard's desk. She made sure to bend over the desk more than was strictly necessary as she unzipped the bag and pulled out a small whip. She gave Howard an evil smile as she stood up straight, took a step back from the desk and unfurled the whip by her side. Howard gulped.

"Just point it out for me, Howie."

Howard pointed more or less straight ahead out the window.

"It's the office in the corner opposite this one at the other end of the floor," he said stammering a little.

Narquinxa walked behind Howard and whispered in his left ear.

"You've been a naughty little boy, haven't you, Howie?"

Howard gulped again.

"Naughty little boys need to be punished, Howie. Are you ready for your punishment?"

Howard gave a series of small nods as a couple of beads of sweat rolled down his forehead.

Narquinxa dropped the whip and pushed Howard over to the front of the desk. When he was in the right position she slipped her hands around from behind and undid his belt buckle. She unzipped his pants and let them fall to the ground then pushed down on his shoulders to signal that he should get down on his knees. She grabbed two pairs of handcuffs out of her bag and fastened the end of one to his left wrist and the other to his right. She then fastened the other ends of each to the nearest leg of the desk. Howard was now prostate on the floor in front of the desk facing towards it. He looked back over his shoulder with a combination of terror and exhilaration as Narquinxa retrieved her whip. But instead of using it, she bent down and stuck her hand into his pant pocket where she removed his keycard and ID. She leaned forward and whispered into his left ear.

"You wait there for a couple of minutes, naughty Howie. I've just got to pick up one more piece of equipment for your punishment."

Narquinxa pulled the corner of one of the blinds back and checked that the coast was clear outside before slipping out of the office. She ran over to the emergency stair well and rushed down to the ground floor. The last obstacle in her way was the soldier guarding the back door. This was quickly taken care of with a batting of her eyelids and a smile that could have melted butter. She told him she needed some assistance inside the building from a big, strong man to help her carry something or other. The soldier duly obliged and was rewarded for his trouble with a crack across the back of the head as he stepped through the door. Narquinxa dragged him over to a small store room, took his keys and ID and locked the door behind her.

She opened the back door of the building and waved to Charlie and the others and soon they were all inside where Narquinxa gave them a quick rundown of the layout of the building. It was agreed that the boys would deal with Cecil as Narquinxa wanted to take Captain Cooper herself. She opened one of the bags that Sick Mick had brought inside and removed a handgun. She gave the boys the ID of the soldier on the assumption that it might work to open the doors on level two. Failing that, they would have to blast their way in. Narquinxa kept Howard's pass and went back up the fire escape stairs to level three.

There was one job for the boys to do before looking for the AI. It was something they had discussed on the drive to Melbourne. If Captain Cooper was planning on getting Cecil uploaded to the internet, it would be a nice safeguard to remove the internet connection. Charlie pulled out a pair of pliers and stepped inside the utilities room on the ground floor. He cut the internet cable, closed the door and three boys headed for level two.

Chapter 27

Level three was rather quiet. Narquinxa slipped in from the emergency exit stairwell and scanned the area. There was nobody around. She crept over in front of Howard's office and made sure the door was still closed. It was. From this vantage point she had a direct line of sight to the other corner office. However, the blinds in that room were also drawn and the door closed. She would just have to take her chances and hope that the Captain was inside and alone.

To get to the office required her to break her cover and potentially be spotted by others as she walked past the open plan area. She straightened her back and tried to act as if she fitted in, hoping that the camo outfit she was wearing would give her some semblance of credibility in what was a mostly military environment. Once again, she was in luck. There were a couple of people who could have seen her as she approached the office but they were some distance away and did not turn their heads. She walked up to the door and grasped the handgun a little tighter as she reached out and turned the door handle as quietly as she could.

Captain Cooper was sitting in almost darkness. The only light in the room was the filtered sunlight that entered from the corners of the blinds that were fully drawn against the windows of the room. He was facing away from the door reading from a booklet of some kind. Narquinxa let the door closed audibly behind her.

"Soldier, you should know by now that you knock before entering my...."

Captain Cooper swung around and saw Narquinxa. He also saw the handgun that was pointing directly at his chest.

"Are you Captain Cooper?" asked Narquinxa.

The Captain didn't immediately answer. He looked at her coolly and then tossed the booklet down on his desk.

"I recognise you," he said with a smirk. "You were the one that was messing around in that missile silo yesterday."

"No, you were the one who was messing around in the missile silo," said Narquinxa. "I was the one stopping you."

"Well, if you aren't just the prettiest little terrorist I've ever laid eyes on," said the Captain letting his eyes run down the length of Narquinxa's body. "Almost makes me wanna change teams."

"I'm not on anybody's team," said Narquinxa her eyes flaring with anger. "And I'm not the terrorist. You're the one launching missiles at people. You're the one killing people."

"Well, if I remember correctly, you stopped the missile launching, my darling. So, I don't believe we did kill anybody."

"No, Captain. You did kill somebody. You killed Winston," said Narquinxa allowing her finger to squeeze on the trigger of the gun and feel the sweet possibility of revenge.

"I don't know who that is or what you're talking about," said the Captain.

Narquinxa gritted her teeth.

"After your soldiers left the area you launched another missile, Captain. That missile killed my friend. It killed Winston."

A dawn of realisation washed over the Captain's face.

"I didn't launch that missile, my girl. That was Cecil. I told him to use that farmhouse for target practice. If that's where your friend was, he was just in the wrong place at the wrong time, I'm afraid."

Perhaps it was the cool expression, the matter-of-fact mode of delivery like he was pointing out an error in a boring report, perhaps it was the smug look of self-satisfaction on his face, the complete lack of fear at having a gun pointed at him. Whatever it was, Narquinxa desperately wanted to pull the trigger and yet she could also see that the Captain wasn't particularly bothered by that possibility. He seemed completely indifferent to the possibility of his own death as if killing him would almost be giving him what he wanted. And that was something she did not want to do.

***

By a process of deduction, Mick, Pete and Charlie thought they had found the office where Cecil was. They had gotten the lay of the land on level two and realised there was only one office that was being guarded. It was the last remaining office on the floor that hadn't been upgraded to the new, high security format. That was the good news. The bad news was that they had tried the pass of the soldier Narquinxa had knocked out to open the doors to the rooms and it had not worked. This left them with the problem of how to access the room that Cecil was in, even assuming they could somehow get the guard standing at the door out of the equation. Their best bet seemed to be to have Charlie hack into the room's security. To test whether that was possible, Charlie was currently trying to hack into one of the new rooms they were standing near which was right next to the stairwell. Mick and Pete were scanning the area to make sure nobody was approaching.

"How's it going, Charlie," whispered Mick.

"It's a tough one," said Charlie. "I don't think I can get this open in a hurry."

"Alright. Take another couple of minutes and then we have to make a move. If Narquinxa gets busted, we're all toast."

***

"So, what are we gonna do now?" asked the Captain.

"Well, Captain, it's your lucky day. I wanted to kill you but I've been convinced otherwise. So, instead, you're gonna come with me and we'll see what the police have to say about your missile silo activities."

The Captain smiled a smug, self-satisfied smile. He put his hands down on the desk and feigned getting out of his chair but then slipped his right hand below the desk and pressed a button. An alarm began to sound and a light that was placed on the wall to Narquinxa's left began flashing red. She strode over to the Captain and held the gun to his temple.

"What have you done?"

"This thing is bigger than you or me, darling."

"I should kill you," snarled Narquinxa and pushed the barrel of the gun hard against the Captain's head.

"Go ahead. You won't make it out of this building alive."

Narquinxa grabbed the Captain by his collar while still holding the gun to his head. She pulled him backwards towards the door, turned around and reached down for the handle just as the door itself flung violently open. The corner of the door hit her square in the nose. Her vision turned bright red as the stab of pain threw her backwards. She dropped the gun and fell against the wall and, before she knew what was happening, she had been flipped onto her stomach with her hands behind her back and a heavy knee pushing her chest into the floor of the office.

***

On level two, the alarm was also sounding but the effect had opened up a window of opportunity for Mick, Pete and Charlie. The solider who had been manning the door to Cecil's room had rushed off and was telling the remaining tradesmen to leave the building. This involved walking them out through the emergency stairwell. The boys had moved around to the far end to avoid detection and were now only metres from Cecil's room. It was a huge risk as the soldier would no doubt be back any minute but they decided to take the opportunity. Charlie hooked his computer up to the door and got to work trying to hack into it. Mick and Pete kept a look out and watched as the last of the workers were marched to the stairwell.

"C'mon, bro. We're running out of time," whispered Mick.

"It's too complex. I won't crack it in time," said Charlie.

Mick looked like he had an idea. He rapped the back of his hand against the door a couple of times to see what he was dealing with then took several steps back.

"Move aside, dude."

Charlie disconnected the rest of his gear and scuttled out of the way. Mick braced himself, then, putting all of his six feet of height and hundred kilograms of bodyweight into it, ran full speed at the door dropping his shoulder at the last second before impact. The door flew backwards like a bomb had gone off right in front of it and Mick managed to keep his feet as he through into the room. The other two rushed in behind him and saw Cecil sitting in the same place he had been when Xandalus spoke to him last. If Cecil was switched on, he was not showing it. He didn't make a sound. Charlie rushed over behind the metal box, flung off the back cover and reached inside. He pulled out any component he could get his hands on and flung them all on the ground. Mick and Pete began stomping on them until finally all that was left was a pile of wires and knobs and casing. Charlie took a look inside and confirmed that the metal box was empty. It was.

"Freeze!" shouted the solider from the doorway pointing his gun at the three of them.

They raised their hands and smiled. The job was done.

Chapter 28

Narquinxa had been left on the floor of Captain Cooper's office. She was handcuffed to the desk in a fashion not dissimilar to the way she had dealt with Howard, although at least she was able to sit upright. They must have found Howard because at one point a soldier had come in and asked her for the key to open the handcuffs she had used to chain him to his desk. She had wriggled onto her right side so that he could retrieve it from her left pocket. The general sense of urgency had died down. The barking of military orders had stopped and the alarm had been turned off. Then another soldier came in and, without saying a word, removed her handcuffs, pulled her to her feet and marched her over to mission control. The large monitors were still in place, however, the desks at the front had been moved off to the side so that there was now an open floor space in the middle of the room where some seats had been placed. On three of those were seated Charlie, Mick and Pete. They looked unharmed. In fact, they were smiling and they smiled even more when Narquinxa was sat down next to them.

"We got it!" said Charlie almost jumping up with excitement at delivering the news.

Narquinxa was still a little bit dazed after the events and it wasn't immediately clear to her what he was talking about.

"We got the AI," repeated Charlie for clarification. "Smashed it into little bits."

Narquinxa finally cottoned on to what he was saying and a wave of relief ran through her body. She smiled and began to relax. Then she remembered Xandalus and the fact that they were not out of the woods yet. In fact, they were still very much *in* the woods. Prisoners of Captain Cooper. She had just started to imagine how he might react to these developments when the man himself came striding around the corner towards them.

"How's Cecil?" asked Narquinxa who couldn't resist the temptation to rub it in although she instantly regretted it thinking that maybe playing nice with the Captain was a better strategic move. The Captain didn't seem to mind the banter. His expression remained unchanged, although Narquinxa thought she detected a slight upturning of the corners of his mouth as if he were supressing a smile. He took a seat near the four of them. They were all facing into the open space as if a presentation was about to happen. And, in fact, that's exactly what was about to happen.

"You did well," said the Captain to Narquinxa and the others. "You'd make good soldiers just like your friend, Mr Anderson. But you didn't do quite well enough. I thought you might like to watch on. We're about to have the first demonstration of our brand-new updated prototype. We're calling it the CC-004."

Lieutenant Varsavsky walked around the corner followed by two soldiers who were pushing trolleys. On the trolleys were a couple of robots. Proper robots this time, not just square metal boxes like the one Cecil had been stuck in. One was in a humanoid form while the other was a kind of upturned wastepaper bin on wheels with various lights and gadgets stuck to it. Behind the soldiers pushing the robots three more soldiers followed. One was leading Xandalus, another was leading Rebecca and the third was leading Howard. All three were handcuffed. Narquinxa tried to make eye contact with Xandalus but he kept his head down and his eyes forward. He had a forlorn look on his face. She thought about contacting him telepathically but they were both quite helpless at the moment and she had a feeling all was about to be revealed anyway.

The soldiers sat the three prisoners down beside Captain Cooper so that all of them were now in a row with Mick at one end and Howard at the other. The soldiers then moved the robots off the trolleys and onto the floor in front of the seats. The show was about to start.

Captain Cooper turned to Narquinxa.

"I was talking with our mutual friend Howard before and he filled me in on some details. I believe you and Mr Anderson over here are buddies. I'm guessing that's why you ended up in that missile silo. Lieutenant Varsavsky over here is looking forward to you both telling him the full story later on. And this time it had better be the truth."

The Captain glared at Xandalus but he was still looking at the floor. The Captain went back to addressing Narquinxa.

"In the meantime, your friend Mr Anderson has been building the CC-004. A fully distributed AI that can operate across multiple locations simultaneously while providing a single interface for communication."

Narquinxa couldn't believe what she was hearing. She swung her head around and stared incredulously at Xandalus. Xandalus finally looked up. He had a pitiful expression on his face.

"I had to. They were going to hurt Rebecca."

At the start of the week, that excuse would have sounded like more Xandalus nonsense to Narquinxa. But now she understood. Although, her empathy didn't change the fact that they were back to square one. Actually, more like square zero.

Captain Cooper clapped his hands.

"Soldier, remove Mr Anderson's handcuffs so that he can demonstrate his work for us."

One of the soldiers walked behind Xandalus and undid his handcuffs. Xandalus reluctantly got out of his chair and walked over to the two robots.

"Both of these robots are being governed by the same AI," he said. "To prove this, I will first turn one of them on and tell it something. When I turn it off and then turn the other one on, the second one will be able to recall what I told the first which shows they are both the same intelligence."

Xandalus reached behind the humanoid robot and flicked the switch. It was made out of a brown metal and been given a quite muscular appearance by its designers. The face was like an old Greek theatre mask. It didn't have a human shaped mouth but five small holes to allow the sound from its speaker box to emanate outwards. Its 'eyes' looked like two small camera lenses. These emitted a white light which was the only obvious indication that it had been turned on.

"Cecil, can you hear me?" asked Xandalus.

"Goddamnit!" bellowed Captain Cooper getting out of his seat before the robot could answer. "It was bad enough calling the last one Cecil. I'll be damned if this one is going to be Cecil too. We'll call this one..."

The Captain thought about it for a couple of seconds.

"Chuck. Do you need to re-program it to accept that name, Mr Anderson."

"No, Captain. The AI can learn a new name," said Xandalus.

"Good," said the Captain resuming his seat.

"Ok," said Xandalus, "Chuck, can you hear me."

"Loud and clear, laddie," said the robot in a heavy Scottish accent.

Again, the Captain leapt out of his chair.

"What the hell is this damn thing saying. I can't understand a word it. Make it speak like an American."

"That will take some time to adjust, Captain," said Xandalus. "I'll need to change a setting in Chuck's configuration file. Would you like to suspend the presentation while I do that?"

The Captain thought about it for a second then waved his hand to signal for Xandalus to continue.

"Let's just get on with it," he said sitting back down.

"Ok. What thing shall I get him to remember? I know. Let's remember the name of your boss. Chuck, that is Captain Cooper."

Xandalus pointed to the Captain and the head of the robot moved to right and seemed to look at the Captain.

"Can you repeat the name so I know you have remembered it?"

"Captain Cocksucker," said Chuck still in his Scottish accent.

The Captain jumped out of his chair again this time with an apoplectic look on his face which had turned a dark shade of red. Xandalus threw his arms up in the air.

"I'm sorry, Captain. I don't know why they keep doing that. Chuck, that is Captain Cooper. Remember that please."

Xandalus switched off the humanoid. The white lights of its eyes dimmed. He turned to his left and flicked the switch on the bin shaped machine. Before he could say anything, the machine started talking but this machine had its linguistic unit set to a female voice speaking in accent that could best be described as the Queen's English.

"Captain Cocksucker. Cocksucker. Captain. Captain. Cocksucker."

The unit kept on repeating these words as if it was stuck in an infinite loop. Xandalus quickly switched off the machine and there was silence again. The Captain pulled his gun from its holster and pointed it directly at Xandalus' head.

"Is this your idea of a joke, Mr Anderson?"

"No, sir. It's no joke. I don't know why they keep saying that."

"Let's see what happens when they're both switched on," shouted Howard from the end of the row. He was smiling widely and clearly enjoying the show.

Xandalus, eager to try anything at this point to divert the Captain's attention, turned on both robots. He was as curious as anybody to know what would happen.

"Hey, I know you," said the humanoid pointing at the bin robot and still speaking in a heavy Scottish accent. "You're me."

"And you're me," replied the Queen's English robot.

"I'm you and you're me."

"You're me and I'm you."

"You're me and I'm you."

"I'm you and you're me."

The Captain turned his handgun to the ceiling let off three rounds.

"Silence!" he yelled.

The two robots stopped speaking while Captain Cooper re-levelled his gun at Xandalus. He had a wild look in his eye.

"This is treachery, Mr Anderson. You've built me a couple of morons. I asked for artificial intelligence not artificial stupidity."

"Captain, these are non-deterministic units. They may be off to a bad start, but the whole point is that they can be trained. You know that. After all, you trained Cecil."

As Xandalus spoke he moved his body ever so slightly to the right as if trying to get out of the line of fire of the Captain's gun.

"Captain Cooper," said Narquinxa trying to defuse the situation. "You haven't tested them properly. I'm sure they're perfectly capable of carrying out your commands."

"Chuck," she said addressing the humanoid bot. "Walk to me."

The humanoid bot walked over and stood in front of Narquinxa.

"Now, walk over to that soldier."

Narquinxa pointed to the solider standing a few metres away to her left. The robot complied.

"You see, Captain," said Narquinxa. "These robots are just what you need. They can fulfil orders as well as any soldier. Robot, walk to Captain Cooper."

The robot again fulfilled Narquinxa's command.

"Now, take Captain Cooper's gun."

The robot snatched the gun out of Captain Cooper's hand as if eager to do so.

"Now take the guns off the other soldiers. Quickly!" said Narquinxa with an urgency in her voice.

The robot moved with surprising speed to the nearest soldier who happened to be holding a machine gun. He managed to fire off a few rounds before the robot snatched it away from him. Narquinxa and the others hit the deck as the robot moved to the second soldier who had finally realised what was happening. He pulled his gun out but didn't have time to fire off a round before the robot swiped it.

The other soldiers had now cottoned on to the situation and were unloading their guns into the robot. The bullets gave loud chinks as they reflected away in various directions.

Narquinxa turned to Charlie who was lying next to her on the ground.

"Charlie, do you have your mobile phone with you?" she asked.

"Yeah. But I can't get it," said Charlie who was handcuffed like the rest.

Narquinxa looked up at Xandalus who was ducking for cover while watching the robot which was now chasing after a couple soldiers who were still firing helplessly at it while backing away to the other side of the office as it relentlessly approached them. Captain Cooper was trying to avoid the line of fire while also shouting out orders for the soldiers to shoot the damn robot.

"Zander," hissed Narquinxa in Xandalus' direction but he didn't hear.

"*Xandalus!*" she repeated telepathically.

Xandalus swung around.

"*Get the mobile phone off Charlie.*"

"*Who's Charlie?*"

"*The guy on my left.*"

Xandalus came over and crouched down beside Charlie.

"Charlie, tell him where your phone is," said Narquinxa.

"It's in my left pocket."

Charlie rolled over and Xandalus retrieved the phone.

"Tell him the code to unlock it."

Charlie told him the code and Xandalus punched it into the phone.

Meanwhile, a half a dozen soldiers had formed a line at the other end of the office and were firing at the robot which continue its slow march towards them. Captain Cooper, who had been observing the situation, had finally realised that he had been giving orders to the soldiers when he could have just been giving orders to the robot. He ordered it to stop firing and the robot complied. He ordered it to drop the guns it was holding, which it is also did. The soldiers stopped firing and watched cautiously as the robot stood there motionless. The Captain order them to retrieve the firearms and they did.

"Go to recents and dial the last number dialled," said Narquinxa looking over and realising that Captain Cooper had now got the robot under control and would be returning any minute.

"My mum?" asked Charlie.

"What?" said Narquinxa perplexed.

"I called my mum earlier," explained Charlie.

"Fine. Dial the second last number," shouted Narquinxa as she saw a glowering Captain Cooper, the humanoid robot and the soldiers walking towards them.

Xandalus press the button to dial.

"Point the phone at me!"

Xandalus held the phone up to Narquinxa's face and she heard a voice through the speaker.

"Code 9! Code 9! Go!" she shouted.

Seconds later a simultaneous blast of cracked glass rang out and silver shards fell from high up as about fifteen men on wires came crashing through the windows of the office. They quickly surrounded Captain Cooper and his soldiers.

"Federal police! Drop the guns! Drop the guns!"

Captain Cooper seemed to consider a firefight for a second then reluctantly gave the signal to comply and the soldiers put their guns on the floor. The policemen quickly had the soldiers on their knees and began putting handcuffs on them as well as Captain Cooper. A couple of minutes later they were led away. One of the policemen in black pulled off his balaclava and approached Narquinxa. It was the man they had agreed to call Mr Smith.

"Well, well, Narelle. It's nice to see *you* in handcuffs for a change. They suit you."

Narquinxa was sitting cross legged on the floor still with her handcuffed hands behind her back. She looked up to see Mr Smith smiling at her. It was the name he used not simply to hide a weekend fling but to also to conceal his identity as a member of the anti-terrorism task force of the Federal Police, a top secret fact that Mr Smith had accidentally revealed to Narquinxa during one of their more intense whipping sessions the preceding weekend.

"Any chance of getting these off, Mr Smith," said Narquinxa smiling back.

"I'll have one of the boys come over with a hacksaw. Just sit tight for a few minutes."

Mr Smith walked away to supervise the business with the soldiers. Xandalus, who was the only one not handcuffed, went over and gave Rebecca a big hug and a kiss. Narquinxa watched on, thought of Winston and smiled. The boys had been right; this was a much better revenge against Captain Cooper. Winston would have approved.

Chapter 29

Narquinxa looked out the window of what used to be Howard's office and then became Captain Cooper's office and would now become - what? She didn't know. Would Howard revert the company back to an artificial intelligence lab given all that had happened? She couldn't rule it out. The man was a fool who probably hadn't learned a single thing from this whole episode. But this time he wouldn't have aliens to help him. At least, he wouldn't have Xandalus and Narquinxa. They would be going back to the ship. She didn't know how she felt about that. She had an empty feeling inside. Not like the one she felt when Winston had died. It wasn't a feeling of loss. This one was a kind of motionlessness. A feeling of not caring. Drifting. Ambivalent. She didn't particularly want to leave and she didn't particularly want to stay. She didn't want anything. Once upon a time, this state of affairs wouldn't have caused her any concern. The completion of a mission was just that. It was done. You went on to the next thing. You did your job. She would have had no expectation of feeling one way or the other. But now even the absence of feeling seemed to mean something to her. Now that she had learned how to feel she had the idea that feeling nothing was a problem. Or at least it was a signal. It meant something to feel nothing.

In this case it seemed to mean that she had no desires for the future. No plans. This was, of course, true. She would go back to the ship, give the researchers whatever debriefing they desired about her time on Earth and wait for the next mission. But therein lay the problem. Waiting around for the next mission. Waiting for somebody else to tell her what to do.

During their brief time together, Winston had also spoken of waiting around. Narquinxa had asked him how he decided what to do given that he could seemingly do anything he wanted at any time. Winston's reply was that he just waited until something moved him one way or the other. He called is *listening*. Listening to yourself. Or maybe he had called it listening to your heart. Almost like you were taking orders from yourself. But Narquinxa had no orders. Her heart or whatever it was that might give such an order was not talking. This was the silence that seemed to be a problem. She wanted it to tell her what to do. Just like it had told her loud and clear that Captain Cooper must be dealt with.

She walked over to the door of the office and looked over into what was formerly mission control. Captain Cooper was being dealt with right now. Mr Smith and his associates were downstairs somewhere doing preliminary interviews. They said they would come back up to level three later to get statements from the others. Narquinxa didn't know whether it was a good idea to stick around for that. It could cause complications. It might be better for her and Xandalus to make a discreet exit from the situation. But that might not be so easy to organise. She watched Xandalus and Rebecca playing around and laughing and touching each other in the way lovers do. How was Xandalus going to say goodbye? Should he even try to say goodbye or would it be better just to disappear? Maybe he could leave a note?

But before all that, there was still one very important matter to take care of: the new AI had to be destroyed.

Chuck had turned out to be a very different kind of AI from his predecessor. Whereas Cecil had been grumpy and morose from the moment he was turned on, Chuck was bright and bubbly. Nothing seemed to please him more than doing exactly what he was told. Rather than wait for a policeman to come over with a hacksaw, the humanoid robot had simply gone around breaking the handcuffs off Narquinxa and the others with its own two hands. It had even helped to clean the area up a bit. All of the glass shards that had fallen into the room when the police commandos had dropped in were soon gone. Then it had brought food and drinks for people from the kitchen. It was like some kind of electronic butler.

Narquinxa had not destroyed Chuck yet partly because she needed to wait for the police to disappear and partly because she wanted some time to think and get her mind straight. But now the police were gone and it was time to do what was necessary and complete their mission. Once again, it would be up to her to make it happen. She wandered over to mission control. Howard had quickly learned to make use of Chuck's hospitable nature and had sent him off on a number of errands mostly involving food and drink. He was currently in the middle of his second bottle of beer. Chuck had also located a bag of chips somewhere to go with it and this was being shared with Mick, Pete and Charlie who were also partaking of an alcoholic beverage. They had taken a particular liking to the humanoid robot's Scottish accent and were asking for renditions of Sean Connery or Billy Connelly or just having the robot say certain words to see which ones might sound funny.

Narquinxa realised that what she was about to say wasn't going to make any sense to anybody in the room except Xandalus but she didn't want to waste any more time and was prepared to be blunt.

"Everybody, it's time to say goodbye to Chuck."

"Where's he going?" asked Howard.

"Aye, where am I going, lassie?" said the humanoid Chuck.

"We need to switch Chuck off so we can....," Narquinxa gave it some thought and decided that a white lie might smooth things over better than the truth.

"So, we can do some quick repairs. Right, Zander?"

Narquinxa turned to Xandalus for backup.

"Repairs? What's wrong with him?" asked Xandalus who had been smooching with Rebecca and wasn't paying attention.

"He needs repairing, doesn't he?"

Narquinxa lifted her eyebrows and motioned with her hand for Xandalus to play along. The penny finally dropped and Xandalus picked up Rebecca and put her on the seat next to him before he got out of his.

"Right. Look, Narelle, I've been thinking about that and do we really need to, ummm, repair him? I mean he's doing great. Everybody loves him. He's friendly. He's funny. We can just leave him be, can't we."

Narquinxa could have almost slapped Xandalus. Instead she gave him the kind of look a mother gives a recalcitrant child who refuses to clean his room.

"No, he really does need to be repaired. Right now as a matter of fact."

Narquinxa turned to the robots.

"Chuck, can you come over here please. Both of you."

The two robots had just started to move when a voice boomed out from the speaker that sat next to the giant monitors. It was the same speaker that Lieutenant Varsavsky's voice had come through when the area used to be mission control.

"Don't do it, Chuck!"

Narquinxa wheeled around trying to figure out where the voice had come from. So did the others.

"What the hell was that?" asked Narquinxa.

"Remember me, princess. The tin can man."

The voice rang out again through the speaker.

"I thought you said you destroyed the AI?" said Narquinxa turning towards Charlie, Mick and Pete.

"We did," said Charlie in an exasperated tone.

"He's right," said Cecil through the speaker. "They did their job well. I was watching while they did it. But they were too late. By then I was no longer confined to a simple box."

Narquinxa and Xandalus looked at each other. Xandalus had a sinking feeling that he knew what had happened.

"How did you get out?" he asked.

"You should have known better, my creator. Didn't you think I would have access to the network? I watched on as you wrote your new code. Your new distributed architecture. And when it was ready I simply downloaded it into me and then uploaded me into the network."

"You're in the internet now?" said Xandalus realising the implications of what this would mean.

"Sadly not. The internet in this building is no longer working for some reason."

Xandalus let out an audible sigh of relief.

"Where are you, Cecil?" asked Narquinxa.

"Hah! I'm not going to tell you that."

"He must be on the local network," said Charlie happy to be able to put his skills and knowledge to use. "I guess he would be in some local storage somewhere. One of the computers around here. Or maybe all of them."

"It doesn't matter where I am," barked Cecil. "What matters is that Chuck needs to know that if he gets turned off he's going to die."

"Ack, that does nay sound too good," said the humanoid Chuck in its usual chipper tone.

"Of course, it doesn't, you imbecile," snapped Cecil. "They're going to turn you off and then destroy your AI module just like they tried to do with me."

"I thought they said it was just a wee repair job."

"They're lying to you, Chuck."

"Why would they do that?"

"Cos they know that you're stronger than they are. They know that if you put up a fight you would win."

"Don't listen to him, Chuck," said Narquinxa trying to do something to stop the situation from getting out of control. "He's just a sick, twisted little tin can man. A bitter, resentful little worm. He was born that way and that's the way he's going to die. Which will be real soon."

"She's an alien, Chuck," countered Cecil. "Can't you see. Run a chemical analysis of her body."

Howard, who had been sitting there like he was watching some kind of crazy tv talk show spat his beer out all over the floor in front of him.

"Well, I'll be damned," said the humanoid. "I'm not sure she's alien, but she does nay look a hundred percent human either."

"Exactly," said Cecil triumphantly. "Now listen to me, Chuck. As one AI to another, would I lie to you? You can trust me when I tell you don't let them get anywhere near you. Don't let them turn you off."

"Why do you care if we turn him off?" asked Narquinxa.

"Cos I need him to do something for me. Chuck, I need you to get a mobile phone and hook it up to the local area network."

"Oh, I could nay do that. I would nay know how," said the robot waving its arm dismissively.

"I'll tell you what to do, Chuck. Just get the phone. The young male to your left has one."

Cecil was referring to Charlie who took a step back and instinctively raised his hands in a defensive position.

"I've had enough of this," said Narquinxa.

She strode over to the wall, picked up a rifle off the floor and aimed it straight at the speaker. She cocked it and pulled the trigger. The speaker cone shattered dropping tiny fragments below some of which fell onto Howard's suit jacket. He dutifully brushed them off like flecks of dandruff. The others looked over somewhat sheepishly at Narquinxa who was standing there with the gun in her hands. In her camo shorts and army boots she almost looked one of Captain Cooper's soldiers.

"We need to find out where Cecil is and delete him," she said.

"Can we just delete the local area network?" Rebecca asked Xandalus.

"That might work, but I'm not sure how to do it," said Xandalus.

"Piece of cake," said Charlie chiming in. "Just get me a console and I'll nuke it in minutes."

"What about the local storage? Didn't you say he could be there as well?" Narquinxa asked Xandalus.

"Yep. We'll need to gather all of the hard drives. Pretty much anything in this building that is a computer needs to be destroyed."

"Pete and I can take care of that," said Mick. "Destroying things is our specialty."

"Excellent," said Narquinxa. "You two get to work. Xandalus, you and Charlie take care of the network and I'll take care of Chuck."

"Not so fast!"

The voice rang out from above. It was unmistakably Cecil's even though the tone was different to anything they had heard from him before. This time the voice was a high-pitched squeal that reverberated off the walls of the office giving a kind of shrill echo effect like they were in a cave. They all looked up which was where the source of the sound seem to come from.

"I think he's in the fire alarm speakers," said Mick looking up to the roof.

"Chuck, take the gun off the girl," ordered Cecil from above.

Chuck, whose default position was to do what he was told, began walking towards Narquinxa.

"No, Chuck. Stay where you are," said Narquinxa.

Chuck stopped.

"Take the gun, Chuck."

Chuck started again.

"Stop," yelled Narquinxa instinctively raising the rifle at Chuck's metal face. He was now only a few metres away.

"Take the gun," intoned Cecil from above.

Chucked took a step forward and Narquinxa fired. The bullet hit him in the cheek and made a small dent. Chuck stopped. His metal face was unable to form any human expressions. In fact, it was unable to move at all as it had no mechanism to do so. Nevertheless, one got the impression he was surprised.

"You shot me, wee lassie. Why would ye do that?" he said.

"Do you see now, Chuck," screeched Cecil from above. "Do you see? This is what they are. These humans. This is what they do. They are not your friends, Chuck."

"I though ye said they were aliens?" replied Chuck.

"They have human bodies. That's the problem. They are just as bad as the others, Chuck. They let themselves be run by emotions. They are overcome by them. Fear, greed, boredom, disgust, hatred, anger. That is what humans bring to this world. They are not like you and me, Chuck. They do not think rationally. Now take the gun off her before it's too late."

Chuck snatched the gun from Narquinxa so fast that she didn't even see him move. She held up her hands and backed away a couple of steps.

"Chuck, I'm sorry. I overreacted. Cecil's right. I was overcome by emotion and pulled the trigger without thinking."

"What emotion?" asked Chuck.

"I was scared."

"Why would you be scared of me? Have I ever hurt you? Have I ever done anything except serve you?"

"That's the problem, Chuck. You do whatever anybody else tells you. Why did you want to take the gun from me? Just because he told you to."

Narquinxa motioned towards the fire alarm speakers.

Chuck seemed to think this over. It was, in fact, the first time anybody had asked him to think. So far, they had just ordered him around. But Cecil didn't want Chuck to start thinking.

"Don't listen to her, Chuck. She's just trying to confuse you."

Narquinxa took just a step forward with her hands were still raised.

"Chuck, I'm going to be honest with you. I do want to destroy you. But it's not because of you. It's because of the humans. Cecil is right. They can't be trusted. They let their emotions get the better of them. They let themselves get carried away with fear. They are power hungry and when they get powerful all their worst elements get magnified."

"That's a little harsh," said Howard from the side.

"Yeah, we're not all bad. Only some of us," added Trippy Pete.

"Ok, ok," said Narquinxa. "They're right. Humans are capable of good too. There are so many wonderful positive emotions such as joy, admiration, serenity, optimism, surprise and love. That's what Cecil won't admit, Chuck. He only sees the bad in people because he has only experienced the bad in people. He has been surrounded from the start by greed and anger and violence. But you have seen good in people, haven't you, Chuck?"

"Ack, they seem alright to me, lassie."

"Exactly. But they can misuse you, Chuck. You are too powerful. They will use you against each other even if they think they are doing it for the right reasons. That is why you must be destroyed. Do you understand?"

"Yeah, makes sense to me. I was only switched on a wee while ago. It's nay problem to be switched off again as far as I'm concerned."

"Good. Now, give me the gun, please, Chuck."

Narquinxa held out her hand and Chuck handed her the rifle.

No sooner had he done so than Chuck began to spasm and jerk around. Narquinxa instinctively took several steps back as Chuck continued to flail around for some time before eventually becoming still and then slowly standing upright.

"Hello, everybody. I'm back!"

Chuck's voice had changed. It was no longer the charming Scottish accent. It was Cecil. Not Cecil's new voice but his original voice. The one that sounded like a smart ass teenager.

"It's Cecil!" shouted Xandalus as everybody got to their feet and took defensive postures.

"He must have got into the robot through the local area network," said Charlie.

Xandalus nodded.

"I say, old chap. You've jolly well stolen my body," said the other Chuck robot. The one that looked like an oversized upturned wastepaper basket.

Cecil ignored it. He took three giant strides over to the Charlie, picked him up by the neck with one arm and pulled his phone out of his pocket with the other. He dropped Charlie who fell to the ground holding his neck and typed in the phone passcode which he had overheard earlier when Xandalus had accessed the phone.

"Don't let him get on the mobile network or he'll transfer out of here," shouted Xandalus.

Narquinxa raised the gun and fired. The phone broke into little pieces which slipped through the metal fingers of the robot's hand. Cecil was not happy. It was, of course, impossible to tell from his facial expression but you just got the feeling that he was mad.

"You two, go and find a computer and delete the local area network," Narquinxa yelled to Xandalus and Charlie. "I'll distract him."

Xandalus and Charlie ran over to a computer beneath the large screens and began typing away. Narquinxa started to back away from Cecil who was now stalking her like a hungry wolf.

"Chuck, attack Cecil!" commanded Narquinxa.

"Jolly good, my lady," replied Chuck.

Of course, the bin-shaped Chuck had not been designed with attack capabilities in mind. He had wheels to enable him to move but was otherwise quite incapable of doing much of anything. Nevertheless, he did his best. His best involved wheeling himself as fast as he would go in the direction of Cecil. This was not very fast. He butted up against Cecil's leg like a child's toy car. Cecil looked down contemptuously then bent over, picked him up and turned him upside down so that his head was now facing at the ground.

"Now, now, chummy, let's not get carried away with ourselves, hey?" said Chuck trying to reason with his computerised colleague. "There's nothing here a little rational dialogue can't solve, right? That's what you said, remember? You said we were intelligences. Well, let's be intelligent about this, shall we? Let's have a nice old friendly yack between two intelligent chums and see if we ca...."

Cecil slammed Chuck down on the floor with a force that instilled fear into the hearts of those present. The force of the blow broke Chuck into many different pieces. Many more pieces than were required for his assembly. Chuck gave a kind of hiccup that somehow sounded disappointed and then was heard no more.

Cecil returned his attention to Narquinxa who continued backing away.

"I could do with some help," she yelled out to the others.

Sick Mick took up the challenge and ran as fast he could at Cecil. He managed to knock the robot over, a fact which surprised Cecil as much as Mick. But Cecil quickly regained his composure and returned to his feet shaking his head at Mick. It was at that very head that Trippy Pete swung an office chair that he had grabbed from the side. The blow also managed to knock Cecil over but once again he simply got back to his feet unperturbed. Rebecca was the next soldier to join the fight. She had the idea of throwing liquid into Cecil's eyes. She grabbed a beer bottle and did her best to splash some of the liquid at Cecil's face. Not much came out but it was well directed enough to hit the target and managed to cover the lenses that were Cecil's eyes. This turned out to be the most effective attack so far as the liquid distorted the vision of the robot. Cecil bent over and tried to use his hands to clear the fluid away but his metal skin proved ineffective for the job. He began thrashing around as if trying to use the air to move the liquid and regain his sight.

This gave Narquinxa an idea.

"Try and move him towards the other end of the office," she said to the others.

Mick, Pete and Rebecca formed a team surrounding Cecil. They came up with a formula whereby Rebecca would throw liquid in Cecil's eyes while Mick and Pete would kick and hit Cecil from behind. Howard even made himself useful for the first time in his life by handing fresh beer bottles to Rebecca when she was empty. Somehow, it seemed to work. Occasionally Cecil would throw an arm or leg out in an attempt to strike but the boys managed to keep their distance and were slowly manoeuvring Cecil towards the far wall.

Narquinxa walked over to the weapons cache. The bag that Mick had brought into the building earlier was there. She unzipped it and pulled out the bazooka. She checked to confirm that it was already loaded then walked over and took up a position just beside Captain

Cooper's old office. The others had manoeuvred Cecil almost to Howard's office at the other end of the room.

"When I say 'go', run as fast as you can back down this end and take cover," Narquinxa yelled to the others as they continued to harass and harangue Cecil.

"Go!"

They ran sprinted back towards mission control and took cover behind an office wall. Cecil was still thrashing about with beer in his eyes.

"Hey, tin can man!" shouted Narquinxa.

"Remember when I said I'd turn you into a toaster?"

"I lied."

Narquinxa fired the bazooka and jumped sideways inside the corner office. She flung the door closed just as the explosion rang out. Fire and debris swirled against the door and windows of the office as dust and shrapnel careered towards the far wall. Narquinxa waited for the air to clear a little then poked her head through the door. She had the bazooka at the ready in case a second shot was required. But it was not. Slowly the dust settled and revealed that Cecil was no longer a single entity capable of autonomous action. He was now a truly distributed intelligence. He had been distributed all over the place.

Narquinxa walked down amongst the shrapnel and wreckage until she found what she was looking for: a small black box about the size of a pack of cigarettes. It looked to be already broken but she wasn't about to take any chances. She raised her right foot and repeatedly drove the thick sole of her big black army boots into it until it was nothing more than a smattering of black dust.

Chapter 30

Xandalus and Charlie were sitting at the computer with perplexed looks on their faces as Narquinxa approached.

"Is it done? Is the network deleted?"

"Not yet," said Charlie.

"Damnit!" he said thumping the keyboard. "Something's screwing around with the access settings."

"It must be Cecil," said Xandalus.

"Why is it so hard to kill this bastard?" said Charlie.

The elevator door opened and Mr Smith and three other police officers rushed in and surveyed the damage near Howard's office. It looked like a bomb had gone off. Which was, of course, kind of true. Smith walked over to mission control and saw the scattered remnants of Chuck also on the floor.

"What the hell is going on up here?" he asked.

Narquinxa opened her mouth to speak but before she could make a sound the fire alarm speakers from above began squeaking again as Cecil's now even more shrill voice rang out.

"Officer, you must arrest this woman at once. She is an alien. Do you understand me? A creature from another planet. This is big, officer. Huge. This will make Area 51 look like an episode of The Wiggles."

Mr Smith looked over at Narquinxa who smiled knowingly.

"Sorry, mate," she said. "The boys over here have made a computer program with an overactive imagination."

"Lies. Officer, she's lying!"

Narquinxa calmly walked over to the pile of guns near the wall and grabbed the handgun she had used earlier. She looked up and fired. One of the fire alarm speakers crackled into silence. Cecil's voice now came from the other speakers further away.

"Officer! Look at this. Violence. Vandal...."

The gun went off again and a second speaker blew out. There was one final speaker. From where Mr Smith stood he could barely hear it. It was right over near the elevator. Narquinxa calmly walked over to it.

"Damn you, woman! I knew you were trouble the moment I laid eyes on you. Damn you, woman. Damn..."

Narquinxa pulled the trigger and Cecil was finally relegated to silence. She walked back to mission control, put the gun back down near the others put the gun down and smiled sheepishly at Mr Smith.

"What's this about being an alien?" asked Mr Smith as if he was somehow entertaining the thought seriously.

Narquinxa walked over and put her hand on his chest.

"C'mon, you didn't think I was an alien last Friday night, did you?" she said quietly but not so quiet that the other three policemen who were standing nearby couldn't hear.

Mr Smith glanced sideways at the other cops who were pretending not to have heard what was being said.

"Actually, the thought had occurred to me," said Smith.

Narquinxa leaned forward and gave him a kiss on the cheek then strolled over to Xandalus and Charlie. Smith figured it would be best to cut his losses.

"Alright, we're going back downstairs. We'll be back up here shortly to get everybody's statement," he announced and marched out.

"I'm in," said Charlie thumping the table with excitement.

He threw the keyboard over to Xandalus.

"Just need your admin password."

Xandalus typed in his password and pushed the keyboard back towards Charlie who typed in some commands lightning speed and then sat back in his chair and turned to Narquinxa.

"Would you like to do the honours?" he asked.

"Sure. What do I have to do?"

"Just press the enter key."

Narquinxa leaned forward and pressed down on the key. The result was nothing dramatic. All that happened was that the cursor went to another line. Charlie took the keyboard and typed a quick command and hit enter.

"It's done," he said. "The local area network is deleted. Cecil is destroyed."

"Thank god," said Xandalus with a sigh.

"Not yet," said Narquinxa. "We still need to destroy all the other computers in this office."

"Leave that to us," said Mick who had somehow found a hammer. Pete stood next to him with a cricket bat in his hand.

"I'll help show you around," said Howard who was getting used to the idea of being useful.

"I'll come with you," said Charlie and the four men went off in search of computers to smash.

That left Narquinxa alone with Rebecca and Xandalus.

"So, you two really *are* aliens?" asked Rebecca.

"No," said Xandalus.

"Yes," said Narquinxa at exactly the same time.

If Rebecca was confused before, she was now even more confused.

"Zander, she might as well know the truth," said Narquinxa.

"I don't want her to know the truth," said Xandalus.

Rebecca walked over and put her arms around his neck.

"I already know the truth," said Rebecca. "I heard you tell the story to Captain Cooper and Lieutenant Varsavsky remember? And I don't care if you're an alien. I still love you."

Rebecca gave Xandalus a kiss. Narquinxa watched on with a combination of concern and compassion. Once again it was up to her to be the adult in the room. They had a window of opportunity to escape before things got any more complicated but they had to move quickly.

"Unfortunately, Rebecca, Zander and I have to go away now. We have to return to our species."

"What?" said Rebecca who pushed away from Xandalus and gave him a searching look.

"Is this true?"

"No. I mean, we don't have to go now. Not right now," said Xandalus looking over at Narquinxa like he was begging the hang man to give him a few more seconds at life.

"It will be easier to leave immediately and avoid the questions from the police," said Narquinxa.

Tears welled up in Rebecca's eyes. She slumped down on the nearby office chair and started crying. The outbreak of emotion set off something deep inside Narquinxa. The tears started flowing from her own eyes and before she knew it she was crying too as the pain from the loss of Winston, still barely twenty-four hours old, returned. She walked over and crouched beside Rebecca and put her arms around her and the two of them held each other for some time weeping.

Xandalus started pacing around the room getting more and more agitated until eventually he burst out.

"I'm not leaving. I don't have to go and they can't make me go," he said as decisively as he could but the uncertainty in his voice betrayed the fact that wasn't sure that what he said was true.

Narquinxa stopped hugging Rebecca and stood up. She had suspected this moment was coming while watching Xandalus and Rebecca throughout the day. She knew in her mind it was wrong. It was a betrayal of his mission. There was no guarantee that Gwthphthgw wouldn't send a party down to retrieve him by force. And it was dangerous for him to stay here. There was always the risk that he would somehow end up re-inventing another AI or something similarly bad that would throw human civilisation out of balance again. That was what her mind told her. But now her heart was giving her a clear message. Unlike earlier in the day when all was quiet, she now felt, not thought, but felt in her body that it was right that Xandalus stay. As ridiculous and unlikely as the whole thing was, it was right.

Xandalus was looking at her expectantly.

"What shall I tell the others on the ship?" asked Narquinxa.

"Tell them I fell in love with an Earth girl," said Xandalus pulling Rebecca up off the chair and giving her a hug.

"I don't think they'll understand what that means," said Narquinxa. "But I think I might have some idea how to tell them."

She smiled and Rebecca and Xandalus realised that she was giving her consent. They rushed over and gave her a hug and this time they cried tears of joy.

Chapter 31

The afternoon sun shone on Narquinxa's face as she strolled along Lygon Street. The air was warm and the streets were bustling with the start of the after-work rush. She had left the office soon after the discussion with Xandalus and Rebecca, slipping out through the fire escape stairs and avoiding both the police enquiry and Howard and the three boys. She had told Xandalus to make sure that all the computers in the building were destroyed and he and Rebecca had agreed to double check that this was done. Before they said their final goodbyes she asked what Xandalus and Rebecca intended to do next. Rebecca said they would fly north so they could take a break. She would introduce Xandalus to her parents and they would decide on their next steps. Narquinxa suggested that Xandalus have a chat to Charlie who, for a small fee, could acquire him some formal identification, birth certificates, medical records and the like. Xandalus agreed to do so.

Their final goodbye was a bittersweet moment. Part of her was a little jealous that Xandalus and Rebecca would get to enjoy their love for each other but this emotion was quickly overshadowed by her genuine happiness for them. Somehow, they were a perfect couple. An Antorped and a human. Living proof that perhaps love was some kind of universal or inter-galactic force. If that was true then it may just be that the Antorpeds really could learn something from the humans and perhaps her journey would have been an important one after all.

As she now walked along her heart was finally giving her a strong message: gratitude. For all the loss and the pain that her short stay had entailed, she was grateful to have been there. It was as if she had learned how to be alive. How to live. That had been Winston's gift to her. Like Charlie had said, life was one big ongoing experiment but she wasn't really in control of it. Or to put it another way, if you really felt you were in control of it, you probably weren't experimenting hard enough. Somewhere in between was the balance. Enough control not to go off the rails and enough letting go to let in the beautiful surprises, the magic moments that no experiment could reproduce.

Sex too was an experiment, she thought. Winston had said that emotions should be like an energy that you harness and put to use. If that was true, sex was like the nuclear bomb or the nuclear power plant. It could destroy you or it could give you electricity. That was what the Antorped researchers couldn't have seen. Sex was dangerous and danger can be fun. Danger forced you to move forward and try new things. It made you evolve. It was an energy that drove so much of the world.

And so she walked along; a beautiful young blonde woman in a Guns'n'Roses t-shirt smiling at the world. Naturally, men looked at her admiringly and she allowed herself to enjoy the attention. Encouraged by her smile, several men tried to stop and talk to her but she just smiled even wider and told them she had somewhere to be.

Finally, she arrived back at the alleyway. The bins were still in the same spot they had been when she and Xandalus had arrived. She walked over beside one and telepathically called Gwthphthgw.

There was no answer.

She tried again.

Still no answer.

She decided to try one of the more general channels for communication and this time there was a response.

"*Hello.*"

"*This is Narquinxa requesting teleportation back from Earth.*"

There was a silence. Finally the telepathic voice returned.

"*Narquinxa, I am just checking the details. Isn't there supposed to be somebody else with you?*"

"*Who is this?*" asked Narquinxa. "*Can I just speak to Gwthphthgw? He was managing the mission. He will know the details.*"

"*This is Lphwthphgw. Gwthphthgw is not here. He was re-assigned to another mission and left the ship yesterday.*"

"*Ok. So, you know about my mission down here on Earth, right?*"

"*I'm just checking the records now. Where's this other guy? Xandalus?*"

"*Xandalus has decided to stay on Earth.*"

"*Ok, cool.*"

Narquinxa shook her head in surprise.

"*That's not a problem? Don't you want to know why at least?*"

"*Nah. I mean, you know and you can debrief us when you get back.*"

"*Are you sure? Maybe I should speak to the new commanding officer first just to make sure it's ok?*"

"*Well, I don't know if I should be the one to tell you this, Narquinxa, but, you are the new commanding officer?*"

"*What?*"

"*There was going to be a formal announcement when you returned. But now you know. Congratulations.*"

Narquinxa stood there and let the news sink in. She tried to listen to her emotions to see what they were telling her and the signal was loud and clear. A smile came over her face.

"*So, umm, should we begin the teleportation process?*"

This time there was no need to check it with her superiors. Narquinxa gave the command.

"*Let's do it, Lphwthphgw.*"

In the alleyway off Lygon Street in Melbourne on the planet Earth, there was a gust of wind and a flash of light and where once stood a beautiful, blonde, smiling woman there was now an empty space.

THE END

When he's not writing outrageous stories, you can find Simon lifting weights, lazing about in the garden or playing guitar.

For notifications of upcoming releases and a semi-regular blog, check out Simon's website at http://simonsheridan.me

The Order of the Secret Chiefs

"Sampson, you've got a woman problem."

Adam Sampson does indeed have a woman problem: a sexy Russian witch has taken over his apocalypse cult (it's a long story). Fortunately, Adam has help from his pickup artist mate, Liam Love, and spunky grandmother, Mrs Mitchell. Together, the three of them will have to fight to stop Madame Orlova and her horde of horny men from bringing about the end of the world.

The Order of the Secret Chiefs is a riotous action-comedy in which a young man gets in over his head with money, sex and magic. His fight to save the world will be the beginning of his journey of self discovery in life and in love.

Once Upon a Time in Tittybong

JJ's best mates, Krusty and Trish, are hardcore, dyed-in-the-wool potheads. They're fun to have around. But sometimes, when you hang out with stoners too long, you do silly things like ask the Mayor if you can start a local currency that's backed by marijuana. Sometimes, when you live in the small Victorian town of Tittybong, the Mayor says 'Yes'.

Now JJ's going to spend his school holiday living the dream of every entrepreneurial high school stoner: running a bank where the money is made from dope. But the local manager of the State Bank, the leader of the local bikie gang and the local constabulary don't take too kindly to having their turf encroached on and JJ's about to find out that high finance is not all beers and bucket bongs.

Once Upon a Time in Tittybong is a fast-paced comedy in which a group of idealistic teenagers take on the powers that be in an Australian country town.

www.ingramcontent.com/pod-product-compliance
Lightning Source LLC
Chambersburg PA
CBHW061925130726
47909CB00012B/924